THE LOVE DETECTIVE:

neXT LeVeL

To Emma,

best wishes

[signature]

Also by Angela Dyson

The Love Detective

THE LOVE DETECTIVE:
NEXT LEVEL

ANGELA DYSON

Matador
9 Priory Business Park,
Wistow Road, Kibworth Beauchamp,
Leicestershire. LE8 0RX
Tel: 0116 279 2299
Email: books@troubador.co.uk
Web: www.troubador.co.uk/matador
Twitter: @matadorbooks

ISBN 978 1838590 574

British Library Cataloguing in Publication Data.
A catalogue record for this book is available from the British Library.

Printed and bound by CPI Group (UK) Ltd, Croydon, CR0 4YY
Typeset in 11pt Adobe Garamond Pro by Troubador Publishing Ltd, Leicester, UK

Matador is an imprint of Troubador Publishing Ltd

This one is for my sister, Claire Dyson.
With much love and thanks for everything, Clairabella!

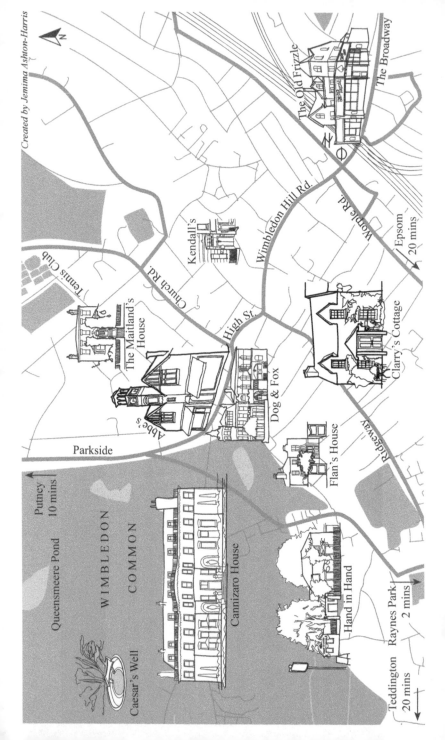

CHAPTER ONE

Evidently, I wasn't making a good impression.

The woman sitting across the desk from me flicked a dismissive eye over the one neatly typed page of A4 paper that makes up my CV.

"I'm afraid that we have nothing for you," she sniffed, looking again at my resume, "because, as I'm sure you'll agree, it is rather thin."

Harsh, I thought, but basically true. So, all right, at the age of twenty-six, I wasn't exactly what you might call a high-flyer, but she must have something for me.

"I believe that your last temping job for us was cut short after only three days." There was an edge of enquiry to her tone. "The notes we have on file are rather unclear as to the reason for this."

I winced at the memory. Things had been going pretty well at the marketing company in Victoria, until a somewhat unfortunate incident involving my take-out cup of Grande Latte and a computer server. Apparently, there's something in a double shot of caramel syrup that doesn't quite agree with all its delicate little components. The system went down for two days with many thousands of pounds of potential business lost, I was informed by the managing director as he personally escorted me from the premises.

I cleared my throat. The woman was awaiting an answer.

"I was so efficient that I dispensed with the company's workload in record time."

Hoping that this would be enough to satisfy her, I flashed what I like to think of as a frank and engaging smile. She didn't smile back. In fact, she appeared to be growing testier by the minute. Well, I reflected, I'd probably be out of temper too if *I'd* got up that morning and actually chosen, of my own free will, to wear a heavily ruched tunic top in a particularly bilious shade of green. It would be enough to ruin anyone's day.

I took a swift glance at the laminate badge bearing the name *Marion* that was pinned to the offending tunic, and then widened my eyes at the accompanying slogan which promised that she was *Here To Help*. When was she going to begin? By her manner of barely suppressed irritation, I was guessing that it wouldn't be any time soon.

"I only need a couple of days a week, Marion, to fit in with my waitressing shifts."

I did my best to look bright and responsible and waited expectantly.

Marion sighed and sat back, tapping one of her long synthetic nails on a pile of folders.

"Part-time work is always much sought after, especially here in Wimbledon. And of course, we have plenty of other applicants. What is it about you that makes you different? Something that would incline me to put you forward as a candidate over all the rest? What's your USP?"

My what? What was she talking about? What does *USP* stand for? Unusual Sexual Practices? I think I'm relatively normal in that department but how could I ever be sure? I made a mental note to ask the very next guy I slept with. Come to think of it, it was a very interesting question and one that deserved further consideration, but it did seem a bit odd somehow to have it asked by a recruitment agent.

"Hmm," I faltered.

"Never mind," she said, and the nail tapping upped a level. "Let's look at it from the other way around. Let's consider your weak points."

I opened my mouth, about to explain that I wasn't a big fan of routine, that I didn't like taking orders and wasn't a particularly organised person, when it occurred to me that this might be a trick question.

"Well," I floundered, "I'm very flexible and I'm... um... good with people."

I attempted another winning smile. "People like me."

She didn't look convinced. "They *do*?"

"Yes," I added firmly, because that was just plain rude. "Usually they do."

There was a pause as we eyed one another, and I decided to give it one last shot.

"I have recently developed some new skills."

The nail tapping stopped for an instant as she again looked at my CV.

"No," I explained, "it's not on there. It's not really the sort of thing that..." I hesitated. I was on the verge of telling her just how much I'd learnt in the last couple of weeks from my first stab at private investigating, or what the more narrow-minded may refer to as poking my nose into other people's business, when I broke off. What was the point? Somehow, she didn't strike me as the kind of person likely to be stirred by tales of stake-outs and surveillance. I got to my feet.

"Forget it. I doubt you'd consider the experience relevant. Anyway, you have my number."

From her look of relief, it was clear that we were neck and neck in our desire to bring the interview to a close. As I headed for the door, Marion called out, "I don't hold out much hope."

I turned back. Was she still speaking to me? No, I decided. She was merely expressing her own view of the world. Must be the influence of the tunic.

*

I stepped out into the warmth of a beautiful May morning and strolled up the hill towards home, resolving to put all thoughts of my pitiful lack of office experience out of my mind. Here I was on a Friday, feeling the sun on my face and the sense of freedom that comes from knowing that I didn't have to answer to some ego-inflated jerk of a boss. I liked my ad hoc lifestyle. I had my waitressing shifts and still some slack on my credit cards and so, all in all, life was pretty good. And as for getting another part-time job or landing my next assignment, well, something would no doubt turn up.

Something did. And much sooner than I could ever have expected.

CHAPTER TWO

As I let myself into the house, I could hear the phone ringing. Dashing into the sitting room and flinging aside my bag, I made a grab for it whilst simultaneously trying to shrug myself out of my jacket.

"Clarry? It's Tara."

"Hi, Tara. How are you?" I asked distractedly into the receiver, whilst struggling to free my left arm from my sleeve. Tara is one of my fellow waitresses at Abbe's Brasserie and, although we occasionally work together, we hadn't particularly struck up a rapport and had never gone out together socially. I waited for her to continue.

"Is there a shift you want me to cover for you?" I finally asked, presuming that was the reason for the call. "I can probably help you out."

"No. No, nothing like that," she offered hesitantly. "It's just that… well… you know what a talker Ian is."

I certainly did. My co-worker, Ian, or Iris as he prefers to be known, is one of my best friends. He's wildly irreverent and utterly indiscreet. I adore him. He, in his turn, is very fond of me and I don't think the fact that he also has size eight feet and can borrow my silver sling-backs for his drag queen act at the Jezebel Club, has anything whatsoever to do with it.

"Yes," I agreed. "Once he gets started, it's almost impossible to shut him up." I finally managed to yank my arm clear and sank down onto the sofa. "So, what's he been on about now?"

"It's just that he mentioned," Tara sounded a little embarrassed and I wondered what was coming next, "just in passing conversation, that you undertake private investigations, and so, I wanted to know if you could take on a job for a friend of mine."

Typical Ian! He'd played a minor part in my recent adventures as a first-time amateur sleuth and now he was setting himself up as my agent.

"Actually, what he did say," continued Tara, "was that although a highly experienced investigator, you keep the waitressing on as a cover story."

I bit back a laugh at the absurdity of his exaggeration. I'd had one case, very nearly screwing it up.

"Tara. Listen," I protested, "Ian is prone to, well, to be nice, let's call it sensationalism, because in truth I haven't much—"

"Much time? That's such a shame. But what if my friend could pay more than your usual fee? Do you think you could fit her in?"

Fee? She had all my attention now.

"Perhaps I might be able to squeeze something in. What's the story?"

"OK." Tara sounded relieved. "My friend Caroline is worried about her sister."

From her delivery, she seemed to assume that this statement said it all.

"And?" I encouraged.

"Vanessa is younger than Caro and I, she's twenty-one and recently she's become involved with some people that…" She cleared her throat. "Well, the fact is, Caroline and her family are a bit concerned about the group she's got herself mixed up with."

"What's the problem with them? Are they into hard drugs? Or crime? Because if so, it's not me you should be talking to, but someone who knows about these things—"

"No, no, nothing like that," she cut in. "It's just that her family don't exactly approve of…"

"Tara, my family have hardly ever approved of any of my friends and why on earth should they? You're telling me that this girl is twenty-one and—"

This time it was Tara who interrupted.

"There's more to it than that. I can't really explain over the phone. Would you agree to meet Caroline and talk it over?"

I thought for a moment. "Sure, if you think I can help."

"Great. Thanks so much. And I'll be there too. Oh, and you'll like Caro's mother, Diana Maitland."

"*Mother?*" I yelped. "Who said anything about mothers?"

Mothers, in my opinion, being one of life's natural hazards, are best avoided. They can be very tricky to deal with. My own mother doesn't exactly come highly recommended, so I know what I'm talking about.

"You don't happen to be free today, do you?" continued Tara, blithely ignoring my interjection, "because I'm seeing Caro this afternoon at Mrs. Maitland's."

I held the receiver away and rested my head back against the sofa cushions, taking a moment to deliberate. It would probably prove to be a complete waste of time, but as I had nothing else planned for the next few hours, what did I have to lose by checking it out?

"Fine with me," I replied. "I'm not due at the restaurant until six. So yes, let's do it."

"Right," said Tara, "give me five minutes and I'll call you back," and she hung up.

CHAPTER THREE

t three o'clock, I pulled into the long gravel drive of a grand double-fronted house in Wimbledon Village. Thick woody stems of a well-established wisteria clambered up the white stucco walls, its fountains of cascading lilac flowers stirring restlessly in the afternoon breeze. A pair of great stone urns flanked a flight of stone steps leading up to the front door. I parked my battered old Renault between a smart Volvo and something that was all black metallic lines and shiny chrome detailing and hoped it didn't look too out of place. This family must be loaded, I thought, trying to smooth some of the creases out of the cream jacket that I'd flung over the black vest top and jeans I was wearing, in the unshakable belief that a jacket always gives a woman an air of confidence.

I took the stairs at a trot and rang the bell. Almost immediately it was opened by a woman in her late fifties. She was wearing one of those fitted shift dresses that designers claim will serve you for any occasion. In this case, they were right. In a shade of soft caramel, expensively cut and teamed with low-heeled pumps, the look appeared relaxed and effortless but was clearly anything but. With her immaculately coiffured honey-coloured hair and a necklace of heavy linked gold gleaming dully around her throat, this woman was every inch the old-money Wimbledon Grandee. I was glad I'd decided on the jacket.

"Hello, I'm Diana Maitland." Her voice was low and perfectly pitched. "And you must be Clarissa? How kind of you to come at such short notice."

She extended a beautifully manicured hand.

"Actually, everyone calls me Clarry."

"Clarry then," she replied smoothly. "Do come in. We're just about to have tea. I gather that you are a local girl?"

"Yes, I'm just off the Ridgeway," I answered, as I followed her across pink-veined marble flooring and into what I believe estate agents refer to as a Formal Reception Room. And formal it certainly was. High ceilinged, with a huge marble fireplace, it was decorated in tones of richly glowing honey and amber. There was an antique desk, fragile-looking tables with spindly legs and two long apricot velvet sofas. Perched upon a window seat that curved along the length of the southernmost wall, was Tara. Her lank hair, colourless face and slight body, bearing living testimony to the fact that it *is* possible to be too thin. Beside her sat a tall woman of about twenty-eight who appeared to have either got dressed in a hurry or whilst undergoing a sudden outbreak of nerves. She had the look of a badly bound scrapbook, all wisps and patches of material; a flash of shirt poking out through the buttons of her long navy cardigan, a corner of hankie showing above the line of a pocket and her fine brown hair escaping the confines of a tortoiseshell clip.

I greeted Tara, was introduced to Caroline Maitland and furtively dusted off the seat of my jeans, before taking my place on a high-backed chair proffered to me by Diana, who then sat down opposite me. Above her, on the wall, hung an imposing portrait of an elegantly dressed woman of some bygone age, squinting down her straight and disapproving nose as if certain that anything the forthcoming centuries could offer would never meet with her approval. I thought that in Diana, I could detect a family likeness, but I might have been wrong.

"Will you pour, Caroline, please?"

Dutifully, Caroline rose and approached a white clothed table, set with primrose and gold-ringed china. Now, my idea of tea is a mug of supermarket brand. Things, I could see, were done differently around here. There were platters of thin-cut sandwiches and a three-tiered cake stand bearing tiny little chocolate éclairs and something golden and sponge-like that oozed cream. In this display, as in the perfectly arranged spray of yellow roses on a nearby console table, the plumped-up scatter cushions on the sofas and the highly polished parquet flooring, the presence of an army of staff was felt, if not seen.

Caroline handed us cups of fragrant tea and then indicated the sandwiches.

"I won't," Diana demurred and then turned to me. "Do please, Clarry, help yourself." The coolly assessing gaze she bestowed upon my generously proportioned size fourteen figure was not lost upon me. I hadn't planned to eat anything but now, shooting her a dazzling smile, I stretched out and placed just two of the egg and cress crustless triangles on my plate. I wanted to save room for the cakes.

"I trust that you have been enjoying this delightful weather, Clarry?"

Diana kicked off with that most predictable of subjects.

"Yes, hasn't it been lovely?" I answered inelegantly through a mouthful of sandwich.

"But it does bring so many strangers into the village," she sighed, "leaving their mess about on the common and commandeering the parking spaces."

"And there are precious few of those," remarked Caroline.

I wondered how long this stilted conversation would run and how much I would be expected to contribute, and noted that Tara, who at Abbe's, chats away endlessly about the latest diet fads and exactly how many minutes' aerobic exercise it takes to burn off however many calories, said next to nothing. She didn't eat anything either.

From beneath the puffy swathes of the blinds that dressed the windows, some glare of unforgiving daylight still managed to filter through into the room and I could see now that Diana was older than I had first taken her to be. It must be sheer force of will, I thought, that kept her back so straight and her knees demurely set together at the slight angle that maintains a certain tautness in the thigh. There was no doubt that she was what was generally described as a handsome woman, but the dignity of her carriage, the understated elegance of her dress and the gracious condescension of her tone could not disguise the fact that this woman was deeply irritated and put out by something or someone. I could only hope that it wasn't me.

Having eaten my way through two of the éclairs and a slice of the sponge, and small talk not really being my thing, I was now eager to get to the reason for my summons.

Something of my impatience must have communicated itself to Diana.

"Time, I think," she rested her cup back on its saucer, "that we got down to business. Now, Clarry, how much has Tara indicated to you of the… situation… that we find ourselves in?"

"Not a lot," I said. "Just that your daughter is hanging out with some people that you don't…" I hesitated, searching for the right word, failed and finished lamely "…think suitable for her to associate with."

"Indeed," replied Diana.

"So, who are they?" I was really curious now. "Are they travellers? Or eco-warriors? Or bikers? A street gang?" At her lack of response, I pressed on and joked, "Or a terrorist cell? Some kind of cult?" Then stopped abruptly as I caught the look exchanged between Tara and Caroline.

"Really? A *cult*? Some weird religious sect?"

"It is not a cult," Diana snapped, "I believe it's a group of women interested in…" The pause was loaded, and I realised that I was leaning forward in my seat and holding my breath. "…In folklore, alternative religions and paganism."

I sat back in surprise. "Paganism? I know absolutely nothing about that sort of thing, but I don't get what the big deal is here. Loads of people are interested in all that stuff. It's probably just a fad."

It was Caroline who answered. "We don't know much for sure. Nessa is being very secretive about it—"

"She's always been like that," cut in Diana plaintively, "even as a child, she hid things from me. Me, her mother."

She seemed to expect some expression of condolence from me, but I asked, "So, what *do* you know? And why is it worrying you so much?"

That sounded reasonable enough, and Diana seemed to think so too for she appeared to relax a little in her chair and crossed her ankles.

"I trust that anything we say to you shall be kept in the strictest confidence?"

"Yes," I nodded and then felt a pang of remorse as, of course, I would be telling Flan, my sidekick in my previous investigation, all about it.

"Vanessa is rather young for her age in some ways," continued Diana. "She was never strong physically as a child and so we didn't send her away to school like our eldest daughter. Nothing like boarding school to toughen one up and set one on the correct path, is there, Caroline?"

"No, Mother." Caroline sounded docile, but I caught the quick flash of a mutinous look pass between her and Tara.

"Vanessa is easily led," brooded Diana, "and in the past has got herself embroiled in dubious company and entangled with some particularly unfortunate men."

"But I thought you said it was a group of women," I interjected.

"It is as far as we know," said Caroline, "but the thing is—"

"The thing is," interrupted Diana, "after dating several quite frankly appalling creatures, she now has a very decent prospect before her."

She must have caught my look of bewilderment and explained.

"A highly suitable young man that both Vanessa's father and I like very much, but we are concerned that if she persists in this…" and here she dropped her voice to a shuddering whisper "…*pagan* business, then Charles may well—"

"Take fright and dump her," cut in Caroline with an unmistakable edge to her voice.

"May decide that she is not the young woman for him," corrected Diana with a reproving look at her daughter.

At this, Tara, speaking for the first time, offered, "Oh, I'm sure he won't. He seems such a nice guy and really into Vanessa."

"Charles wants a wife that will be an asset to him," returned Diana crisply. "To be by his side and help further his career and to entertain his friends."

I blinked. This was all sounding too much like an episode of *Downton Abbey* to me. What century did Diana Maitland think she was living in? I turned to her.

"I'm not clear what it is you want me to do."

She shifted uncomfortably in her seat before answering. "I was thinking that you could perhaps check out the lie of the land, see what you can find out and even keep a discreet eye on her movements."

"Spy on her, is what Mother means," volunteered Caroline.

"Now, Caroline, that's not at all helpful."

"OK then," amended Caroline, "ingratiate yourself with her and perhaps she might invite you along to one of their meetings."

Suppressing a mounting impatience with their thinly veiled sniping, and deciding there and then to turn down what seemed to me an absurd request, I asked, "But why don't you simply talk to her about it? If you feel you really have to."

"I've tried several times," admitted Diana, and for the first time I noted a tinge of genuine anxiety in her voice. "But she just tells me to stop interfering and trying to run her life."

Nice one, Vanessa, I thought.

"I only want her to be happy and not mess up what may be her last chance to make the best of herself and her potential." Her voice had risen a little. "And that's what she's doing. I'm sure of it."

To fulfil her potential by getting *married*? And last chance at *twenty-one*? By this woman's reckonings, at twenty-six and single, I might as well just shoot myself now. But, however ridiculously outdated Diana's notions may be, they were stirring echoes of my own mother's constant criticism of what she calls my bohemian lifestyle, and I felt a flash of compassion for Diana. Because in my mother's own, and utterly maddening way, with her nagging and her transparent attempts to limit and control my choices, she is only showing that she cares about me. And Diana evidently cared about Vanessa.

"I suppose I could give it a try," I muttered, more to myself than for general consumption, but Diana pounced upon my words.

"Good." She was brisk now. No trace of her previous emotion.

"How do you propose to begin?"

Various possibilities suggested themselves and I was just about to ask for a photo of Vanessa and some details of her day-to-day movements, when Caroline suggested, "I've been thinking. How would it be if we invited Clarry to the party tomorrow evening? It might be the perfect occasion for her to meet Nessa without it looking like a… well, too staged," she explained.

Diana nodded to me with a gracious smile. "An excellent suggestion, I think. Clarry, Caroline's father and I are having a cocktail party, nothing too grand, just a modest affair at Cannizaro House, to celebrate our wedding anniversary. I won't tell you how many years because I am sure that you will be able to work that out for yourself."

I was indeed grappling with some mental arithmetic. "Slight problem, I'm afraid. I'm working tomorrow night and it'll be too short notice to—"

Tara cut in. "It's all right; I'll do your shift for you."

"But aren't you also invited?"

"She is, of course," Diana returned smoothly, "but I think that on this occasion she won't mind foregoing the pleasure. Will you, Tara dear?" She turned and fixed Tara with a look.

"No, of course not," Tara coloured, "that's why I suggested it."

"Well, that's settled then." Diana sat back and again turned to me. "Now, all that remains to be discussed are your terms, Clarry."

My terms? I really hadn't thought this through. I had no idea what to ask for, but before I could think of a number and then double it, I found myself saying "Let's leave that on hold for the moment. After all, I don't even know if I can help you yet."

I could have kicked myself. Here I was, seriously in need of some cash, and I had just talked myself into doing something for free. And I'd be losing the money for tomorrow night's shift.

Diana acknowledged the offer with a slight incline of the head.

"By all means, we can discuss that at a later date, but whatever arrangement we come to, I shall certainly expect you to report back to me every day."

"No," I said flatly, "that's not how I work."

It wasn't? Since when did I have a modus operandi?

"But then how will I be able to monitor your progress?"

"You won't."

In the silence that followed you could have heard a Ming vase drop.

"I will, of course, keep you informed at intervals, but I have to be free to work in my own way. Or not at all."

"Well, really," puffed Diana, the experience of not instantly getting her own way being apparently new to her. "I hardly think that will be at all suitable."

I shrugged and made as if to rise to my feet.

"One moment, please." She raised a detaining palm and my eyes flickered from hers to those of the censorious woman in the portrait above her. Definitely an ancestor, I decided, and then sat back, curious to see Diana's next move.

"Very well. I am prepared to give your methods a try. Whatever they may be."

How magnanimous of her, I thought. She seemed to have conveniently forgotten that they approached me, but I bit back any retort and waited.

"I am willing to pay for two weeks of your time." Here she caught my look of protestation. "Yes, I am aware of your *waitressing* commitments." She made it sound like a criminal act. "And so, I understand that you will have to work around them."

This sounded all right and I was wondering again what I could decently charge, when she rose from her seat.

"We won't take any more of your time. Caroline will telephone you tomorrow morning to discuss the financial issue and I will see you at the party."

It was Caroline who walked me to the front door. "I'll get your number from Tara and talk to you tomorrow. And thank you, Clarry."

I let myself into the Renault. *Hmm,* I thought, as the engine spluttered into life and I shifted into first. *Looks like I've got my next case.*

CHAPTER FOUR

"Hi, Dave," I called, as I entered the restaurant at five minutes to six. "What have we got tonight?"

He looked up from the reservations book.

"Full house, including a rugby club do. Table of sixteen in the basement at eight o'clock."

I groaned. "Who's with me?"

"Steph. I reckon you two can handle it. And there are three parties of six and one of seven. Jason can cover those."

I made my way to the kitchen.

"Evening, Chef," I said respectfully.

Laurence paused in filleting something large and pink with scales and sketched a wave, just as Stephanie stomped in and greeted us.

"Hi, y'all." The twang was heavy. "How y'all doin'?"

I stopped short. Stephanie is from south London.

"What's with the voice?"

"I got to rehearse, babes," she explained, reverting to her usual slightly nasal tone. "I've got an audition coming up and I've got to lock down an American accent."

She peeled off her leather jacket as we made our way through the kitchen.

"You see, I reckon…" and we were back with the Daisy Duke drawl "…that if I immerse myself in the character twenty-four seven then I'll be—"

"You'll be immersed in my *bouillabaisse* in a minute, if you don't get out from under my feet," scolded Alec, the *sous-chef*, crossing our path with a steaming tureen. "Mind you, I'll be happy to give you a good rubdown after," he winked.

"Pervert," Steph and I chorused in unison.

He grinned and shooed us away.

There's a lot of competition in Wimbledon Village, but at Abbe's Brasserie the food is reliably good, offering timeless classics with a modern twist. This keeps the locals coming back. And, although relaxed in atmosphere and not overpriced, the restaurant has a certain celebratory feel, making it a favourite for anything from a casual mid-week dinner to more special birthday parties and anniversary dos. Dave, an experienced manager, knows how to get the best out of the staff. He pretty much gives us a free hand and wants us to enjoy what we do, but on the understanding that the customers are always our priority and must be made to feel welcome and looked after. And it works. There's a warmth and a vitality about the place. I love being a waitress here.

Having set up the tables and waiting for the first of the customers to arrive, I was polishing glasses at the bar when I felt two hands grab me by the waist from behind.

"Hi, Gorgeous."

It was Jason. Lazily charming, he was good-natured, had a seriously fit body and facial features regular enough to make him most women's type, but boyfriend material he most certainly was not. He was a player. In his early thirties, he attracted everything and anything female, from girls in their teens to grandmas in for a family Sunday lunch. It was something to do with the way he gave each and every one of them his complete and undivided attention. It may only be for a few seconds, but the effect of his direct eye contact never failed. They went down like ninepins. And, as he regularly regaled us at our after-shift lock-ins with stories of his sexual conquests, going down wasn't all they did. Steph had been there, I hadn't. Although we had once had a serious snog in the stores cupboard. I have my weak moments. Dave claimed that the Jason Factor had contributed to repeat custom from the Wimbledon Businesswomen's Association, the New Mums' Survival Group and the Ladies First Eleven Cricket Club, all of whom had their monthly lunch meetings with us. Alec called him a lucky bastard. Steph and I called him a man-whore. He answered to both.

"Jose says do you want him to save you some of the risotto for later? It's the one with the saffron and pancetta."

This was not really allowed because the staff were only supposed to get anything that was left over at the end of the night and that would not be reused the following day, but Jose, being a real sweetie, and knowing I loved this particular dish, would hide a plateful for me at the back of the pudding fridge. In his fifties, as kitchen porter he took most of the brunt of chef Laurence's fitful temper but remained resolutely cheerful. He said it was having five kids that did it. He had his favourites, though. Tara, he wasn't a big fan of because she didn't eat, but me, he loved. Briefly, I considered the sandwiches and cakes I'd wolfed down earlier and thought maybe I should say no to the risotto. But, I persuaded myself, that was hours ago, and besides, after midnight when we'd finished, I'd be starving.

"You bet," I told Jason and picked up another glass.

*

It was a busy night. By quarter to nine, I'd finally managed to get the rugby club party, who had the basement to themselves, to look at the menu. They'd eaten their way through eight baskets of bread, and Steph and I had been up and down stairs to the bar so many times for more drinks that my legs were beginning to ache, and we were only halfway through our shift. Laurence had been sending out increasingly tetchy messages requesting the food order, but with the amount of beer these lads were knocking back, one or other of them would disappear off up to the loo and then get waylaid chatting up women on other tables, and so it was proving nearly impossible. Controlling them was like trying to get a litter of kittens into a carrying basket. Just as you think you've got all the little tails and all the little paws safely in, a head pops up making a bid for freedom and you end up chasing it around the house, leaving the others free to escape. It was time to get tough.

"Listen, guys, if I don't get your orders in soon, the chef will come after me with a meat cleaver."

This cued a volley of cat calls and offers to get out, for my inspection, their own equipment. I eyed the group. Although there were a few in their mid-twenties, mostly they were in their thirties and forties. Must be the veteran team. My eye settled upon a stocky guy of about thirty with thick dark hair, at the far end of the table. He wasn't conventionally attractive, but he was burly and strong and looked like he could heave my five foot eight frame over his shoulder and take me back to his lair, and so I gave him the once-over. I'm big on the caveman type.

"I'll protect you," he mouthed, and I flashed him a smile.

Back in the kitchen, glad to catch a breather, I panted, "One chicken, two lamb shanks, three monkfish and ten steaks." And spiking the order form onto the counter, added, "Five medium rare, three medium, one rare and one incinerated."

"Took your time," growled Laurence, pushing two plates of *spaghetti vongole* towards me. "Table twelve. *Now,*" and I was off again.

*

"How *are* yuuuu?" demanded Steph an hour later as we collided at the service station. "I mean… oh my Gaaaad… like… totally…"

She was now sounding very LA.

"Have you really managed to keep that up all evening?" I asked, grabbing a handful of napkins.

"Yeah, but I think I need a little more practice. You know how Americans often end a sentence as if they're asking a question? Well, when I repeated her order to a woman on table five…. *'Chicken?'*"

And her voice creaked with enquiry. "She asked me, why not? Wouldn't I recommend it? And what was wrong with it? Was it off? She didn't want to get salmonella and…"

I laughed and pushed past her.

"Puddings about to go down in a minute. Ready?"

The rugby team were all pretty drunk by now and we could hear warblings of "*Swing looooooow, sweet chariooott*" as we made our way down the stairs, arms laden with chocolate brownies, ice creams and parfaits. Steph was ahead of me and I nearly cannoned into her, only just managing to retain hold of the plates, as she came to an abrupt halt at the bottom of the steps.

"Blimey," she breathed, all trace of Americana having vanished.

"What is it?" I asked curiously because Steph's not easily fazed. Peeping out over her shoulder, I could see what had stopped her so thoroughly in her tracks.

In a really smart restaurant, a formal table plan is drawn up and food choices added in at place of order. This means that when the waiter brings out the plates, he doesn't have to ask who's having the soup? Who the duck? Etc. It's more professional. At Abbe's, like most places, we rely on memory and a few visual clues. And this was what I'd done with the rugby crowd. Caveman was having the brulee; the guy in the blue polo shirt, the cheese; the older chap in the jacket, the crumble, and so on. But now a difficulty presented itself. When I'd last checked in on them and topped up their wine, ten minutes earlier, they'd been boisterous and a bit lairy but still manageable. Since then, things had gone decidedly downhill and matching the clothing to the puddings would be a problem. The jackets and the polo shirts had been discarded. Along with nearly everything else. Most of them were now wearing nothing but their club ties and their socks. They *had* got their equipment out after all.

I rolled my eyes at Steph and we started to giggle. It was one of those situations where you know you shouldn't stare but can't help yourself. So many penises in so small a space. And what a variety. Without a haze of alcohol-fuelled lust, the male member looks a little defenceless. Although there was one that belonged to a floppy-haired guy in the corner, that was spectacularly... I dragged my gaze away and catching the eye of Caveman, was relieved to see that he was one of the few who remained fully dressed.

"What's going on?" I gestured.

"That's just rugby!" he shrugged, with a laugh.

And here was me thinking it was two teams running about with a funny-shaped ball and knocking each other over. Although, come to think of it, there did seem to be an element of chase-me-chase-me to the game, and so perhaps it was just a natural development for them to get their kit off when pissed.

"*Swing low*" drunkenly bellowed a man with short brown hair and a penis that kinked to the left.

"*Sweet chariot*," tunelessly crooned his mate, lifting his wine glass and simultaneously crossing his legs so his genitals flapped like a jellyfish.

At this, Caveman took charge.

"Come on, guys. Game over. It's not fair on the girls. They've seen enough."

"Or have we?" whispered Steph in my ear. "I was just beginning to enjoy myself."

"I think we'll leave the puddings and let you help yourselves," I said briskly, and saluting Caveman with a thank you, Steph and I dumped the dishes on the table, threw down some more spoons and escaped back up the stairs.

At nearly half past twelve, when all the other customers had left, the rugby party settled the bill. It may have been a combination of alcohol and shame, but they left a huge tip on top of the in-built twelve and a half per cent. Either that, or Caveman had bullied them into it.

"I'm Ed," he said, shepherding the others through the door and buttoning up his jacket. "Who are you?"

"Clarry."

"Nice to meet you, Clarry." He stuck out his hand and I shook it. "And thanks for handling the scene back there so well. It can't have been…Whoa…"

He broke off as two of his mates were seen stumbling into the path of an oncoming night bus.

"Better get this lot into some cabs before they end up as road-kill. Can I call you?"

I nodded "OK. Why not?"

He grinned, and I liked the way his eyes crinkled up at the corners.

He fished out his mobile. "Quick, give me your number."

*

"I hear that the boys downstairs put on a bit of a show," smirked Jason, as later, with the closed sign up at the window, we were all sitting around drinking the customers' half-finished bottles of wine.

"Anything worth seeing?"

"You bet your sweet aaaaassss there was," replied Steph, the accent making a comeback but this time snappier and more edgy.

"And Clarry might get a private show, cos she's just given her number to some big guy in a reefer jacket. I saw you."

"Where are we now?" I asked, ignoring her knowing wink. "State-wise, I mean,"

"New York. I'm going old school and channelling my inner Monica from *Friends.*"

"What's the part you're up for?" Alec asked as he and Jose joined us, bearing a plate of the pancetta and saffron risotto, a handful of forks and a large bowl of chips.

"A touring production of *Chicago.*"

"Then why are you bothering with New York?"

Alec swung his long legs over the back of a chair and reached for a glass. "Give me some of that, Jase. I'm dying for a drink. Some of us have been sweating hard all night, not just swanning around eyeing up the talent."

Jason chucked a chip at him.

"Because," explained Steph, "I have no bloody idea what a Chicago accent sounds like, and mostly, it's singing and dancing, anyway."

"I didn't know you could dance," I remarked, forking up a mouthful of risotto.

"I can't," she admitted, "but I'd put it on my resume when I first got my agent and I haven't got the heart to admit now that I'd made that bit up. Along with being able to ride a horse and sword-fight."

"I'm going to Cannizaro tomorrow night," I said, suddenly remembering my promise to Diana Maitland. "Know anyone that works there?"

"Too swanky for the likes of us," observed Alec.

"My friend Jonian washes up there," chimed in Jose. "He works at the weekends. Tell him I said hello if you see him."

"I don't think for one moment that I'll meet him as thankfully, tomorrow, I'm not one of the hired help but an invited guest," I grinned, and said in mock grandeur, "going to a cocktail party, don't you know."

"Ooh," crowed Stephanie, "what are you going to wear?"

CHAPTER FiVE

On the following morning, as I jogged my way through the woods of Wimbledon Common, it was Steph's question about what I was going to wear that evening that occupied my mind. It was a beautiful day and still early enough for the dew to sparkle on the grass like Swarovski beads on an A-lister's Oscars dress.

Birds were up and about, cheerfully noisy; doing whatever it is that birds do. Raising their young, I supposed, at this time of the year. Troupes of rabbits were cropping the grass in companionable huddles, only to flee instantly back to the safety of their warrens as they caught the vibrations of my thundering footfalls. Bracken shoots were thrusting their insistent spurs up and out through the undergrowth, and I could see the pale yellow faces of buttercups in and amongst the moss that lined the edge of the trickling stream that wound its languid course down from Caesar's Well.

Negotiating my way along the paths and trying to avoid brushing through the gossamer threads of baby caterpillars, hanging from tree branches, that can get in your hair and down your back, I felt a return of strength to my legs and the quickening pulse of energy as I hit my stride. I lacked the self-discipline required to work out at a gym, but reluctantly accepted that I had to do something to keep even vaguely in shape, and so had settled on jogging a few mornings a week on the common.

Maintaining a steady pace, I allowed my thoughts to stray away from the contents of my wardrobe and to focus upon Caveman, or Ed, I suppose I should call him, from last night. *Now that's something to look forward to,* I thought. It may have been only a week or so since I'd broken off the casual relationship I was having with Tim, one of my fellow waiters at Abbe's, but I saw no reason not to check out what was available and try it… *him*… on for size.

Dimly, I became aware of a slight movement on my left shoulder. Slowing down to a walk, I looked down to find the tiny green wriggling form of a caterpillar intent upon making its way down my chest. Now, the rabbits and the birds are one thing, and I appreciate them. Really, I do. But this was way too up-close and personal with nature for me. I flicked the thing off in distaste. Sorry and all that, but there would now be one less butterfly in the world.

*

The trick, I decided, as I walked through the bar area and up several flights of stairs to the Hotel Du Vin Cannizaro House Queen Elizabeth Room where the Maitland cocktail party was being hosted, is to wear an old and inexpensive outfit with as much self-assurance as if it were new and designer labelled. A little black dress *is,* after all, just a little black dress. So, I'd slung a couple of long ropes of fake pearls around my neck and pinned some strands of my hair in a half-up-half-down do and told myself that I might just pull the whole thing off if I assumed a convincing air of confidence.

Caroline, when she'd telephoned earlier, had instructed me to turn up at seven o'clock, but I had decided to leave it until a little later so as not to look too conspicuous arriving on my own. Now, at half past seven, the room was full of elegant, if conservatively dressed, women flashing discreetly expensive jewellery (their pearls presumably were the real thing) and men in dark suits, all with that unmistakable complacent bearing of those who enjoy both money and success. A respectable party, mostly late middle-aged, affluent and civilised. It would be a stretch for me to fit in.

Diana Maitland, stately in midnight blue silk, and flanked by a tall serious-looking grey-haired man wearing glasses, was standing in an attitude of welcoming reception by a pillar bearing an extravagant display of white roses and something green and feathery that, at the angle I was viewing from, appeared to be growing out of her ear. Doing my best to assume the relaxed manner of a *bona fide* guest, I approached her.

"Good evening, Diana."

"Ah, Clarry, how nice to see you." Her eyes bored purposefully into mine.

"I don't think you've met my husband, Clive, have you? Clarry is a friend of Caroline's, darling."

Clive stuck out his hand.

"Jolly good of you to come. We are very lucky to have so many well-wishers here with us tonight, celebrating our anniversary."

His smile was sincere, but his words were a little mechanical, as if he'd polished and perfected his greeting and wasn't going to chance a deviation from the script.

"Thank you for inviting me," I answered politely, and then more from the desire to have something to say than a request for information, I asked, "Where is Caroline?"

"My daughters are over by the fireplace," said Diana with a significant look, and gesturing towards the middle of the room, "Do join them."

It was a command not an invitation. Taking a couple of steps forward, I was waylaid by a waitress bearing a tray of Champagne flutes. I took one and, straightening my long ropes of pearls that kept hiking up over one bosom, eyed the assembled throng with a fluttering of anxiety. *OK then, here I go. Cast off.*

There was a lot of noise in the room. Voices were pitched a tad higher than normal everyday conversation in the back and forth of small talk. Tinkling laughter from a woman in structured black velvet seemed as brittle as the stem of the glass I held in my hand. Her companion, a heavy-set man with a sweating forehead, hee-hawed back at her.

Elbowing politely past them, I greeted Caroline.

"Nice party."

"Oh hi, Clarry. Glad you could make it."

Although wearing what was clearly an expensive evening dress, she still managed to retain that air of having dressed in a wind tunnel. One of the spaghetti straps of her chiffon shift had slipped off a shoulder, her hair, in a precarious-looking top knot, was beginning to droop and the navy blue liner she'd applied inexpertly around her eyes gave her a

33

smudgy startled look. I turned to the girl beside her. Vanessa Maitland wasn't as tall as her mother and sister, maybe five foot five or six, and it was apparent that, unlike Diana, clothes did not interest her. The black jersey dress with a full skirt she wore was ageing and unflattering. Her hair was the dirty blonde colour that in the salon costs a fortune to reproduce, but in her case was natural. It looked like she was growing out a bob. It was at that in-between length, just above her shoulders. The Maitland nose, straight and patrician, was set on a childlike face where the bright brown eyes were positioned slightly too wide apart.

"Nessa, this is Clarry. I know her through Tara."

"Hello," I said and nodded amiably in Vanessa's direction.

Vanessa's eyes briefly scanned me, but whatever she saw was evidently of not much interest to her.

"Hi," she said, and there was an uncomfortable pause.

Caroline and I both tried to fill it at the same time and then laughed awkwardly. Vanessa, doing nothing to ease the social tension, merely gazed about the room and looked as if she'd much rather be someplace else. Well, wouldn't we all? I tried again.

"So, your parents' wedding anniversary? Mine have been married nearly thirty years. My dad claims that locking himself away in the shed for long periods of time makes all that togetherness bearable. Who knew the importance of an outbuilding to a marriage?"

Caroline laughed, genuinely this time, but there wasn't a flicker from Vanessa, who continued to look about her. Now, I know I'm no comedian, but still, it wasn't a bad effort and didn't deserve to be completely blanked. I gave myself a mental shake. *Don't try too hard,* I told myself. *Be natural.*

"Actually, the thought of being married at all freaks me out," I continued. "The idea of becoming some amorphous mass, with no beginning of one person and no end of the other. Of becoming one of those women who say *we* like it, when asked her opinion on a new film, or a bar or restaurant. Like she's never been an individual with her own tastes and her own views."

I was speaking more vehemently than I felt, but from Diana's disclosure about the eligible Charles as a prospective husband for Vanessa, I hoped to strike just the right mutinous note. And it looked like I may have scored, as she turned directly to look at me, but it was Caroline who spoke first.

"Not all marriages are like that," she observed, and it occurred to me that I didn't know if she was married or not. Somehow, I had assumed that she still lived at home. The bickering between her and Diana seemed longstanding, and integral to a relationship lived in too close a proximity. I glanced down at her left hand, where a beautiful square-shaped diamond engagement ring sparkled against a plain gold wedding band. Question answered. And her husband was presumably here somewhere.

"No, I'm sure you're right," I said. "Some of them must work, or else why would anyone do it?"

"Not even fifty per cent," Vanessa cut in quickly. "That's what the statistics say."

I laughed. "I must remember to tell my mother that, when she next tries to guilt-trip me with the 'When am I going to be a grandmother?' routine."

"Does she really do that? Pressurise you, I mean?"

I had her attention now.

"Sure. Don't all mothers? They can't help themselves. It's something primeval."

"It's a form of control," said Vanessa, and her voice was strident. "They want to live their lives through us."

"It's because they love us," said Caroline quickly, "because they care."

"Care about how we reflect upon them, you mean," snapped back Vanessa. I had obviously hit on a bloody big nerve. Interesting maybe, and certainly an angle to work on as a way in, if I wanted to get this girl on side. That's if I was, in fact, going to take the case. And I hadn't quite made my mind up about that yet.

"Because if we don't appear successful in their eyes, then they think that they've failed somehow or that we've let them down?" I offered. "That's a pretty big weight to put on anyone. Let alone someone you love."

"Yes, but if the intention is good…" Caroline began.

"Oh, fuck the intention," said Vanessa.

"Not the language for a cocktail party," I said, in mock disapproval.

Vanessa looked surprised and then gave a snort of laughter.

"Right," she smiled at me. "What was your name, again?"

"Clarry Pennhaligan." I stuck out my hand. "Twenty-six years old, single, and the despair of my mother."

She shook it. "Vanessa Maitland. Twenty-one years old, single, and the despair of everyone. Nice meeting you."

And she turned and made off through the crowd.

I looked at Caroline. "Well, I think that broke the ice, don't you?"

CHAPTER SIX

Half an hour later, I was thinking about calling it a night. There didn't seem much more I could achieve for now. Caroline and I had chatted for a while, and although I had spotted Vanessa talking to her father out on the terrace, I hadn't been able to get near her.

I'd eaten several of the canapés that were being offered by discreetly efficient waiters and wondered whether Cannizaro might be taking on more staff and what the hourly rate might be. I'd exchanged social niceties with a pleasant barrister and his wife, had discussed the plight of honey bees in crisis with a myopic gent in a bow tie, and learnt rather more than I'd have wished to about the treatment of sewage, from an enthusiastic member of Merton District Council's environmental team. Time to get out of here.

I decided against saying my goodbyes to Diana and Clive, choosing instead to make a discreet exit. Not polite maybe, but I was done with chit-chat.

I needed the loo and so made my way down a long, winding corridor with numbered guest rooms and suites, in the hope of finding one on this floor. I did so, and it was plush with soft lights and tissues in fancy boxes. I was just washing my hands, when out of one of the stalls came

Vanessa, dressed in jeans, T-shirt and a pair of Converse, and stuffing her black jersey dress into a backpack. I noted that these clothes flattered her shape and that she looked much more at home in them.

"Making your escape?" I asked, "Good plan. I was just doing the same."

She opened her mouth to answer, when from outside came the unmistakable voice of her mother.

"Vanessa, are you in there?"

Vanessa shot me a glance and shook her head. I went to the door and, holding it only slightly ajar, attempted to head Diana off at the pass.

"No, she's not here," I said evenly.

"Are you sure?" She looked at me suspiciously. "I've been looking for her everywhere. Charles has just arrived. Caught up late with business, I gather, but he's here now, and so naturally, Vanessa chooses this moment to up and disappear."

Her exasperation was tangible and, rather than have her barge past me to investigate for herself or, even worse, blow my cover, I improvised hastily.

"I'm not sure, but I think I may have seen her further along the corridor."

"Thank you," and before I could say anything else, she made off in the opposite direction from the Queen Elizabeth Room.

I closed the door. "Close one."

"Thanks, Clarry. That was cool of you."

Yes, it was. And now was the time to capitalise on it, but Vanessa was already at the door, peering out.

"Trouble is, if I go back that way," she gestured along the corridor towards the party, "I might bump into Dad or Caroline. And if I go that way…" She pointed in the other direction. "…I'll probably bump into Mum."

"Don't worry; I'm pretty sure that I passed an exit along the way. Come on, and if we meet any opposition, I'll come up with a diversion tactic."

From the look of relief on her face, you'd have thought we were hiding from the Gestapo, not sloping off to avoid a parental reprimand. I led the way and swiftly we paced along the hall and came to a grey utilitarian door I'd spotted earlier, that obviously didn't lead into a guest room, when we heard footsteps behind us and the plaintive call of "Vanessa, is that you?"

"Quick," I said and yanked at the door, pulling Vanessa through, just as her mother rounded the corner. Diana could certainly move fast for a woman in a long dress and heels. We found ourselves on a stone staircase that presumably had once been the servants' stairs when the hotel had been a grand private house. It was now a service entrance.

"Come on," I hissed and set off down the stairs. We had shot down one level and then another, when we caught the strain of Diana's voice from the top landing. Would she actually give chase? I had to admire her tenacity. Pressing ourselves against the wall, we held our breath, catching each other's eye, as laughter bubbled up between us. Then, we raced down the remaining two flights of stairs, hurtled through another grey door, and abruptly found ourselves amongst the dishwashers and towering crockery stacks of the hotel kitchen's utility room, and under the glowering scrutiny of a kitchen porter in yellow plastic clogs.

"You are not supposed to be here." His voice was gruff. "Guests aren't allowed."

He eyed Vanessa's jeans. "If you are guests, that is. If not, I'll have to call the manager."

"Of course we are," I said, with as much self-possession as I could muster. I felt red in the face from clattering down four flights of stairs in stilettos, and my double set of pearls had looped themselves one over each breast.

"We took a wrong turn. It's a simple mistake that anyone could make. We've been at a party in the Queen Elizabeth Rooms and we decided to look about and…"

Suddenly I remembered Jose's friend who worked here. In fact, right here. Washing up. What was his name, Jan? Jon? No. Jonian.

"We were heading, before we lost our way, to ask at reception if Jonian was working this evening as he… as he has been highly recommended to me, to assist at an event I'm throwing. Are you Jonian?"

I fervently hoped that he wasn't.

"No."

"Is he here?" I persisted. I was warming to my role of imaginary hostess. "It's important. The right staff are so difficult to get nowadays."

"Yes, he's on shift now," the man grunted. "I'll find him, but you'd better make it quick or you'll get him in trouble."

As he stomped off in his clogs, Vanessa whispered, "What's going on? Who's this guy you mentioned, and how are we going to get out?"

I shrugged. "It's either back up all those bloody stairs, face the manager, your mother and God knows who else, or we get out through here somehow. And I have a friend who knows this Jonian."

She looked at me doubtfully. "Well, have you got a better idea?" I demanded, just as the porter returned.

With him, in a stained apron, was a guy in his mid-twenties with dark close-cropped hair and a gentle face. He regarded us curiously.

"You were asking for me?" He had an Eastern European accent.

"Yes," I smiled reassuringly. "I wanted to talk to you about…"

I broke off and looked pointedly at his colleague who was blatantly eavesdropping. He got the hint and reluctantly disappeared off into what I presumed was the main body of the kitchen.

"Hi. I'm Clarry and this is Vanessa," I explained quickly. "I work at Abbe's restaurant in the village with Jose. He mentioned that you work here. We're in a bit of a fix and need to get out of here in a hurry but not through the main entrance. Do you think you might help us?"

He looked at us in alarm. "Have you stolen something? Or are you trying to leave the hotel without paying? Because if so, then no, I won't help you. Definitely not. I can't afford to lose my job."

"No, honestly, it's nothing like that," said Vanessa, stepping forward and lightly touching his arm.

"Really, it's all a lot of fuss about nothing. You see, we've been upstairs at my parents' cocktail party and… well, it's complicated… I changed out of my dress in the loo and wanted to escape my mother and…" She trailed off. "No, it's too difficult to explain and I'm being incredibly childish and stupid. I'm sorry. We should never have bothered you. Come on, Clarry."

"Wait." Jonian held up his hand. "It's OK. Come with me. I will take you out through one of the back doors."

"You will?" Vanessa smiled warmly at him. "Thanks so much."

"You don't look like a thief. And you…" He gestured to me. "You really are a friend of Jose's?"

"Yes," I nodded emphatically. "I'm one of his favourites. Because I have a healthy appetite, apparently."

"That sounds like Jose. Right, follow me."

The kitchen was on a massive industrial scale, making the one at Abbe's seem like it belonged in a doll's house. And everywhere was abuzz with energy. We received barely a glance as we followed Jonian around the perimeter of the work stations. With so many chefs on duty and so much going on, the scene looked chaotic, but I knew that only a highly structured and organised system could make it all come together. We were taken out through a swing door that led to another series of doors then through several twisting unpainted corridors, until finally, we arrived at a fire exit. Jonian eased open the push-bar.

"This goes out into the park. I have to get back to work now." His dark eyes took in us both, but it was Vanessa they lingered upon.

We thanked him profusely but, as we turned to leave, Vanessa called him back.

"Where are you from?"

"Albania. Have you ever visited there?"

She smiled at him. "No, but I've always wanted to."

"*Have* you?" I asked, as he left us.

CHAPTER SEVEN

I'd only ever been in Cannizaro Park at night when they used to host a music festival. The whole place would be lit up by coloured lanterns and be alive with the strains of jazz or opera. Now, it was quiet and gloomy, and we made our way in silence along the path.

"Right, here we are," I said, as we came out front. "One successful, if slightly bizarre, escape accomplished."

I looked at my watch and was surprised to find that it wasn't even ten o'clock. It felt much later but I wasn't ready to go home yet. I had a job to do. Ah! So, it looked like I would be taking the case after all.

"Fancy a drink after our adventure?"

Vanessa looked hesitant.

"It's still early," I pressed. She owed me, and this seemed a great opportunity to gain her confidence.

"I would, but it's just that I'm meeting some people."

Trying to look disappointed and expectant at the same time is no easy matter. The effect I was looking for was that of a Labrador who's been told categorically that she won't get any more treats, but still fixes you with a wistful expression in her big brown eyes. My eyes are blue, but something of my inner doggie must have communicated itself to Vanessa.

"You know what?" she said, "I think you and my friends would get along. They're over at the Hand in Hand now."

The Hand in Hand is one of two lovely old pubs that squat side by side, just a five-minute walk away from Cannizaro.

"So, you work at Abbe's?" Vanessa asked as we set off. "I've been there a few times. It's a great place."

"It's fun," I agreed. "Crazy busy some nights, but I really enjoy it."

"So is that… like… your career?" she continued.

I never like this question and so I hesitated, unwilling to explain or justify to her what must seem a shattering lack of ambition.

"Well, let's just say that I haven't really found myself yet."

Even under the semi-darkness of the street lamps, I could feel her regarding me curiously. Time to turn the spotlight on her.

"And you? What do you do?"

"At the moment, nothing. I graduated and I'm applying for jobs, but there's not much out there. And so I'm back with my parents. They've been great, and I do know how lucky I am, but it can be a bit of a strain sometimes. Mum especially. I don't always handle her well."

She shot me a rueful glance. "Like tonight. I meant what I said to Jonian about behaving childishly."

"I wouldn't worry about it. Mothers have a way of getting under our skin. I think they must all go on some kind of course: How Best to Antagonise Your Daughter."

She laughed. "He was nice, wasn't he, Jonian?" There was a pause before she added, "Did you notice how long his eyelashes are?"

46

I wondered how Diana might view an Albanian pot-washer as a rival to the eligible Charles.

"So, who's this Charles that your mother seemed annoyed that you weren't there to meet? Some kind of blind date?"

"Not exactly. We've been out a few times. He's nice but…"

"He just doesn't do it for you?"

"He's quite good-looking. But he's so straight and kind of uptight."

"Jonian was a bit uptight," I pointed out, "when he thought we were trying to rob the place."

"That was just because he was trying to protect his job," she protested, and then caught the smirk I was doing nothing to disguise.

"You have to admit," she continued, but she was smiling now, "he is pretty fit."

We reached the pub and were about to push open the door, when I looked down at my chest. "I think it's about time I lost the pearls." Shoving them into my bag, I followed her into the pub.

On most evenings you would find a handful of old gents enjoying their single malts by the open fire, one or two of whom will have a sleeping spaniel or collie at their feet, alongside lively groups of twenty- and thirty-somethings, knocking back drinks and exuding a miasma of boisterous energy, before going on to a party or a club. Tonight, being Saturday, it was particularly busy. And it was couples night out. I spotted clutches of twos and foursomes tucking into bar food at corner tables and chatting companionably.

Vanessa elbowed through the throng and introduced me to two women sitting on pews at the back of the room. Sarah, who looked to be in her early forties, had short wavy red-gold hair, a pronounced chin and intelligent hazel eyes. She was substantially built and draped, rather than dressed, in a long line skirt and layered tops of charcoal and cream linen, the kind of fabric that looks like a dishcloth five minutes after you put it on but is actually fiendishly expensive. Polly was somewhere close to thirty, with brown curly hair clipped high back from her forehead and a bright, lively face, completely bare of make-up. With her clear pale skin and long, thin nostrils, she looked like she had stepped out of a Renaissance painting. Her clothes, however, did not echo the theme. She was wearing a mid-thigh length dress of a washed-out purple cotton over black leggings, with a pair of chocolate suede ankle boots. Wound twice about her neck was a long flowery scarf in shades of cream and rust, and grazing her shoulders were dangly silver and turquoise earrings in the shape of owls. By my way of thinking, this look absolutely should not have worked. But on her, somehow, it did. Vanessa offered to get the drinks, including refills for her friends, whilst they made room for me at the table.

"Sorry to gatecrash," I offered. "I hope it's OK with you?"

"No problem." Polly's smile was welcoming. "Happy to meet you. Do you know this place?" Her gesture took in the room. "It's got a good feel to it. And I like the flowers. It's a nice touch."

She was right. The stripped pine tables each held a small china jug in which a handful of daisies lifted their upturned faces. Just then a chatter of conversation broke out loudly about us. Someone was celebrating a birthday, and from across the bar came gusty but tuneless singing.

"Yes, it's a local for me," I replied, raising my voice above the din. "Have you been having a good night?"

"Yes, but perhaps not quite as fancy as yours." The older woman, Sarah, looked me over.

"You're rather dressed up for a pub. Been somewhere interesting?"

I was just about to explain that I'd been to the Maitlands' anniversary party when Vanessa, returning with the drinks, cut across me.

"Oh, Clarry just likes to look glamorous."

I blinked. I did? Since when? So, OK then, it was clear that she didn't want these two to know about her family party. Why not? I made a mental note to find out.

I shrugged. "Well, Saturday night and all that." And then, to change the conversation, I turned to Polly. "Fabulous earrings."

"I made them," she said simply. "I make all my own jewellery."

I groaned inwardly. Of course she did.

"That's great," I said, doing my very best to look suitably impressed. "I'm completely useless with my hands. Can't even sew on a button properly, but you obviously have talent. Did you make your scarf as well?"

"I did. I'm very creative. We all are. It's just that many of us don't ever release it. For me, it's a form of self-expression."

Her eyes gleamed as she went on to tell me about the spare room she had turned into a home studio. And whilst her description of beads and baubles arranged in size and hue, of silver crimps, clasps and chain-nosed pliers, of multi-coloured threads and beading wire, left me feeling that I'd just been hurtled in a frenzy, twice around a haberdashery department, her enthusiasm for her craft was engaging. If her idea of having a good time was getting busy with a soldering iron, so be it. I found that I liked her. It was only when her weighing up of vintage trims versus contemporary fastenings had been exhausted, that I realised that Sarah and Vanessa had been talking together in low voices.

"The next meeting?" asked Vanessa. "When is it?"

"Not sure yet," replied Sarah, "but it will be the usual place and time, and Zoe says that…"

But she broke off on becoming aware that Polly's and my conversation had come to a close. What meeting were they talking about, I wondered? Was this something to do with the group Diana was so concerned about? But whilst I racked my brains as to how, without asking directly, I could find out, the conversation became general once more. At a loss for something to say to prompt them back into discussing it, I gave up and went off to buy another round of drinks.

As the evening went on, we chatted about the latest American blockbuster, a new bar Vanessa had been to in Battersea, my job at Abbe's and a guy that Polly worked with and was crushing on, which, naturally, led us on to whether it's ever a good idea to get involved with a colleague. Throughout, Sarah said the least and offered nothing in the way of personal information. And, on asking her how long she had known Vanessa and Polly, it was the latter who explained.

"Oh, I've known Sarah about a year, and then we met Vanessa quite recently."

She turned to her. "Only a couple of months ago, wasn't it?"

But before I could ask how and where they'd met, Sarah had batted the topic away. I thought now would be as good a time as any to take my leave.

"I think I'll be off home. Thanks for your company. I enjoyed it. Hope we meet up again soon. Vanessa, let's swap numbers, shall we?"

We did so, and I was just wishing Polly continued luck with her jewellery-making, when she said, "You must come and see it. Give me your number and we'll set it up." Once again, I scrabbled in my bag for my phone. "Or you can check it out at Sarah's shop. She sells them for me."

"Shop? Is it local?" I looked at Sarah. "Clothes? Accessories?"

"Not exactly." Sarah's chin seemed more pronounced than ever as she regarded me, coolly. Again, it was Polly who volunteered the information.

"It's in Teddington and it's called The Nook. It's an amazing place."

The owls bobbed and twinkled as she nodded emphatically. "You'd love it."

*

I'd had too many drinks to drive and so decided to leave the Renault at Cannizaro. I rummaged in the boot for the pair of trainers I always keep in there and changed out of my shoes. My feet were still smarting from the race down the hotel stairs. As I set off on the ten-minute walk home, it was

Sarah who dominated my thoughts. She hadn't been rude exactly, more unwelcoming. And what was this meeting that she'd said would be at the usual time and place? I was certain that I hadn't imagined her reluctance to continue discussing it when she knew I was listening in. Why was that? Well, I decided, she and that shop of hers deserved closer inspection. I'd visit it tomorrow. Sunday is always a good day for pootling about an area, and casually browsing around the shops. And, to make sure it would look convincing, I would need a companion. I knew just the woman for the job.

As I undressed and took off my make-up, I thought over the evening. Although pleased with the progress I'd made and with the plan I'd formed for the next day, reflections prompted by Vanessa's query about my lack of a career would insinuate themselves. I am usually pretty adept at avoiding introspection. What good comes of asking yourself a lot of uncomfortable questions and brooding over your failings? But sometimes, like tonight, such thoughts would come. I really enjoyed being a waitress, but was it something I wanted to do for the rest of my life? Should I be pursuing a profession? Was I lacking the confidence to make real decisions and follow them through? Or was I just too lazy? Drive and ambition seemed to have passed me by. I'd always envied some of the girls I went to school with, including my best friend, Laura, a solicitor, girls who had known that they wanted to be a vet or a doctor or an actress, from a young age. It gave them focus, and a clear course of action to follow. I didn't have that.

Stooping to pick up my dress from where I'd flung it over a chair, I hung it up in the wardrobe left to me by my grandmother. A thin slice of moonlight gleamed through a gap in the curtains and, as if with new eyes, I looked about my bedroom, taking in the duck egg blue walls, the Victorian bedstead and the gilt-framed pictures on the walls. And it soothed me. But deep down, and in a place I rarely ventured to delve into, I knew that the answer to my lack of ambition lay right here in this room, in this house, on Hillside. My father's mother, Grandma P, had not only left me her wardrobe, but she had also left me her home. This cottage, built in the mid 1800s, located just a few minutes' walk from the centre of the Village, and which my grandmother had loved deeply and been happy in, had been her special gift to me. But had it acted as a buffer against the real world? Was this why I hadn't got my act together? Because I didn't have a mortgage or rent to pay? All I had to do was cover my bills; and that made an enormous difference to what I needed to earn. It meant I hadn't really needed to forge out a place for myself. I was bloody lucky. I knew that. And spoilt, as I suppose many people might consider me. Not for the first time, I wondered if, in receiving this good fortune, I may have lost something else. A sense of purpose.

I felt low as I pushed back the duvet and crawled into bed, but as I stretched to turn out the lamp, I glanced at my mobile and realised I had a text from a number I didn't recognise. It was from Caveman.

Hi Clarry, this is Ed. You are probably either out and about this evening or working, and so I thought I'd give you a call tomorrow, if that's OK with you?

It certainly was. I drifted off to sleep in a much happier frame of mind.

CHAPTER EIGHT

The phone rang at 8.30am. On a Sunday. It could only be my mother.

"Clarry?" Diana Maitland was brisk. OK, so not *my* mother but somebody else's.

"Was that you running away with Vanessa last night?"

"Hello, Diana. Yes, it was."

"I thought so. Well, if this is how you conduct your investigations, I am not at all sure that this arrangement is going to work. Not a good beginning, I must say."

"On the contrary. It was a very good beginning."

"I don't see how," she retorted. "Careering about the hotel and deliberately aiding my daughter in running away from—"

"No, you don't see, Diana. That's why you hired me."

Silence at the end of the line.

"But," I continued, "if you've changed your mind and want to forget about the whole thing, then you only have to say so."

"No, no," came the reluctant reply. "Since, as you claim, you have started to make progress," the pause that followed was heavy with unspoken irritation, "then we will leave things as they are."

"Good." It was my turn to be brisk. "I will contact you in a few days," and I rang off.

I had just put on the kettle when the phone rang for a second time. This time it had to be my mother. I was wrong again.

"I knew you'd be a morning person," chirruped a bright and cheerful voice that took me a few moments to place.

"Polly, is that you?"

She was right, I am a morning person. And a late night person. I'm just not a mid-afternoon person. That's another reason why I'm not best suited to office work. I've found that bosses aren't very understanding when, at four o'clock, I'm found with my head on the desk happily napping, when apparently there are a lot of important duties still left to perform.

"Yes, it's me. I said I'd ring and so I thought that I would straight away because it's so easy not to, and then lose out on the chance of making a new friend. And I think friendship between women is so important, don't you?"

I did. I couldn't argue with her there. But so much effusive cordiality first thing in the morning took me a little aback.

"Absolutely," I agreed weakly. "Great to hear from you."

"I've been thinking, Clarry. About what I said… about releasing the creative urge."

I tried to recollect our conversation.

"Oh, about self-expression and all that?"

"Exactly. And I think you are a very creative person. I do. I have a feeling about it."

"No," I laughed. "Really, Polly, I'm not. But nice of you to say so."

"I mean deep down," she persisted, and I wondered if she had on the owl earrings of last night, and whether they were nodding in agreement. Who *says* owls are wise?

"Well," I admitted grudgingly, "it must be buried very deep down indeed. But either way, why was it you were thinking about that?"

"Because," she replied, "I think that you might benefit from coming to one of our special meetings."

"Special meetings?" I was on the alert now. "What kind of meetings? What's special about them?"

"Just a few of us getting together and opening up our ideas on how to draw out the creative force. We do keep them pretty private, but I think you might be an interesting addition. A balancing force. So, what do you think? Shall I phone you when I know when the next one's planned? It'll be sometime this week."

Vanessa and Sarah had been talking about a meeting. Was this what they meant? Some kind of homespun craftwork circle exchanging tips on stitching and stencilling? So much for paganism. It would probably be something along the lines of the Women's Institute, just without the jam and Jerusalem. On second thoughts, considering the nation's current baking craze, there might well be jam.

"Yes. Count me in."

We hung up and I considered how different the two phone calls had been. From Diana's frustrated irritation to Polly's good-natured enthusiasm. And all this before my first mug of tea of the day.

*

An hour later, after that mug of tea and some toast, I was again on the phone, but this time I had dialled out.

"Flan. It's me."

"Clarry. How lovely. I was going to telephone you this morning for a chat."

Flan is my honorary aunt and close confidante. Strictly speaking, it should be honorary *great*-aunt as she had been Grandma P's best friend. At seventy years old, she is elegant in a completely different way from the younger Diana Maitland. Flan exudes glamour. That timeless glamour of old movie stars, which somehow makes other women seem smaller, dimmer, slightly out of focus. She had always attracted men, and that gift had not diminished with the passing of the years. She usually has several men vying for her attention, presenting her with flowers, taking her out to dinner and… staying over. She is always utterly frank about sex. This, I admit, had been a little embarrassing when I was at that awkward self-conscious age of thirteen or so, when just the idea of grown-ups hopping in and out of bed was grotesque, but now, I simply admired her. There are times when she's seeing more action than I am.

"Are you busy today, Flan?" I asked. "Because I was wondering if you'd care to join me on a fishing expedition?"

Her laugh was knowing. "Now, as I'm quite sure that that can't possibly be a reference to angling, I can only assume that *The Love Detective* is back in business?"

She and my best friend, Laura, had coined this pseudonym for me when I had solved my first case. And it looked like it was going to stick.

"Something like that. Not that *love* seems to have anything to do with it. I'll explain all when I see you. Can you make it? I was thinking in an hour or so."

"I had said I might go out for lunch with Harold, but you know, one has to be in the right mood for Harold. And I don't believe that I am today. And besides, I am now simply agog with curiosity. And so yes, darling, I'd be delighted to accompany you."

Harold Babcock, a retired undertaker, was one of Flan's pair of ardent admirers. The other, George Huxtable, who had helped in my previous investigation, was a bit of a favourite with me, and I'd rather hoped that she had dropped Harold. But Flan likes to keep her options open. And let's face it, where men are concerned, that's probably a good policy.

*

After retrieving the Renault from the car park at Cannizaro, I nipped around to Lauriston Road to pick up Flan at just after eleven. Tall and lean, she was dressed in a long pale pink lawn shirt over cream trousers and was expertly but discreetly made-up. I was struck, as I always am, at how she didn't look anywhere near her seventy years of age. She greeted me with a hug and then gestured down at her trousers.

"You didn't say where we were going, so I wanted to be ready for anything, and that meant it had to be slacks."

"You look perfect. But then you always do. It's a very annoying trait of yours."

She took in the jeans and plain white collarless shirt I was wearing and shrugged.

"Yes, I do see how it must be maddening for you," and laughing, she got into the car.

As we drove away from the Village and through Raynes Park, I filled her in on my new investigation.

"And your plan is what precisely?" she asked, after listening attentively through to the end of my account.

"Haven't got one," I replied cheerfully, as we nosed through the traffic onto Kingston Bridge.

"So," Flan nodded gravely, "your intention is to just blunder about, ask a few questions and hope that, by kicking up the dust, something will be revealed that will be of use to you?"

"That's about the size of it," I admitted.

"Marvellous." She clapped her hands in excitement. "I couldn't have come up with anything better myself. And, as I may have mentioned before, I'm quite sure that if I'd started on the career earlier, I would have made an awfully good sleuth."

"Yes," I said dubiously. "So you say."

"I certainly would have. I have just the right combination of intelligence and daring."

She grinned rakishly. "And of course with a certain degree of irresistible charm thrown in."

"It's the world's loss," I agreed, and then braked sharply to avoid rear-ending a taxi that had slowed practically to a halt in front of me.

"Concentrate, Clarry, please. Or our careers will have ended before they've had a chance to get going. Now, this meeting that Polly phoned you about. Do you think Vanessa will be there?"

"I've no idea, but it's likely, given that she and Polly are friends, and that she and Sarah mentioned a meeting."

"Ah, Sarah," Flan said thoughtfully. "Why do I get the feeling that you don't much like her?"

"That's putting it a bit strongly. It's more that she seemed to deliberately deflect questions. But I could be wrong about that."

"So," asked Flan, "when we find her shop, are you hoping that she will, or she won't be there?"

"I haven't really thought that through. Let's just wing it."

"I can do that," said Flan happily. "Improvisation is my middle name."

We had now reached Teddington and, with Flan on the lookout for a parking space, we cruised down the High Street.

"This was always a nice area," remarked Flan, as I laboriously manoeuvred the Renault in between a Land Rover and a Mercedes.

"I used to know a chap here rather well in the old days, and we would go to a lovely pub by the river. Many a moonlight walk along the towpath we had. I wonder what happened to…" she broke off with a sigh.

"Him or the pub?" I asked, switching off the engine.

"Oh, I know what happened to *him*. Married a domineering dental nurse and moved to Wales where, no doubt, if he is still alive, she is dominating him still. No, I meant the pub."

"We can go and look for it afterwards if you like," I said, "and have lunch there. Poking about asking questions always gives me an appetite."

"What doesn't?" she asked with a sideways look and then climbed gracefully out of the car.

We found The Nook just off the High Street in a quiet road containing a restaurant and a couple of shops, but where the rest of the properties were residential. Its name had been handwritten in swirly old-fashioned script above the door, and its window display presented an eclectic miscellany of items. Books, some of which appeared to be second-hand, fanned out alongside glass jugs, decorative bowls, packets of writing paper, artificial flowers, boxes of lavender and rose soaps and a pair of oversized onyx hands bejewelled with rings and bangles of an ethnic style. I wondered if any of them were designed by Polly.

"Nothing there I'd want to buy," muttered Flan.

The tinkling of wind chimes announced our presence when we pushed open the door and entered the shop. The interior was dark after the brightness of a midday sun, but I could make out that the ceiling was low and timber-beamed. Instinctively, I ducked my head. The building must be pretty old, I thought, glancing about at the white wattled walls. A scent of something deep and resiny with a hint of flowers emanated from the gloom. It made me think of summer afternoons in the garden at home when, as a child, I'd have my milk sitting at an ancient wooden latticed table that Dad must have thrown out years ago. Funny how a smell can instantly conjure up forgotten memories, and with a pang, I remembered that I hadn't spoken to my parents for over a week. I'd call them tonight, I decided.

A woman, who wasn't Sarah, appeared from behind a counter and greeted us warmly in a strong West Country accent.

"Welcome Be. Feel free to have a good look around."

I exchanged a quick look with Flan. *Welcome Be?* Was this a West Country thing or had we just stepped back through the centuries to Ye Olde England? Reassured by the sight of a calculator and a mobile phone on the counter, I relinquished the time machine theory and put it down to a linguistic quirk.

"It never does anyone any good to rush on a Sunday," the woman said, "and so, please do take your time."

I guessed her to be in her late sixties. She had a broad, gently smiling face and long pepper-and-salt hair dressed in plaits. In her long crinkly cotton skirt of a deep wine colour, knitted waistcoat and sturdy sandals, she looked like she had once, at the music festivals of the nineteen sixties, danced with her arms raised to the sky in joy and sheer abandon.

Flan gestured about her.

"What a treasure trove. Where should I start? All that clunky jewellery…" she said, pointing at the onyx hands in the window

"…is not for me, I'm afraid, but I do like a notelet. So useful for thank-you cards. I expect you have some?"

"We do," replied the woman. "Let me show you the selection we have."

She ushered Flan over to a table stacked with boxes of illustrated cards and velum stationery. She then turned to me. "Is there something that you are particularly interested in?"

I looked about me. "I'm just happy to browse."

On a stand near the window, I spotted sets of dangly earrings in the shape of butterflies, worked in silver filigree with turquoise beading, which I felt sure had to be Polly's. I walked over and pretended to examine them. Should I mention that I knew the designer? I picked up a long chain, its owl pendant blinking up at me, which confirmed my guess. Setting it back down, I continued to look around.

Arranged on one broad shelf was an assortment of figurines, all of them representing fairies. I took an instant dislike to them. In watery pastel shades, with long garlanded hair, the fairies, with names like *Serafina* and *Delphinium*, displayed their gossamer wings and teeny-tiny elfin ears, whilst kneeling gracefully in the open petals of a flower or with slender arms wrapped about the trunk of a tree. There was a particularly nauseating tableau depicting three of the little freaks entwined in each other's arms, called *Fairy Friends*. Who buys these things? I wondered, pulling my gaze away from that of a vaguely sinister-looking character in a woodland princess get-up. She had a pointed chin, a sickly smile and she'd been given the name, quite mistakenly in my opinion, of *Serenity*.

I moved across to a display of candles, oil burners and incense sticks, wondering what on earth Flan and I were doing here. I presumed that the woman with the plaits worked for Sarah. Should I tell her that I had met her boss, and try and pump her for information? I was about to bring up the subject when I realised that her attention was no longer on me but was focused back upon Flan.

"You are a very beautiful woman," she remarked, as Flan idly inspected a packet of cards depicting a chocolate-box image of a rustic farmyard scene complete with ducks, geese and frolicking lambs.

"If you don't mind my saying so, that is?"

Flan put down the cards and beamed at her. "How could I? Thank you."

"And what age would you be?"

"I'm seventy," replied Flan easily.

Another thing I admired in Flan. She was always up front about how old she was. "Why ever not, darling?" she would say. "It's tiresome and ultimately fruitless to pretend to be anything other than the age one is. The trick is, to make friends with the changes that the years bring. Grace in acceptance is the way forward."

I hoped that in this, as she was about so many things, she'd prove to be right when my turn came around.

"You have been blessed," said the woman simply. "Have you used the gift wisely?"

Flan pursed her lips gravely, giving this extraordinary question her full consideration, and then after a pause answered. "If you mean, have I been aware of the power that it sometimes gave me, and did I exert it kindly? Then no, probably not. Particularly when I was young."

She broke off and shook her head slightly, as if to dispel the vision of her former self bestowing her beauty as a benevolence that she could proffer or withdraw as she chose.

"And now I enjoy the little that remains, causing harm to no one."

The woman nodded and intoned, "An' it harm none do as yee will."

And then she turned to me. Her eyes, of a deep blue, gleamed brightly through the shadowy dimness of the room, and I had the distinct feeling that she was about to ask me some awkward uncomfortable question too, when my mobile rang. I fished it out of my bag and, gesturing to Flan, stepped gratefully out of the shop and pressed Receive.

"Clarry?" came a male voice down the line. "It's Ed. Are you OK to talk for a minute?"

"Hi, and yes, now's fine."

"Great. Well, I was wondering if you'd like to get together? For a drink, or something? If you're free sometime?"

I smiled into the phone, not saying anything.

"Whenever suits you," he added.

He had hit just the right note. Not too cocky. None of that arrogance of tone that a lot of guys adopt, implying that of course one would accept straight away, because any woman must be grateful to be asked out by him. Nor too hesitant. Nothing apologetic. Just a straightforward invitation.

"Yes," I said, moving absentmindedly away from The Nook and down towards the corner of the High Street. "That would be nice."

"Great," he said again. "How are you fixed this week? Or…" and then paused, before asking, "I don't suppose that you are free tonight, are you?"

I thought quickly, as I paced up and down outside a French bistro. The Rules of Dating say never accept an invitation made on the same day. It makes you come across as too eager, suggesting that you have a diary as empty as the streets of a ghost town in one of those old Westerns, where tumbleweed blows and twists through the dead leaves, and the swing doors of the abandoned saloon eerily creak backwards and forwards in the echoing silence. You are supposed to imply that you are a social butterfly, flitting from one interesting event to another, and that if a man wants to catch you with a free evening, he must book well in advance. The perceived wisdom is that the harder he has to work, the more he values the prize. That's you. A good strategy, but the problem here was that I didn't know what shifts I would be doing at Abbe's in the coming week, and I wanted to be free to go to the meeting with Polly whenever it turned out to be.

"Actually, I could do tonight," I said, because rules are meant to be broken sometimes.

We agreed on a time and a place and rang off. Then, suppressing a flash of excitement, I turned and retraced my steps back to the shop to find Flan handing over some cash and accepting in return three boxes of notelets from the woman with the plaits.

"Ah, there you are," said Flan, taking me by the arm. "Time we were going, I think."

"But," I protested, "I wanted to—"

"You've lost track of the time, my dear," insisted Flan, steering me gently but firmly towards the door. "Don't forget our lunch reservation."

She called back over her shoulder, "Thank you so very much, Shelia, for your help, and for the interesting discussion. Goodbye. I'll be seeing you."

The woman nodded and there was something enigmatic in her smile that made me think fleetingly of the fairy figurines. She lifted a hand in farewell. "Merry part and merry meet again."

CHAPTER NINE

"What on earth was all that *Merry Meet Again* business?"

I asked, as the door closed behind us with a trill of wind chimes.

"We don't have a lunch reservation, so why did you rush me? I wanted to ask her a few questions. And how did you get on to first-name terms with that lady? That's quick work even for you."

Flan, who had been ignoring my questions as we headed towards the High Street, stopped walking and turned to face me.

"What does Sarah look like?"

"Biggish," I replied. "Short red-gold hair. Mid-forties."

"Ah."

"Why? Did you meet her?"

"I saw someone fitting that description, wearing a singularly unflattering kaftan-style affair in navy blue linen. She'd have looked so much better in something tailored. If you get the opportunity, *do* tell her that, Clarry. You'd be doing her a favour. She'd thank you for it."

"I very much doubt that," I said. "So, what happened?"

"She was acting most suspiciously," said Flan, as she resumed walking.

I stared after her and then hastily caught her up.

"What do you mean, *suspiciously*? What was she doing?"

"Furtive and suspicious, that's how best to describe it."

"Describe what?" I demanded, as we reached the car.

Flan's look was arch. "I'm hungry. Let's have lunch and I'll tell you all about it."

*

The pub was still there, and although it had been extensively refurbished and gentrified, it retained, according to Flan, its atmosphere of old-world nautical charm. We sat in its pleasant garden overlooking the lock, on benches made of old ship planks stencilled with anchors. In white wooden tubs scarlet geraniums stood stiffly to attention.

A man at the tiller of a narrow boat, whose weathered paintwork depicted garlands of faded roses along its flanks and up and over its hatches, sketched us a wave, and we waved back as it ploughed its ponderous progress upstream.

"I think I'll have the garlic prawns," said Flan, having considered the menu.

"Me too. And a glass of white wine. Great. No, you stay here; we have to order at the bar. And put that away, it's on me."

"Thank you, darling. I'll be sure to send you my written thanks on one of these notelets." She gestured to the three packs she had just bought. "Hideous, aren't they? I can't wait to inflict them upon all my friends."

Inside, I was just about to request the prawns for two when I remembered my date with Ed and selected a chicken sandwich instead. Garlic-fish breath was not what I needed tonight.

As I carried the drinks back through to the garden, Flan called to me.

"I've just been reminiscing about Philip, darling. Such a sweetie. But it would never have worked out between us, long-term. He wasn't a sensual man. Sexual but not sensual. An important distinction, wouldn't you agree?"

I would. But judging from the raised eyebrows and curious expressions on the faces of the other diners at nearby tables, I wasn't sure everyone else did. Flan has a voice that carries.

"Just as well he married that dental nurse then," I said, sliding onto the bench. "Nothing very sensual about a lady with a plaque scraper. Now, tell me about Sarah."

"Well," said Flan, "I was over by the window looking at some placemats with Sheila, when… *she,* by the way, is a very pleasant woman, if somewhat unusual in her conversational habits. She said some highly—"

"Hold that thought for now, Flan. Get back to Sarah."

"Rightio. The woman, Sarah, came in, called out a casual greeting to Sheila, and was just moving behind the counter when she caught the strap of her handbag on something. One of those large bucket-shaped bags. A black one. And all this money fell out."

"So? Maybe her purse wasn't shut properly. What's so suspicious about that?"

"Clarry, it was a lot of money. Wads and wads of notes." She took a thoughtful sip of her wine before continuing.

"She tried to shield her hasty shovelling of it all back into her bag, behind that hideous kaftan. Furtive, you see? As I said. Then she went behind the counter and disappeared behind a curtain of a particularly violent shade of purple. Not a colour I have ever cared for. Makes me think of the robes of Roman emperors. And bishops. Or is it Monsignors?"

"I don't care if it's the Pope, Flan. What happened next?"

Flan eyed me.

"Patience, Clarry, was never your strong suit. I therefore suggest that you attempt to familiarise yourself with its art if you are to succeed in this new line of work."

"I'll get right on it," I said and grinned across at her.

There was never any point trying to rush Flan. I knew that. And why should I try? It was a beautiful day and we were looking out over a tranquil river. I was on a case that looked promising and I had a date tonight. What more could I want?

"All right. I give in. Tell it to me in your own way."

"Very wise of you." Flan's eyes gleamed with humour and intelligence. "And it looks like now is your opportunity to develop a little patience," she replied with a laugh, "because here comes our lunch."

And so, it was only when we were settled with our plates and had batted away the offers of more lemon, bread and drinks, that she continued.

"The answer to your question is that nothing happened next. But what was she doing with all that money? That's the real question."

"Hmm," I thought for a moment. "Probably just the takings from the shop. She was going to the bank, maybe?"

"She was coming *into* the shop, not going out. And do you really think that The Nook does that much business? And in cash?"

She had a point. "How about staff wages?"

"In cash?" she repeated. "That much?"

"Maybe Sarah doesn't work there herself, and so she would need at least a couple of people—"

"Aha," broke in Flan with a triumphant laugh. "That's where you're wrong. Sarah does three days a week at the shop." She blotted her lips with her napkin. "Sheila, as I said, whilst having some conversational eccentricities, which frankly, darling, I couldn't make head nor tail of, and a somewhat direct approach in the way of addressing strangers, was nevertheless quite open when casually questioned about her role at the shop. She's worked there ever since it opened three years ago and is the only other member of staff."

She set down her cutlery. "That's what I found out. I think I did rather well, don't you?"

CHAPTER TEN

I hadn't overthought my outfit and so in jeans, heels, and strappy white top, I felt comfortable and relaxed, or as relaxed as anyone can feel on a first date. I arrived, deliberately ten minutes late, at the Old Frizzle, a lively, well-run and friendly place on Wimbledon Broadway.

Ed was standing at the bar. As he moved towards me, I mistakenly thought he was leaning in to give me a kiss on the cheek, and there was an awkward moment when we both lurched hesitantly from side to side before settling on a clumsy handshake.

He laughed. "Nice to see you, Clarry. Shall I get us a bottle of wine?"

His gaze scanned the room.

"Look, there's a couple just leaving. Why don't you grab the table? White or red?"

"Happy with either," I said and scooted off to secure the table.

It had flashed through my mind earlier in the day that when I saw Ed again, I might not find him attractive. That can happen sometimes. You meet a guy, think he's cute and agree to meet for a drink. You dress up. You're excited. You get to the bar and... ah... there he is. There must be some mistake, you think. This can't be the same man. How could I have missed those enormous ears and unnaturally prominent Adam's apple? Ed, thankfully, was just as I'd remembered him.

"Thanks for coming," he said, as he poured the wine. "And great that you happened to be free tonight."

Does he think I'm overeager? I wondered. About to tell him that I didn't know what shifts I would be doing in the coming week, I remembered the maxim that Flan always applied in her dealings with men: *There is never a need to justify oneself. Just be who you are.* And as it always seemed to work for her, I merely smiled and asked him about his day.

"I was working this morning," he said. "My job means that I often end up working over at least part of the weekend. Although I do my best to keep Saturday afternoons free."

"Why's that?"

"Rugby." He nodded. "Yeah. Bit of a passion of mine. Strictly amateur. But you saw my teammates and so you probably guessed that."

"I saw a considerable amount more of them than I'd bargained for."

"Yes. Sorry about that." His smile was rueful. "Got a bit out of hand. Nearly always does, actually."

"I'm trying hard to obliterate it from my memory," I said, and took a sip of my wine. "So, what is it that you do?"

"I'm a garden designer," he said, placing his glass back down on the table, "which is really just a fancy way of saying I'm a gardener. I started my own business four years ago. It was a complete change of career for me, but it was something I had always been really interested in. Until finally, I took the plunge and decided to take my hobby and turn it into a business."

"Good for you. That's brave."

He shrugged. "It's not been an easy ride. And I've made a lot of mistakes. But it pays the bills and I am doing something that I love."

"Another passion?"

"Something like that. But what about you? All I know is that you're a supremely competent waitress, able to disarm a bunch of drunken hooligans with a firm hand and a sense of humour. Not something one sees every day. Is this your chosen career or are you paying your way through studying, or something?"

His tone was one of genuine interest and I liked the way that he hadn't shown off about his own job, but I did wish that people would stop asking me this question. At least until I've got a decent answer worked out.

Ed must have sensed my hesitation because he touched me lightly on the arm. His hands were big and square, with short, clean nails. Keeping them clean couldn't be easy, I thought, because in his business, rooting about in dirt and mud must come with the territory. I looked down into my glass.

"I really enjoy my job at Abbe's, but lately I've taken a bit of a trip into the unknown, and I'm not sure how it's going to work out. Or whether or not I'm cut out for it. Sorry. It's complicated, and quite a long story."

He smiled, and I remembered how much I had liked the way his brown eyes crinkled up at the edges. He had a wide face, lightly tanned and with a nose that looked like it had been broken and reset more than once. Not handsome but pleasing in a quiet way.

"Have another glass of wine and tell me. I'm a pretty good listener."

And he was. I gave him the edited highlights of my first investigation, and watched his expression change from one of surprise, to amusement and then to concern. Throughout, he gave me his complete attention, and for a moment I was reminded of Jason from the restaurant. But in Jason, it was merely the tactic of an accomplished pursuer, designed to conquer and seduce. Jason had game. Did Ed? Too early to tell.

"Wow," he said, sitting back. "That puts my worries about planting plans and water features well and truly in the shade. That's a gardening pun, by the way."

As the bar filled up around us, we swapped stories about our jobs, discovered tastes that we had in common, and mapped out places in the local area where our lives could have overlapped. An easy, amusing, light-hearted conversation. Typical of a date. Of a date that's going well. He didn't flirt or pay me compliments, but I felt from the way that his eyes would search my face when he thought I wasn't looking, that he liked me. And I liked him. He was growing on me more and more.

"Are you hungry?" he asked, looking at his watch. "It's after ten. Could you eat something?"

"I can always eat something."

"Great. The food is very good here or we could move on to somewhere else, if you'd rather."

"I'm happy to stay here. The atmosphere's great and the…" I broke off as my mobile rang.

"I'll ignore it," I said. "It won't be anything important. I should have put it on silent."

But a minute later, it rang again.

"I'm sorry. Do you mind if I take it?"

I fished the phone out of my bag and saw that it was Ian from Abbe's. I pressed Receive.

"What's up, babes? Not a great time to talk. I'm just…"

Ian's light falsetto voice came out in a rush.

"Listen, love, you need to get yourself over here. Pronto. Dave's getting tetchy. You know how he doesn't like drunks. Says she's beginning to disturb the other customers. She's been asking for you. Keeps swaying about. Knocked a bottle of wine off the table, and you can guess who had to clean that up, can't you? Yes, little old me. So I thought, since she's a friend of yours, you could come and—"

I cut across him. "Who? What friend? Who do you mean?"

"Young girl. Regrettable hairstyle. Vanessa something."

I blinked in surprise. Vanessa Maitland. Why was she looking for me? And if she wanted to contact me, she had my number. Why go to Abbe's?

"So, love, are you coming or not? I've got a nightmare couple on table six. First, they complained about the crab cakes, then they sent back their steaks, saying they were too tough. I had to beg Chef, who's been in a bit of a mood all night, not to tenderise them by stomping on them. God knows what they'll make of the brulee. So, make it quick, there's a dear."

And he rang off.

"Problem?" Ed was regarding me curiously.

I opened my hands in an impotent gesture. "I am going to have to take a rain check on that meal. I'm so sorry, but I've got to go. A friend, well, she's not actually a friend but more of a… oh, it's hard to explain. I'm supposed to be investigating this girl and she…"

"Ah." He looked disappointed. "One of your cases?"

"Exactly. She's turned up drunk at the restaurant, asking for me. And the manager is getting pissed off, and Chef is having a tantrum. I really need to sort it out."

He regarded me steadily. "This isn't an elaborate excuse to cut short our date?"

I laughed. "No, nothing like that, I promise."

"Right then. Why don't I come with you? For moral support. If you don't think I'd be in the way?"

We picked up a taxi almost instantly and, within ten minutes of Ian's call, we were pushing open the door to Abbe's. Dave waved a finger at me across the bar, and I mouthed "Sorry" as we skirted the front tables to the service station, where I could see Ian stacking coffee cups on a tray.

"Oh, 'ello," said Ian, eyeing Ed's big shoulders and sturdy frame appreciatively. "Who's your friend, Clarry?"

"Ian, this is Ed. Ed, this is Ian."

Ed stuck out his hand, but Ian tapped it away.

"Call me Iris, Sweets. Everybody does. Right, Clarry, she's on table twelve and getting maudlin. Tears next, I shouldn't wonder."

Vanessa was on a corner table with a bowl of pasta in front of her. It didn't look like she had eaten much. A couple of prawns had fallen onto the tablecloth, and a basket of bread appeared to be untouched.

"Hi, Vanessa," I said, approaching her. "What's happening? Is everything OK? You look a bit…"

I had to stop myself from saying *wrecked*. Her gaze was bleary and her mascara was smudged under one eye. She had clearly knocked back a bucketload.

"Oh hi, Clarry." Her voice was slurred as she blinked up at us. "Fancy seeing you here."

"I work here," I said, trying to keep a note of impatience from creeping into my voice. "You know that. And apparently, you've been asking for me."

She ignored that. "Who are you?" she demanded of Ed, who stood a little behind me.

"I'm a friend of Clarry's," he said, stepping forward. "And I think maybe we should help you find a taxi to take you home." He glanced at me for approval and I nodded.

"What do you think?" His voice was gentle and coaxing. "Good idea?"

Vanessa appeared to consider the question for a moment and then retorted loudly and very distinctly: "I am *not* going home with you." Heads turned at the other tables as she said, sounding remarkably like her mother, "I don't *know* you."

I waved frantically at Ian to bring her bill, as Ed tried to explain that that was not what he meant at all. Vanessa put up her hand dismissively as if trying to wave him away.

"All prepared." Ian skipped lightly up to the table, fanning himself with the bill.

"OK, Vanessa," I cajoled, "you need to settle up now."

She looked up at the three of us standing over her and gazed helplessly about her. I could see tears forming in her eyes. My impatience with her changed swiftly to pity.

"All right," I said gently, "where's your bag?"

Unsteadily, she twisted around to retrieve it from the back of her chair and, after what seemed an endless time rummaging in her backpack, produced a purse, from which she extracted some notes and thrust them at Ian.

"Keep the change," she said, in another unconvincing attempt at hauteur, as she stumbled to her feet.

"Thank you," he said, in a show of mock deference. "All of a pound. However will I treat myself?"

As we escorted her to the door, he couldn't resist flapping his hands in the parody of an air flight attendant, and calling in a sing-song voice, "For immediate evacuation, there are emergency exits through the back of the kitchen and out through the lavatory window. Please make your way in an orderly fashion. We thank you for dining with us. We always remember that you have a choice."

I glared at him and was rewarded with a knowing wink at Ed's retreating back.

Again, we were lucky and flagged down a cab almost straight away.

"Where to?" asked the driver, as we ushered Vanessa inside.

I nearly gave the Maitlands' address but remembered just in time that I wasn't supposed to know it. I turned to her.

"He wants to know where to take you."

She didn't reply but just looked moodily out of the window.

I eyed the meter ticking.

"Vanessa?"

She flopped disconsolately back in the seat and then stared at me, looking much younger than her twenty-one years.

"I don't want go home." Her voice was plaintive. "They don't understand me there."

"My wife doesn't understand me either, love," called the driver. "But I still have to go home to her. And I'd like to get back there sometime before midnight. So, make up your mind, will you?"

She shook her head stubbornly and then her eyes fixed on me.

"I know, I'll come and stay with you."

"No!" I squeaked in alarm. "No, not a great idea. I only have a small…"

But I didn't get any further. Vanessa had turned to the driver saying, "Good, that's settled. Take me to wherever she's going."

I turned helplessly to Ed, who had been patiently waiting by my side and was trying to choke down a laugh.

"You should see your face," he whispered, and then clambered up into the taxi. "Come on. I'll see you both safe in the door."

*

Getting her up the stairs was not an easy job, but finally we managed to settle her into my small guest room. I lent her a T-shirt to sleep in and left her to get undressed, whilst I said goodbye to Ed.

"Sorry about all this. What a night," I said, leaning against the front door and facing him as he stood on the step. "And thank you for being so… well… good about everything," I finished lamely.

"I enjoyed it," he said and then, on seeing my expression, "no, honestly, I did."

He looked down at his feet and then back at me. And for a moment, I wondered if he was going to kiss me. Then felt a flicker of disappointment when he didn't.

"So, goodnight then," he said, and there was another pause whilst I waited for him to say something about seeing me again and rearranging the dinner that we'd missed, but he said nothing.

"Goodnight," I said, eventually. "Thanks again for the drinks."

He turned, walked down the path and was through the gate, before looking back over his shoulder and calling, "Good luck with the case."

Great, Clarry. Just great, I thought, as I locked up and filled up a pint glass of water to bring up to Vanessa. How to blow a date and scare off a nice guy in one easy lesson. Expose him to the hapless, stumbling attempts of my amateur sleuthing. Job well done.

I made my way upstairs and knocked softly on the door of the spare room. No answer. I knocked again and then poked my head around the doorjamb. Vanessa was spark out and snoring. She'd only managed to get half undressed. I could see that she was wearing my T-shirt, but one jean-clad leg stuck out from under the duvet. Well, at least that was something, I thought, as I placed the water on the bedside table. She'd be safe until the morning. I'd deal with her then.

My relief was short-lived. On going into the bathroom to take off my make-up, I found that not only had Vanessa used my toothbrush and dumped my towels into the bath, but she had been copiously sick all over the floor.

CHAPTER ELEVEN

The air smelt sweet and full of the promise of summer as I sat in the garden the next morning, drinking a steaming mug of tea. My garden is small but sheltered and had been lovingly tended by Grandma P. It was crammed with cottage-style plants which, luckily for me, mostly looked after themselves. Sitting at the old stone table, I could see the white bells of a cluster of lily of the valley peeping out between a clutch of yellow tulips. Spires of hollyhocks nodded their double pompoms gracefully in the light breeze and I wondered what Ed would make of my garden. Then, firmly, I steered my thoughts away from him, vowing instead to sweep away the dead leaves from the path and root out any stray weeds.

It had taken me nearly an hour the previous night to clean and disinfect the bathroom, but when I had finally crawled into bed, tired and swollen with indignation, I found that I couldn't sleep. I had watched the hands on the clock tick by until nearly three, when I had fallen into a fitful doze. When I awoke, after eight o'clock, I had expected to feel groggy and heavy-limbed, but my frustrations of the previous evening appeared to have magically dispersed with the dawn. I felt clear-headed and ready to face whatever the day had to bring.

There'd been no sound coming from the guest room as, in PJs, I'd made my way downstairs. I'd wondered if Vanessa had let herself out during the night, but the safety chain was still on the front door, as I had left it.

I took another long look around the garden before realising I was starving. I'd had nothing to eat since the chicken sandwich at the pub yesterday lunchtime, and that felt a very long time ago.

I'd put some tomatoes to roast in the oven and was cracking eggs into a bowl, when the door pushed slowly open and Vanessa appeared, looking white-faced and peaky.

"Morning," I said neutrally. "Tea or coffee?"

"No, it's OK, thanks. I don't want anything. I just…" She broke off and bit her lip before continuing "…wanted to say thanks for putting me up. I don't remember a whole lot, but my head is really throbbing. I guess I had a bit too much to drink last night."

Now there's an understatement, I thought but said merely, "Sit down. You need fluids. I'm having tea. OK for you?"

She nodded gratefully and took a seat at the table. I didn't speak as I passed a mug and the sugar bowl to her, but continued with the preparing of scrambled eggs, putting slices of toast under the grill and laying the table for two. When all was ready, I set down her plate and then took a seat opposite her.

"Eat," I said, grating some black pepper over my eggs. "You'll feel better."

Vanessa hesitated a moment and then picked up her knife and fork. When you're hungry, there's nothing better than simple food. I concentrated on enjoying my breakfast and trying to think of how to get her to confide in me about the unsuitable friends that worried Diana so much. That was what I was being paid for, and this opportunity to get her to open up, unexpected and unwanted as it had decidedly been, had fallen into my lap and so I might as well make the most of it. I was on my second slice of toast when I thought it time to break the silence.

"So, what was all that about last night?"

She put down her mug, looking guarded but didn't answer. Some colour had returned to her face and she was looking more human.

"You were in a pretty bad way, you know," I pressed. "Had something upset you?"

Still no answer. And the look she shot me was surly and heavy with resentment. I felt a prickling of irritation. Here she was, in my kitchen, eating the breakfast I'd prepared for her and I was getting the silent treatment. What was she? Twelve years old?

"Well, unless getting roaring drunk and making an arse of yourself in public is usual for you," I persisted, "then it must have been something."

She flushed and pushed away her plate.

"I don't need to account for myself to you."

"No, you don't," I said, fighting to keep my temper, "And I didn't need to look after you last night. But I did."

Her eyes flashed mutinously and I was again reminded of her mother. Whilst I didn't like Diana, I couldn't help but feel a flash of sympathy for her if this was the crap she had to put up with.

"I didn't *ask* you to." Vanessa's voice was challenging.

"No, but the manager of the restaurant did."

That threw her. A struggle between shame and defiance played across her face. Defiance won.

"If you expect me to be grateful, then you can think again!"

That was when I snapped. Sod getting her to open up. And sod the case. Let Diana deal with her own brat of a daughter. I didn't need the money that much.

"Well, fuck you." I flared up at her. "First, you interrupt my date. A date that was going perfectly well, until I had to come and rescue you from being thrown out of the restaurant; and now, chances are, because of *you*, I'll never hear from him again. Then, I had to put you in a cab, which *I* paid for…" I was really warming to my theme now "…because you refused to go home and insisted that I brought you back here. And then… *then*… you were sick all over my bathroom!"

I got up from the table and stomped over to the kettle.

"And so, yes, I bloody do expect you to be, if not grateful, then at least fucking polite."

At this last thrust, Vanessa, whose face throughout my tirade had coloured to crimson and then back to chalky white, looked stricken. There was a long silence and her voice, when she finally spoke, sounded small and cracked.

"I'm sorry."

"About which bit in particular?" I asked, standing with my back to the sink and looking across at her.

"All of it. Especially the sick." She wouldn't meet my eye. "And your date. Oh, yes. I remember him now. Big." And then, she offered hesitantly, "He seemed nice."

"He is," I answered glumly.

"Don't you think you'll see him again?"

"Doesn't look like it." I poured boiling water into fresh mugs. "Oh, well," I shrugged. "I guess some things just aren't meant to be."

"So, you believe in fate?" she asked.

I paused, milk carton in hand. "No. Actually, I'm not sure I do. I think most of us are attracted by the idea as an attempt to make ourselves feel better about the lack of control we have over our lives. There are so many things that we can't do anything about, everything from the state of the economy to cancer, that it's a comfort to believe that there is some Divine Order making sense of things, and ultimately working in our favour. Personally, I don't think there is. We're not that important."

Vanessa looked thoughtful. "That's a pretty bleak view. And a lonely one. As you said, where's the comfort in it?"

Comfort? Was that what she was looking for? At twenty-one years of age? Why? Stop, I told myself. It's way too early to be grappling with such philosophical questions. I sat back down at the table.

"Right. Spill. What happened last night?"

And so, the story came out. After her escape from the party, she had, last night, got into a huge row with her mother. Diana had apparently been very scathing, not only about Vanessa sloping off, and, as she saw it, disrespecting her parents' anniversary, but also her ungraciousness in not staying long enough to meet Charles. The scene had ended with Vanessa storming out of the house. She'd walked through the village and gone into the Dog & Fox, thinking that maybe she'd bump into someone she knew. She'd had a couple of shots and had then ordered a bottle of wine, phoning several of her friends in the hope that they would come and join her, but everyone was busy.

"I felt very alone," she said. "I finished all of the wine. I think. Maybe, I had another glass or two after that, but I'm not sure. A couple of guys came and tried to talk to me but after a while they went away. And then, I remember coming out of the pub, and I saw Abbe's across the street. You'd told me that you work there and I thought that I might…"

"Might what?" I asked.

"I don't know really. I think I just needed someone to talk to…" She trailed off.

Now is the time, I thought, when her defences are well and truly down, to probe a little. A chance to put out feelers and try and discover something about her pagan chums.

"Do you have anyone you feel close to?" I asked. "Is there a special mate or a group of friends that you—?"

I was going to say *confide in* but she cut across me.

"Trust? That's a good question."

Some emotion crossed her face that I couldn't read but, whatever it was, it propelled her into action, and she stood up abruptly.

"And one I don't know the answer to." She slung her backpack over her shoulder. "I'll be off now. Thanks for everything, Clarry. It's weird but I have a feeling that I can trust you. I don't know why, but I do."

But she couldn't, could she? I thought, because I was being paid to get to know her. I was being paid to win her confidence. And, it was only after I had showered, dressed, cleared away the breakfast things, phoned my parents and received a call from Polly inviting me to a Special Meeting the following evening, that I recognised that the uncomfortable feeling I'd been experiencing ever since Vanessa had left, was one of guilt.

CHAPTER TWELVE

I pulled up at seven o'clock the following evening outside a large detached Edwardian house in a quiet residential Wandsworth street. Polly was standing with her back to the gate, having arranged to meet me outside so that we could go into the meeting together. Tonight she was wearing a sprigged cotton dress with her legs bare and her feet in the chocolate suede ankle boots I had seen her in before. Over her shoulder hung a bag made out of a patchwork of flowered prints. Long chains of silver set with egg-shaped stones in a rather ugly shade of salmon wound about her neck and wrists and made a faint jingling sound as we walked up the front path to the house.

"So glad you are here, Clarry." She seemed animated and a bit over-excited. "I really hope that you enjoy the session." She pressed the doorbell and then added with a nervous laugh, "I probably should have asked Zoe if I could invite you but I'm sure, at least I hope that…"

I was never to know what she hoped for, because she broke off as the front door opened to reveal the tall figure of a woman that I guessed to be in her late fifties, wearing a shapeless denim skirt and pale blue blouse, with a pair of steel-framed specs hanging from a chain across a flat bosom.

Her greying hair was dead straight and had been pulled back from her face in an elaborate diamanté clip, an incongruous touch at odds with her workaday outfit. She greeted Polly warmly and then stopped as she took in the presence of a stranger. I stuck out my hand.

"I'm Clarry and I hope it's all right that I'm here? Polly invited me."

The woman looked at me keenly through eyes that were of a deep sea green, very clear and surprisingly lovely in her narrow face.

"Unexpected you may be, but nevertheless you are welcome. My name is Helen, and this is my home. Come this way."

We followed her into a wide hall where flowering pot plants sat in rows along a window ledge and a couple of ancient rain macs and a long knitted scarf were draped over an old-fashioned hat stand. The walls were hung with an array of frameless canvasses in a variety of sizes. Each one was a portrait, and I felt under the scrutiny of at least a dozen pairs of eyes as Helen ushered us into a spacious airy sitting room. Here there were more paintings. Lots of them and all portraits. Several of a man with rust-coloured hair receding from a well-formed face, and whose gaze was both searching and introspective. And half a dozen of a woman with dark auburn hair, fine bones and beautiful sea green eyes. The likeness between her and the red-haired man was unmistakable. It took me a moment to recognise, in the portraits of the woman, earlier incarnations of my hostess, Helen. Self-portraits, I wondered?

The walls, where visible in the spaces between the canvasses, were decorated in a faded cornflower blue. A squat chintz sofa and armchair, heaped with cushions in soft pinks and apricots, looked lived-in and comfortable. The French doors at the far end of the room were open to the evening air, and it was through these that Helen led us. We crossed a curving stretch of lawn and entered, at the far end of the garden, into a low one-storey structure with huge sliding glazed doors, that revealed itself to be an artist's studio. Canvasses were stacked three deep against the walls, revealing glimpses of a disembodied nose, eye or ear. A pair of easels was set up facing out into the garden. Tubes of paint and brushes, of varying sizes and thicknesses, stuck out of old jam jars grouped haphazardly on a broad shelf that ran along the flank wall. There was a square china sink in one corner and on a table stood a kettle, a collection of mugs and glasses and three bottles of red wine. Sitting talking around an oblong trestle table were a group of six women, amongst whom I recognised Vanessa, Sarah and Sheila, the lady with the plaits from The Nook. I waved at Vanessa, who looked surprised but not unhappy to see me.

At first glance, the table appeared to be littered with miscellaneous rubbish: a jumble of odd bits of material, hanks of wool, skeins of thread, twists of ribbon, wooden clothes pegs, sketchbooks and hand-painted plates, until I realised that there was an order to the clutter and that each woman had her own individual collection in front of her. Vanessa, I noticed, kept a protective hand over a thick notebook bound in red leather.

"This is Clarry, a friend of Polly's," Helen introduced me. "And also, I see, of Vanessa's."

There were smiles and hellos and mutterings of *Welcome Be*. I'd heard that phrase before and turned to look over at Sheila only to find her placidly regarding me, a look of benign approval on her face. The nod of acknowledgement I received from Sarah, however, was anything but benign. No *Welcome Be* from her. Dressed, once again, in a layered affair of crumpled linen, her hazel eyes were shrewd and assessing.

"Hello," said a slim girl in a yellow T-shirt, with bouncy brown curls and a nose ring. "Nice to have a new face. I'm Jo-Jo. I handprint fabric using vintage wooden blocks and then make tablecloths and cushion covers."

She pointed down to a calico bag with a drawstring top decorated with a blue lozenge design.

"And laundry bags. I've got a stall at Merton Abbey Mills."

She smiled and there was a flash of a tongue stud. "What are you working on?"

Resisting the urge to say my next pay cheque, I noticed that Polly had opened her patchwork bag and was unwrapping a tumble of bracelets. I wondered briefly what I could offer from my own handbag but decided that a lipstick, a tampon and some small change weren't going to cut it.

"Oh, I'm just here to find some inspiration," I said. Which was true in a way.

I turned to a tall angular woman wearing ropes of chunky amber beads sitting on my left. She was somewhere in her forties with long ash-grey hair, sallow skin and a beaky nose. She wasn't chatting with the others but appeared absorbed in her own thoughts.

"Hi," I said. "Sorry, I didn't catch your name."

"I'm Elaine." Her voice was low and sonorous. "I write." She turned a baleful stare at me as if, somehow, I was responsible for her literary endeavours.

"Oh," I said, "that must be... nice."

"Do you think so?" Her stare intensified. "But then, perhaps you think it's easy being at the beck and call of The Muse?"

"Well, no," I replied. "I don't suppose it is."

Elaine laid a thin hand on a sheaf of papers in front of her and nodded gravely. "She's a hard taskmaster. When she calls I must obey."

"Good for you," I said heartily, and was very relieved when Helen stood up and announced:

"It's now time for the first stage of our meeting. Who would like to begin? Polly, why don't you?"

She sat back down and Polly got to her feet. Bowing her head, she said solemnly, "I thank The Lady for my gifts and graces."

What lady? I thought, taking a swift glance about me. Did she mean Helen? I looked across at Vanessa for guidance but she, like everyone else, had also bowed her head. There was a moment's silence and then Polly, reverting to her usual cheerful accent, continued.

"I've been busy creating these silver bracelets and anklets. As you know, I like to take my inspiration from the beauty of nature and, this time, I've used a leaf motif as my central theme. Leaves are fragile, yet strong. As women are. Leaves, withstanding wind, cold and drought, nourish the atmosphere. As women nourish the world.

She held up a twisty silver bracelet formed in the fronds of a delicate leaf pattern and inset with tiny green beads. She turned shyly to me.

"I thought that you, Clarry, might accept one as a welcoming gift?"

All eyes turned to me. I was taken aback and touched by her thoughtfulness.

"Thank you," I said, accepting it from her outstretched hand and slipping it over my wrist. "It's really lovely. And so sweet of you."

"I have invested it with the Power of Protection," observed Sheila with quiet satisfaction, the warm burr of her West Country accent very pronounced.

Protection? From what? And how? I wondered, and was just about to ask her when Jo-Jo stood up.

"I thank The Lady for my gifts and graces."

Here we go again with *The Lady* business, I thought, and sure enough, it was the same bowing of heads before Jo-Jo showed us a laundry bag and a cook's apron printed with overlapping squares in shades of scarlet.

Then it was the turn of Mary, a girl with cropped pale pink hair, wearing a retro 1950s-style shirt, who made scrapbooks out of... well... scrap material. And they looked it.

Helen exhibited a new portrait she had been working on. It was of the red-haired man. The lines were bold and unforgiving of his flaws but in that frankness, there was tenderness and understanding.

"My dear brother, Gregory," Helen said, and her face clouded. "I know he's gone but sometimes I feel as if he's just stepped out of the room."

I whispered to Jo-Jo, "Did he die recently?"

"Two years ago," she murmured back.

When coffee was passed around, I was pleased to learn that making biscuits was Sheila's particular gift and grace. I knew there'd be baking.

The evening pushed on and the garden beyond the glass became lost in shadowy darkness. Up next it was Elaine, with the chunky amber beads.

"I thank The Lady for my gift and graces," she intoned and we all bowed our heads. "This performance piece is entitled *Of Dirt and Longing*."

This doesn't bode well, I thought, as Elaine threw back her head and began to declaim in a voice of fervent emotion.

'Splatters of white-grey plaster cling to your skin

It is in your hair and upon your shirt

How I long for you to push me down hard amongst the dirt.

Up close the tang of your sweat inflames my senses

The casual graze of your hand on my arm burns through my defences.

I long for the touch of your mouth against my lips

To feel it all over my body's secret hollows and dips.'

Oh, blimey, I thought. Not what I expected. Let's hope it's not a long poem. It was.

'Down amongst the dirt I'd spread wide my legs

You would lick and tease…'

Please make it stop, I prayed. But no, she kept right on going.

'Plaster and dirt would be in my mouth and in the pulsating wetness of my…'

Now, this is getting seriously embarrassing, I decided, as Elaine, beginning another verse, started thrashing about as if in the wild embrace of an unseen lover. A plasterer by trade, apparently. I wanted to look away, but it was strangely and disturbingly compelling. I stole a look at Vanessa, who caught my gaze and hiccupped down a snort of laughter. Elaine's agitations had now reached a point of frenzy, when suddenly she came to a shuddering crescendo as she repeated the word *Spent* three times in a strained and high-pitched voice. Thank God that's over, I thought. Should I clap? But standing with her arms hanging loose and her straggling hair all over the place, Elaine allowed the pregnant silence that followed to stretch on and on. Nobody moved. A ripple of anguish crossed her features and her beaky nose twitched. Oh God, she's having a stroke, I thought, but then with a jerk of her head, she delivered, in a brooding swooping cadence, her final utterance.

'Down amongst the dirt we'd lie trembling together

Down amongst the dirt we'd have known a passion that lasts forever'.

I wondered how much longer it would take for someone to break open the wine.

Sarah passed when her turn came around, and so the final exhibit of the evening was Vanessa's. As she rose to her feet, I thought about the call I would make to Diana in the morning telling her that there was nothing at all for her to worry about. Some of these women may be a little eccentric but there wasn't any harm in them. I'd tell her about Polly's warmth and Jo-Jo's friendliness and of how Vanessa seemed at home in their company. I'd seen no trace of the brat tonight. If it was comfort she sought, she could do a whole lot worse, I'd tell Diana, than find it here. Diana would be reassured. The case would be closed. She would pay me and that would be that.

"I thank The Lady for my gifts and graces," said Vanessa. "I've written a short poem that I've called..." She began.

Oh, crap, not another poem, I thought, when I became aware that someone had entered through the glazed doors behind her and was standing still and silent, framed against the moonlit sky. A tall, slim woman somewhere in her mid-thirties with very long dark hair spilling down her shoulders. Dressed in tight black leather trousers, a body-hugging black top and black stiletto boots, she was striking. Vanessa, sensing a presence, wheeled around and then hesitated before saying, "Hi, Zoe... I was just about to..."

"Your writing is your gift from the Goddess," said the woman. "Share it."

She didn't move to join us at the table, but simply remained standing in the open doorway. Vanessa cleared her throat and started to read but I didn't pay much attention; I was looking at the newcomer. She had good skin, high cheekbones, lips I guessed to be plumped up by collagen and dark eyes emphasised with heavy black liner. It was her nose that let her down and stopped her short of beauty. It was just a little too long for her face, making her features look slightly out of sync, as if a sculptor had slipped with his chisel in the creation of a statue and hadn't had time to correct his mistake before packing it off to his patron. She listened intently and her eyes never left Vanessa's face. There was power in her concentration. And it had a suffocating quality. She seemed to drink in Vanessa's words and, by doing so, it was as if she absorbed all the oxygen in the room.

The final lines of the poem were something about *suppression of the self* and *the woman within* and when Vanessa had finished, Zoe stepped across and placed a hand on her shoulder but didn't speak. There was a pause and then Helen announced, "Now Zoe has arrived, we will proceed with the most important part of the meeting. Ladies, please let us prepare."

The women rose to their feet, swept the table clear of the fabric, beads and scrapbooks and, in practised formation, lifted it across to the back wall, exposing a large area of floor space. Mary, Polly and Jo-Jo lit a host of tealights and positioned them on the table, along the broad shelf and on the floor around the entire perimeter of the room. Helen dimmed the overhead lights, uncorked the wine and poured us each a glass. There was no talking now and, as we all stood there, glass in hand, it was clear that something was about to take place. I looked about me expectantly. I'd been wondering what made these meetings special. It appeared that I was just about to find out.

CHAPTER THIRTEEN

"**P**erhaps the newcomer may not wish to stay?"

Zoe didn't address me directly but threw the question out into the room.

All the women looked from her to me and then back to her again, and it seemed as if they were waiting for her to make some sign. The effect was oddly unnerving, and I swallowed before saying,

"I'd like to, if that's OK?"

I saw Sarah flash a quick glance at Zoe as if about to object, but it was Sheila with the plaits who spoke.

"She will come to find her own relationship with the Goddess, but for now, let us guide her."

Everyone nodded at this except Sarah.

"Make the circle," Zoe ordered.

The women fanned out, forming a loose ring. There were ten of us and I found myself between Vanessa and Elaine, with Sarah directly across from me.

"Goddess of fertility and plenty, we thank you," intoned Zoe. "We accept your bounty and we celebrate all that you grace us with."

She took a sip from her wine and we all copied her.

"We honour your rules."

We all took another sip.

"We enjoy our lives. We do not waste them."

We drank again. This part I was enjoying.

"We live each day as if it were our last."

Another drink.

"We love. We love ourselves unconditionally. Then can we truly love others."

And another sip.

"And now, in the light of her moon, we will focus the life-giving energy of the Goddess," commanded Zoe. "Set down your glasses and join hands."

We all placed our glasses on the table, reformed the circle and linked hands.

"Close your eyes."

I did so but then took a quick peek. Everyone else had theirs tight shut, except for Sarah. She was looking right at me. And, I don't know whether it was the strangeness of the situation or the guttering of the candles in the moonlit room, but I couldn't repress a faint shudder as I snapped my eyes closed again.

"Tune into the energies shifting within you," said Zoe.

I wasn't exactly sure of what she meant by that but, dutifully, I did a quick mental stocktake. I was keyed up and curious. This was some pretty weird stuff, but I had to admit to feeling intrigued.

"We will bring the power of our focus, the power of the Goddess to address a concern from our circle," said Zoe. "Who applies to us?"

"I do," said a voice, and I think it was Mary's.

"Make your appeal."

"It's about Bonnie. My friend's dog," Mary explained. "She's a Westie. And she's lost."

My eyes flew open in surprise. What a let-down. Whatever I had been expecting, it hadn't included anything about a missing pet. I closed them hastily as Mary continued. "Since yesterday. On Wandsworth Common. She disappeared after a rabbit and didn't come back."

"Keep the circle tight," instructed Zoe. "We will now harness all of our forces to ask for the safe return of Bonnie."

I felt Elaine's grip on my hand intensify as Zoe continued in a sing-song voice.

"By our magical practice."

"By our magical practice," everyone repeated solemnly.

"If it be the will of the Goddess to restore the blessed familiar," said Zoe.

"If it be the will of the Goddess to restore the blessed familiar," we chanted.

"Then let it be so."

Again we echoed her. "Then let it be so."

In the long pause that followed as everyone concentrated their thoughts, I tried to keep aware and alert, but the image of poor Bonnie, trotting about looking for her owner and getting more lost and more weary with every hour, was upsetting. I found myself hoping that all this *by our magical practice* stuff really did work and that Bonnie would soon make it home to her basket and her dinner.

Eventually, Zoe asked, "Are there any other applications?"

"Yes," said Elaine and her fingers gripped mine even harder. "My friend Nadine. She has just had a biopsy taken from a lump in her breast."

There was a collective exhalation of sympathy and then Zoe said, "Tighten the circle. Come in closer."

Vanessa and Elaine's hands pulled mine as we took a couple of steps forward. We were all standing very close now. I could hear the women's breathing, almost feel its flutterings upon my face. My body tensed with the realisation that Sarah would be standing just in front of me, but I couldn't bring myself to open my eyes. Then Zoe began again.

"Divine Goddess; The Maiden The Mother The Crone. We offer up our friend Nadine to your protection. We trust in the life-giving energies of the Goddess. You are the Goddess of love and healing. And whilst we know that death is not final but merely another stage of our journey, we ask that Nadine be spared until the learning of her life's lessons are complete. And now, we come together in our strength. In our power."

Suddenly my balance tilted as around me the women began to sway. My hands were held so tightly that I was borne along with the movement.

"By our magical practice," we chanted.

"If it be the will of the Goddess…"

As Zoe led us in the incantation, something in the atmosphere of the room seemed to change. The women had formed a compact with each other and I felt the intensity of their purpose. It was palpable. And, for the first time during this bizarre experience, it occurred to me that they truly believed in what they were doing. It wasn't a game to them or some whimsically unconventional way of spending an evening. It was serious. And this was incomprehensible to me. A lost dog was one thing, but cancer was quite another.

Did they really believe that with their rituals and their weird spells, they could ward off illness?

"Then let it be so," came the final refrain. "Then let it be so."

As the women stopped swaying, their hands still linked, a hush settled over the group, before a voice I recognised as Sheila's said in a matter-of-fact tone, "Time to go home now, I think."

I let out the breath that I hadn't realised I'd been holding in. Whatever it was that had just taken place was over. Normality was resumed. Lights were turned on, candles were extinguished and the table set back in its place. Cardigans and jackets were sought and shrugged into. But I was wrong. It appeared that it wasn't quite over after all.

"Donations, please," said Sarah, producing a round tin that had once held biscuits. "For the cause."

As she shook the tin, her heavy frame shifted slightly beneath her linen draperies. For a large woman, there was no softness to her outline; her bulk was solid.

"The cause?" I asked in surprise. "What cause?"

It was Helen who answered. "Ah," she said with a note of pride in her voice, "We are contributing to a centre for Wellness. For women."

I must have looked blank for Jo-Jo took over the explanation.

"There are so many of our sisters in need of both practical support and spiritual release." Her bouncy brown curls bobbed as she continued enthusiastically. "We are creating a safe place, a haven where we can practise our therapies and find stillness. So, we all give what we can spare," which in her case appeared to be quite a lot because she dug in the pocket of her jeans and pulled out two twenty-pound notes.

"And Sarah has found us a wonderful site." She stretched across and placed the notes in the tin. "It will take time for our vision to become reality, but we are patient. And, in the meantime, we raise as much money as we can."

I looked on as all the women produced cash and placed it in the tin. I was shocked at how high their contributions seemed to be. In the fold of cash Vanessa had passed across, there was definitely at least one fifty. In all, it was difficult to see exactly how much had been collected, but at a guess it was several hundred pounds. I realised then that Helen was looking meaningfully in my direction.

"No cash, I'm afraid," I said, acutely conscious of the forty quid I had in my purse. There was no way I was handing that over.

"Do you take Contactless?" I asked, hoping against hope that they didn't.

"Cash only," said Jo-Jo apologetically.

"Looks like I'm going to have to pass." That's a relief, I thought, just as back-up came from an unexpected quarter.

"Clarry doesn't need to make a donation at all," said Sarah smoothly. "Although I'm sure she couldn't fail to agree that the scheme is a worthy one. And whilst it's been… nice to have her as a guest, we needn't trouble her with our plans. And after all…"

She laughed lightly and the smile she offered was the only one she'd given me all evening. "After all, she's only dipping in."

I was? Well, yes. I was. But *she* didn't know that.

Sarah continued to regard me and then, replacing the lid on the biscuit tin with an air of finality, put it in a large black leather tote bag and swung it over her shoulder. It was an act of dismissal. School was now out. Her *bag*, I thought, remembering Flan's description. The same bag that she'd dropped, spilling fistfuls of notes. Well, now, I guess, I knew where the cash came from.

Goodbyes were said at the front door. That wasn't strictly true. What was actually said was, "Merry Part. And Merry Meet again."

Polly and I were in step as we went down the path just behind Vanessa.

"Wow," I called to Vanessa, "that was some night. Fancy a …?"

I was cut off in my invitation to a late drink somewhere, as Zoe and Sarah appeared at her side and stood wordlessly flanking her. Neither of them acknowledged my presence, but whilst Zoe looked right through me, Sarah's eyes flickered over me in a way that I found faintly hostile. Why? Had she really minded, despite what she'd said, about my failure to contribute to this wellness place?

"Polly and I are going for a quick drink," I said brightly, determined not to be quelled. "Aren't we, Polly?"

"Great," said Polly, who'd been burrowing distractedly in her patchwork bag for something. "Love to."

"Why don't you join us, Vanessa?" I asked, and nodding at Zoë and Sarah, added with the broad fake smile that I usually reserve for traffic wardens, "you two are both welcome, of course."

Vanessa glanced at them and then back apologetically to me.

"Thanks, but I'd better… We've got things to…" And off they walked away down the street together, Vanessa in between the older women, as if escorted by two guards. Something about the image didn't sit well with me. It was then that I realised that my call to Diana would not be so very reassuring after all.

CHAPTER FOURTEEN

Polly and I decided to stick with red, and I ordered a bottle of merlot. Kendall's is one of the best-kept secrets in Wimbledon Village. A cosy bar tucked away in a back street, it's owned and run by a couple in their sixties, Bill and Sally Kendall, and their two sons, Brett and Phil. It stays open late and there's always some mellow jazz music playing. Not on CD or on any form of computerised device, but on vinyl. On an actual record player.

Covering the walls are framed black and white photos of the great jazz musicians of the past: Ella Fitzgerald on one wall, turning a knowing gaze upon Miles Davis on another, Louis Armstrong flashing a lot of teeth across the bar at Charlie Parker hanging over the door to the Ladies'. There's even a dusty trombone suspended over the till. The story is that it was owned by the famous American musician, J.J. Johnson, who lost it in a poker game to Bill after a gig at Ronnie Scott's in the sixties. But I don't know how true that is.

Kendall's, fitted out with private booths upholstered in dark crimson leather, is the perfect setting for a romantic tryst or private conversation. And, if you're a regular, they will even rustle you up something to eat after the kitchen has closed down for the night.

"There's some chicken liver pate and a baguette if that will do you, Clarry?" asked Brett, the elder of the two brothers. He was slim with short brown hair slightly greying along his low sideburns. He wore a pair of those oversized nerdy glasses that look so cool on the right face. And he had the right face, with a chiselled chin and intelligent dark eyes. I'd seen plenty of women make a play for him across the bar, but they flirted in vain. Brett was a devoted husband to his Korean wife and the adoring father of two little girls with shiny black pigtails.

"That would be great," I was about to say, when it occurred to me that Polly might be a vegetarian. But to my relief, she wasn't. I was very hungry. Who knew chanting really sharpened the appetite?

"Mum made it this morning," said Brett. "She adds brandy. That's the trick, apparently."

"How are your parents?" I asked, fishing out my credit card.

"Finding it hard to tear themselves away from the place, as always. I had to shoo them out of the door this afternoon. They need a night off. And besides, nothing much happens on a Tuesday."

He was right. There were only a handful of people at the bar and three occupied tables. "I'll bring it over to you," he said and disappeared into the kitchen.

Polly and I settled ourselves in a corner booth.

"So, did you enjoy it?" she asked, pouring us both out a generous measure of wine.

I took a sip before answering. "Yes… no… I don't know."

She laughed. "It takes you like that the first time."

"What does?"

"The Power," she said simply. "You felt it, didn't you?"

"Honestly," I said, settling myself more comfortably, "I'm not sure that I did."

"But you felt something?" she persisted.

"Well, curiosity, that's for sure. And a little freaked out, maybe, but if you mean, did I experience a seismic shift in my belief system? Then no, I didn't. Frankly, Polly, I don't get it. Those spells, if that's what they were, do you really believe that they work?"

She pushed a hand through her curly hair and closed her eyes for a moment. "Oh, they were spells all right. And I've seen what they can do. I've witnessed the effects. It's wonderful, Clarry. It really changes your perception of the world and of the space we occupy within it."

"Hang on, you're losing me," I said. "What does? What changes?"

"Seeing magic all around you," she cut across me. "That moment when you realise that all life is a form of magic. Just look about you. It's there in the beads of dew sparkling in the web of a spider. It's in the pattern of raindrops sliding down your window pane. It's in the call of the—"

"Right. Right. Got it." I raised a hand. "You're saying that magic is everywhere and in everything."

"If you look with an open heart," she said, "divinity permeates all. Every act we perform therefore becomes a sacred act."

"Because you're *witches*? I mean, I'm assuming that's what you think you are?"

"White witches," she corrected me, just as Brett appeared bearing a loaded platter.

"Witches?" He raised an eyebrow and looked at the food he'd just set down on the table.

"If it's eye of toad and wing of bat that you want, Clarry, then I'll take this back to the kitchen."

"Just try it," I said, planting both hands firmly on the platter. He left us with a grin.

"And not *think* we are," added Polly. "We *are* white witches."

"Blimey," I said, and made my first assault on the pate. With it was some warm sourdough bread, a thick slice of creamy goat's cheese, a dollop of sweet onion chutney and a fistful of rocket leaves.

"And so, this Zoe," I said, swallowing a mouthful of bread, "what's her story? She's your leader? Your guide? Your what?"

"Our High Priestess," said Polly.

"High Priestess?" I said, topping up our glasses. "You don't get to meet one of those every day."

"She's a remarkable person," said Polly. "She guides us to the Goddess."

"Actually, I thought she was rather rude," I observed. "She didn't even speak to me."

"That's just the solemnity of the rite." Polly's tone wasn't in the least defensive as she continued. "Conversation would be a distraction."

"Hmm," I said, not convinced. "And Sarah? Don't tell me she's a High Priestess as well."

"No. She's just one of us. A member of the circle. A devotee."

"Do you like her?"

She looked surprised. "Sarah? Yes, she's cool."

I studied her. "I have the feeling that you think everybody's cool."

"Pretty much," she agreed with a smile. "That's the thing about the Goddess. She brings joy and love into our lives."

I gave up for the moment. Polly might be a bit of a kook, but I couldn't help liking her.

"Thanks again for my bracelet," I said, twisting my wrist this way and that, so that it caught the light.

"I love it. And so, apart from jewellery making, what else is it that you do? I remember you said that you worked in an office, because of some guy you mentioned that night at the Hand in Hand."

"I'm in the publicity department at a local arts charity. We develop all kinds of art projects in the area, working with the council, Kingston Uni and the Rose Theatre amongst others. It doesn't pay much but I really enjoy it."

"It sounds right up your street," I said. "And so, how's it going with the guy?"

"Don't ask." She shook her head and the silver chains with the salmon-coloured stones jingled faintly.

"That bad?"

"I know he likes me. We often take our coffee break together but…"

"But what?" I demanded. "He's married? He's gay? He's on day release from prison? Spit it out."

Polly laughed. "None of the above. I just think he looks on me more as a friend than anything else. Although sometimes I do catch him checking me out."

"So, he's not married but maybe there's a girlfriend on the scene?" I suggested.

"There was. They'd lived together for years. But two months ago, she left him for a rock-climbing instructor with a campervan and went off travelling with him. Adam says that was one of the problems in their relationship. He's a bit of a stay-at-home and she wasn't. He thinks it was the lure of the campervan that was the final straw."

"Really?" I raised an eyebrow. "A *campervan?*"

"It was the thought of all those new places, new experiences. Adam said she couldn't resist the call to adventure."

"The Far East?" I suggested. "The Great American Road Trip?"

"The UK," said Polly. "Following the complete coastline."

"Maybe he just needs time to get over it?" I offered. "And until he has, you have to work on how to change the way he sees you. Vamp it up a bit."

And then a thought struck me.

"Hang on. If those spells really are as potent as you claim, then why not try one out on him? We could have… what's the right word?… *performed…* one tonight."

She shook her head. "Cast. Cast a spell. But no, it would never have worked. Not on a Tuesday."

She picked up her knife. "This cheese is really good. Do you mind if I have the last bit?"

"Go ahead," I said, and then, because I simply had to know, asked, "What do you mean, not on a Tuesday? What's wrong with Tuesdays?"

"Not the right day for a love spell." She popped the sliver of cheese into her mouth. "Fridays work best. If you want to bring a lover to you, do it on a Friday."

I thought about Ed. Our date had been on a Sunday. So, *that's* where I'd gone wrong. And here was me thinking it was something I'd said.

It was as we started on our second bottle of wine that I brought up the subject of the donations.

"That was a lot of cash handed over tonight."

"Yes. How great was that?" said Polly, her face lighting up. "Sarah reckons that we will soon have enough to close on the property she's found for the Centre. She's already put a deposit down."

"Really?" I said in surprise. "Property in this area is very expensive. How on earth can the eight, nine of you possibly raise that much money?"

"There are more of us than that; not everybody can make all the meetings. And besides, it's not just us. Sarah and Zoe are involved with other groups too. One in Richmond, I think, and another in Surrey somewhere. But in our circle, it's Helen that has given the most money. A great deal, I believe. She's wonderfully generous. And so talented. I love her portraits. Especially the ones of her brother."

"She mentioned him," I said, "and he died a couple of years ago?"

"Yes. And it's in his name that she has donated the money."

She looked thoughtfully into her glass. "So sad."

"Poor Helen," I said, before asking, "what's the name of this wellness project? I could look it up and donate online. I felt awful not being able to contribute tonight."

Polly looked up from her glass. "There isn't a website. It was felt that having one would dilute the spiritual influence."

"What's a little dilution if it brings in many more donations? And so they… Sarah and Zoe… collect and look after the money?"

"Oh yes. Sarah has set up a special bank account and she gives us regular updates on the total. It's over £300,000, I think she said a few weeks ago."

I whistled. "And so where is this place? Because impressive as that figure is, it won't buy anywhere sizable around here. Where is this *haven* going to be?" I couldn't prevent an edge of scepticism from creeping into my tone.

"I'm not sure exactly," said Polly. "Somewhere on the Surrey borders, I believe."

"And has anyone seen it?" I asked. "Anyone apart from Sarah and Zoe, I mean?"

She shook her head. "Sarah wants to keep it as a surprise. So that when we go there for the first time and cast the Spell of Protection, our thoughts and impressions will be fresh and will create a really powerful energy."

I let the Spell of Protection pass. I was too bothered about the £300,000.

"That's very trusting of you all."

Polly's smile was indulgent.

"Trust is an essential element in opening up to the Goddess. We receive her power through trust and openness."

And she was off again. I let her talk. When we had finally drained the bottle, I brought up the subject of Zoe again.

"Her look, it seems too studied. The black clothes, the hair. A bit overdramatic. And her manner. Like she was acting a part. In fact, if I were auditioning for the role of a modern-day witch on TV, I'd dress and act exactly like that. Or at least my friend Stephanie would. She's an actress," I explained, "at the restaurant with me."

"Zoe takes her role of High Priestess very seriously. She opens the veil between this world and the spirit world. She is the bridge," said Polly, draining her glass and then replacing it clumsily back down so that a few drops spilt on the table. "And I suppose there is some aspect of theatre in the—"

"That's it!" I exclaimed a little too loudly. It wasn't just Polly that the wine was affecting. "It's all so theatrical."

"You haven't seen a full ceremony! They're pretty heavy, even for me, and the one on Saturday night is supposed to be really full-on. Two meetings in a week is unusual, but Zoe wants us all there as she has something very special lined up for us, apparently, and..."

Wine or no wine, I was instantly on the alert.

"What time?"

"Midnight, of course." She grinned wickedly and then clamped her hand over her mouth. "We're supposed to keep it a secret! Forget I said anything."

"Come on. You can tell me," I wheedled. "Where will it be? At Helen's again?"

She shook her head. And, although I pressed her, she refused to say any more.

CHAPTER FIFTEEN

I awoke the following morning feeling groggy and hung-over. Something I'd have to shake off as I was on lunch shift at the restaurant. Forcing myself into running clothes and trainers, I let myself out of the house, only to remember that I'd left my car at the other end of the village last night. Hoping that I wouldn't bump into anyone I knew, I fast-walked through the streets. I'd brushed my teeth and splashed water on my face but that was about it, so this was no time to bump into an ex.

I'd nearly made it to the car when a woman who looked vaguely familiar crossed in front of me. I gave her a smile and then recognition dawned on both of us simultaneously. She may not have been wearing her *Here To Help* badge but it was Marion from the recruitment office nevertheless. Someone must have once told her that green was her colour, because today she was dressed in another decidedly cruel shade, this time of mint. She should never have listened to that someone. Mind you, this morning I wouldn't be winning any beauty contests either. Or at any other time. I'm not bad-looking in my way; I'm a blue-eyed highlighted blonde hovering somewhere between a size 14 and 16. I have quite good legs, large hands and biggish boobs. I have the occasional very good day but mostly I'm about a 6-7 on the scale. And that's OK with me.

"Hi," I said weakly. "Remember me? Clarry Pennhaligan."

This was unnecessary because it was clear that she remembered me only too well. "Anything come in that might suit me?" I asked.

"No," was the only curt answer she gave me as she hurried on past. But I'm nothing if not optimistic.

"Let's keep in touch," I called to her retreating back, but I wouldn't be holding my breath.

As I made my way through the woods and along a path that threaded through a field carpeted with cowslips, I thought over the previous evening and the ceremony I'd been part of. In daylight, as the birds in the trees about me competed cheerfully in their morning chorus, it all seemed very unlikely and unreal; the shadowy phantoms of a half-remembered dream. But that could have been something to do with the amount of wine I'd drunk.

I jogged on, puffing my way uphill and trying to ignore the protests of pain from my calf muscles. I had to decide what, if anything, I should do next. I was due to talk to Diana. But how much should I tell her? She was paying me to report back, but apart from all the weird witchy stuff I'd witnessed, what else was there really to say? Nothing concrete. Nothing but that feeling I'd had of Vanessa being somehow claimed by Zoe and Sarah. And the money, of course. The money paid by the women in donations. I'd be letting Diana know about the £300,000. I took a breath and then deeply exhaled as I slowed to a walk, wondering exactly how much of that figure had been contributed by Vanessa.

The phone rang just as I was about to leave for Abbe's.

"You'll never guess," exclaimed a voice, "Bonnie's been found. You see! I told you it worked."

It was Polly.

"That's great," I said, genuinely pleased. "That's one lucky little mutt. But come on; it's just a happy coincidence."

"Ah. You say that, but just you wait and see." And laughing, she rang off. As I replaced the receiver, I couldn't help but hope that Elaine's friend, Nadine, would be as lucky as the dog.

*

"I didn't even get a recall for *Chicago*," complained Stephanie as we set up for a table of ten.

"Accent let you down?" I asked sympathetically.

"No, that was fine, apparently. It was my sideways shuffle. And I've never been able to do the splits."

"I can," remarked Ian, waltzing by with a tray of Champagne flutes.

"By the way, I can't *believe* I missed the other night. All those naked guys. You should have called me, Clarry," he scolded crossly. "You really should have."

"She was too busy arranging her love life," Steph smirked. "One of them asked her out."

"Was that the big solid piece of manhood you came in with, on Sunday night?" asked Ian, his eyes gleaming with interest. "Such a to-do on Sunday evening, Stephanie. Some friend of Clarry's was being a nightmare and so, Clarry here, and her hunky, chunky bodyguard had to come to the rescue. I tell you, Sweets, he can watch over me any day."

"What would Ray have to say if he heard you talking like that?" I asked, plonking down ten sets of cutlery and arranging them in the right formation.

"Oh, Ray knows how I am," said Ian. "He says I can't help it."

Ray was Ian's long-term and, some might add, long-suffering partner. A producer of one of those heavyweight political programmes at the BBC, he was as solid and steady as Ian was flighty, but they worked.

*

We were kept busy until after four o'clock. The table of ten turned out to be a fifth anniversary lunch for a local IT business. From a small start-up, they had expanded and had done, if the congratulatory speeches were anything to go by, very well for themselves. By the time they'd got to the pudding course, they had exhausted talk of cyber security and were getting quietly plastered.

Whilst I ferried plates back and forth to the kitchen and served drinks, in my head I replayed the conversation I'd had earlier that morning with Diana.

"Are you actually telling me that my daughter is a… is a… *witch?*" Her voice was shrill with disbelief.

"Not a fully-fledged one," I said. "More one in training."

"This is far worse than I thought," she muttered darkly. "I knew that she was interested in this New Age nonsense.

That's why I hired you. But I had no idea that she'd gone as far as this. Well, I want it stopped," she snapped. "At once."

She didn't give me time to reply.

"I can't believe it. A daughter of mine. A Maitland. A *witch*. What will her father say? What will Charles say?"

Her voice had risen in outrage. "Whatever next? Is she going to turn up on the doorstep on a *broomstick?*"

"Not very likely," I said, but there was no stopping her.

"And fly off the roof with our poor cat, Cuthbert, strapped on the back? He wouldn't like that at all. And what on earth will the neighbours think? We shall have to move. That's all there is to it."

"I don't think it will quite come to that," I said soothingly. "And as for what people will say? It's up to you, of course, but apart from talking to your husband, why mention it to anyone else at all? Least of all Vanessa; it will only antagonise her. Look, Diana, try not to worry. It's probably just a phase. And, as I said, some of the women are really nice and basically harmless. I think Vanessa is feeling a bit lost, that's all. This may be simply an attempt to find herself."

"Find herself?" demanded Diana. "Where? In a *coven?*"

I did my best to try and calm her down and then asked, "So, what do you want me to do now?"

"Make the wretched girl see sense," thundered Diana. "God knows I've tried. But you're right," she said grudgingly, after a pause, "I shouldn't tackle her about it. If I try and interfere, she will only dig her heels in deeper. No. I won't mention it at all, although the effort may very nearly kill me." She gave a heavy sigh. "I don't understand why, if she's looking for an outlet, she can't take up tennis like everybody else in the

Village…? Right." She had herself under control now and it was back to business. "I want you to stay on it. You seem to have won her confidence and are well placed to proceed."

"Stay on it?"

"Yes. Find out more about this High Priestess character and the other one. What did you say her name was?"

"Sarah."

"Yes. And regarding the feeling of disquiet that you mentioned, I…" She hesitated. "…I trust your instincts on that."

She did? I couldn't help but feel gratified.

"If these women have somehow got their hooks into Vanessa, then I want to know more about them. Especially if she's giving them money. That really worries me. Vanessa has a considerable…" She broke off and then added crisply, "I am instructing you to find out all you can."

And that was exactly what I intended to do.

*

I was just walking through the kitchen to retrieve my bag at the end of my shift when I spotted Jose, the porter, standing chatting with someone on the back doorstep. Behind the restaurant is a lane just wide enough for a van to drive down. This is where our deliveries come in, where we store the bins and where some of the kitchen staff nip out for a sneaky smoke.

"Hi," I said, recognising Jonian from Cannizaro House. "Remember me? Clarry, from the other night? You helped me and my friend avoid…"

I left the sentence hanging. Out of his kitchen whites and in jeans and a black T-shirt, Jonian looked fit and lean. And I could see what Vanessa had meant about his eyelashes.

"How is your friend?" he said, "Van*essa*?"

The way he stressed the last syllable of her name sounded very foreign and rather attractive; at least I thought Vanessa would find it so.

"She's fine," I said, and then was struck with an idea. "In fact, she's meeting me for a drink later," I improvised hastily, "and I know she'd like to thank you again for what you did. Are you free to join us?"

I was guessing that by being here at Abbe's at this time of the day, it meant he wasn't on the evening shift at Cannizaro.

Jonian looked at Jose.

"We're just off for a coffee before Jose goes home but after that…" He lifted his hands palms up. "I have no plans."

"You do now," I said, hoping that Vanessa would be able to make it.

I took his number and promised I'd call him within the next half-hour.

The minute I was around the corner and out of sight, I dialled Vanessa.

"Vanessa, it's Clarry. Are you free? Now, I mean. Good. You've got a date. Well," I back-pedalled, "kind of a date."

I arranged to meet her at six in the Dog & Fox, and then I phoned Jonian. I felt pleased with myself. I knew that she liked him, and it was something else to maintain the connection between us.

I needed some key pieces of information to pursue my enquiries, so, I'd show up for one drink, ask a casual question or two and then leave them to it. I looked at my watch. I had enough time to get home, change out of my uniform of white shirt and black trousers, and to phone Flan and update her on last night's craziness.

The restaurant is less than a ten-minute walk from home, and I had just reached my front gate when I stopped abruptly in my tracks. Something looked different. I stared at the hip-high brick wall that encloses the cottage and blinked. I'd noticed last week that the jasmine, having recently enjoyed a significant growth spurt, had started clambering wildly up and over the brickwork in all directions. And, if I was the kind of person that kept a *To Do* list, then cutting it back would probably have featured somewhere at the bottom of that list. But it appeared I didn't need to worry about it anymore. Because either wishful thinking really does translate into action or I'd been hit by some very considerate and green-fingered burglars. The jasmine had now been neatly pruned so that its tiny star-shaped flowers formed a billowing creamy arch above the gate. I gazed at it in wonder and then, still at a loss, unlocked the front door to find a handwritten note lying face up on the mat. Written on the back of a used envelope were the words:

> *I noticed the other night that your jasmine looked a little out of control and in need of a trim, so I thought I'd show it some TLC. Love Ed. Your Guerrilla Gardener.*

My jasmine? *That's* what he'd noticed? Smiling broadly, I made my way into the kitchen and put on the kettle.

My conversation with Flan had taken longer than I'd thought and so it was nearer six fifteen when I got to the pub. Vanessa and Jonian were standing at the bar and looking, I thought, as I made my way over to them, a little awkward. Jonian offered to buy me a drink and whilst he placed the order, I looked significantly at Vanessa. "*So?*"

She coloured faintly and said in a low voice, "How did you wangle this?"

"I have my methods," I said airily. "Still loving his long eyelashes?"

"Shhh," she hissed. "He'll hear you."

She was looking pretty. She'd done her hair and was wearing make-up, and the blue and white shirt she had on with her jeans flattered her. For some reason, this made me feel faintly proud.

Conversation was stilted at first and I was the one working hard at it. I could see that Vanessa's shyness initially inhibited Jonain but, as she relaxed, he expanded and then things flowed more naturally between them.

"My parents came here when I was sixteen," he said. "My English wasn't very good and so school was tough for me and I missed my friends and all my cousins."

He grinned and looked, I thought, very young suddenly.

"I have twenty-two of them," he said.

"Cousins?" I asked.

"Albanians have very large families," he explained. "I went home for a wedding last year and there were over a hundred and fifty extended family members there. And another two hundred friends."

"Sounds expensive," I remarked, but Vanessa was speaking directly to Jonian.

"It must be hard to make a new life in a strange country."

Her earnest gaze was focussed fully on his face. "I really admire the courage it takes."

Jonian held her look. "For many of us, there was no choice, Van*essa.*"

A hint of a blush swept across her face at the way he pronounced her name. I knew she'd like it. He raised his bottle of beer in a toast and I noticed that his hands were long with thin, sensitive fingers.

"I am very grateful to this country. It has given me a great deal. And although I will always be an Albanian, perhaps I grow a little more English every day?"

Vanessa and I smiled.

"Who would you support in a football match between England and Albania?" I asked.

"Albania, of course. But I don't think I will need to choose sides for a while yet. Our national team isn't exactly world-class."

He told us that he was taking a business studies course at night school and Vanessa told him about her job hunting. And by then, I felt I'd done my bit in the interests of budding romance. I had no idea if anything would develop between them but I found myself hoping that it would.

"Oh, Vanessa," I said as I stood up to leave, "I meant to say that I thought Zoe looked familiar somehow."

This was completely untrue, but it was the best I could come up with.

"What's her second name?" I asked lightly. "Perhaps I know her from somewhere? I'm presuming she's local?"

Vanessa's eyes were still on Jonian as she answered. "She lives in Raynes Park. And it's Zoe Thorne."

"Thorne with an *e*?" I queried.

She nodded.

"Doesn't ring a bell," I said, and made another stab at extracting information.

"Maybe I know her from where she works. What is it that she does?"

"She's in sales, I think." Vanessa, clearly wanting to get back to Jonian, added vaguely, "In London somewhere, or maybe she's freelance. I'm not sure. I know she travels a bit."

I had planned to also ask about Sarah, but it was clear that this was as much as I was going to get for now.

CHAPTER SIXTEEN

Twenty minutes later, I was sitting at my computer in my spare room and looking to see what I could find out about Zoe Thorne. I could find no trace of her on social media, and it turned out that there are over a hundred and fifty Zoe Thornes in the UK. Thornes with an *e* that is. By patiently whittling down age group and locale, I finally found her on the electoral register. Her date of birth was there, as was her address in Raynes Park.

At forty, she was older than I'd thought, and I had to admit, she looked good on it. I looked at my watch. It may only have been eight thirty, but what I really fancied was an early night after a hot bath and something to eat in front of the TV. And time to think about my Guerrilla Gardener Ed. The jasmine was a sweet gesture. Unusual but sweet. I'd sent a text thanking him, which he'd acknowledged with a *You're welcome. Ed x* but no mention of seeing me again. Why the hell not? Don't obsess about this, I told myself. Especially not now when you're on the clock and have a job to do.

I never willingly go under-fed, but the contents of my fridge that night were not very inspiring. I really would have to shop tomorrow. Rustling up a sandwich with some cheddar that must have been in there for a while and the last of the tomatoes, I shoved it into my bag with a flask of coffee and headed out.

Zoe lived in a block of flats which was going to make a stake-out difficult. I parked the Renault across the road from the three low-rise buildings and hunkered down in my seat to have a think. I needed to find out which of the blocks contained flat 8 and if there was more than one exit. I ate half my sandwich and thought about it some more. Then, scraping my hair up into the baseball cap I keep on the back seat and pulling a navy sweatshirt over my jeans, I let myself out of the car. It was nearly dark as I crossed the road and walked cautiously across the forecourt of Camford Mansions. The blocks were probably built in the 1970s and looked to be in good repair. The communal gardens were well maintained and, on quite a few of the narrow balconies, there were window boxes. Still, *Mansions* was a bit of a stretch.

I checked the first block. Flats 1-6, which meant that number 8 was in the second block. I was just looking at the intercom, when a couple came out and without any thought for security allowed the door to swing slowly back into position. I stuck out my hand to prevent it from closing and then hesitated. This is the time to admit that, although I'd carried out some surveillance in my first investigation, accomplished and professional I most certainly was not. I didn't have any clear idea of why I was even there. Just the vague notion that if I kept my eyes open, something would occur to me. Or alternatively something would *happen* to me. That idea filled me with misgiving. What if I ran into Zoe? What on earth would I say? I swallowed. How likely was that? I asked myself and then, choosing to ignore the obviously high degree of chance, I stepped through the door and into a clean grey and white painted lobby.

There was an empty umbrella stand in one corner and a fire extinguisher, attached by a bracket, at low level to the wall. That was it. No indications of which flats were on which floors. Gingerly, I pushed open a second door and found myself in a square hallway with a large window on the far wall and with a flight of stairs coming off it at a right angle. The window, one of those that operate on a spring system, was open enough to allow a current of air to circulate through the building. There didn't appear to be a back door. That was good on the one hand, because it meant there was only one exit to keep an eye on, but on the other, very bad, because if Zoe came out of her flat right now, we'd walk slap bang into each other.

I tiptoed down the hall. Flat 7 was on my left and flat 9 was on the right-hand side by the staircase. Number 8's door was at the back, just to the left of the window. And there were lights on. Swiftly, I turned on my heel and scampered back down the hall, through the two doors and out into the night air. Breathing heavily, I had to force myself not to hotfoot it back to the car but instead made my way around to the rear of the building. Here, there was a narrow strip of asphalt backed by the high fence of a neighbouring property. I flattened myself against the wall.

There, was the open window to the ground floor communal hallway. And besides it was another larger window, also slightly open at the top, that had to be part of Zoe's flat. A blind had been partially pulled down but light streamed out at its base. I dropped to my knees and groped my way crab-like, until I was directly beneath it. Heart thumping, it took me a moment before I could bring myself to raise my head and peep over the sill.

I was looking into Zoe's sitting room. I could see a cream carpet with a square of geometric-patterned rug and the low black cushions of a three-piece leather sofa. Did it squeak, I wondered, when she sat down on it when wearing her leather trousers? Wouldn't leather on leather be a bit sweaty? My thoughts flitted about irrelevantly. Nerves were getting the better of me. Concentrate, I told myself sternly and peeked again. There was a matching easy chair and the shiny silver console of a sound system. A light glowed on its panel of buttons and I could dimly hear the strains of music turned down very low. I tried to visualise what the room looked like. Not easy from the perspective I currently had. Were there ornaments and photographs on a mantelpiece and pictures on the walls? Were there flowers in a vase upon a table? The style of rug and the black leather suite didn't suggest a feminine room. I'm not sure what I'd been expecting, but given her role of High Priestess, I'd assumed that her private space might in some way reflect this aspect of her life. I felt a jolt of disappointment. I'd imagined something more dramatic. But who knows? I thought. Maybe, there's an altar in the bedroom lit with candles, and depictions of a crescent moon surrounded by twinkling stars, stencilled on the ceiling? I stiffened and then quickly ducked my head. A pair of bare feet had just crossed the room and disappeared again. Female feet with the toenails painted a sparkly sugary pink. All I'd seen was as high as her slim calves, but I found myself hoping that the woman was fully dressed. The idea of spying on Zoe, or indeed on anyone, when they were partially or fully naked was repellent. Correct that, I told myself. Dressed or undressed, what did it matter? Either way, I was acting like a peeping tom. And would be assumed to be one, if caught out here. I waited and watched. The feet crossed the room again. And this time they were not alone.

A pair of black suede loafers appeared. Black suede loafers in at least a size ten or eleven. Men's loafers, with the cuffs of a pair of dark trousers above. Zoë took a step towards the man but he remained standing with his back to the sofa. They were having a conversation. The window was only open a crack at the top, which was not enough for me to make out what they were talking about, but every now and again one of them would give a low laugh.

Loafers then took a couple of paces towards Zoë but she retreated back. He took another step nearer and again she pulled teasingly back. More throaty laughter and another approach. It was like a dance, I thought. A sexual one. A form of foreplay. And if I'd had a foot fetish, I'd be in heaven right now. But I hadn't and so it only left me feeling embarrassed.

The sugary pink-painted toenails tiptoed towards him again and, this time, stepped in very close. An embrace. If they drop to the floor and start having sex, I told myself, I am so out of here. They didn't. They moved to the sofa, where I could see from the angle of one swinging bare foot, that she had laid her legs over his.

Suddenly I felt something lightly brush my thigh and I had to bite down the scream that threatened to explode out of my lungs. Was someone standing behind me? I could hardly bear to look. Whilst I'd been so intent on watching Zoe, had someone snuck up behind me and was now watching *me*? I felt the hairs rise on the back of my neck. Then, like a ghostly hand running its fingers across the small of my back, I felt the touch again. I spun around and looked wildly this way and that but no one was there. I shot to my feet, heedless of the shadow I might be casting against the window. What was out there? What had touched me? Straining my eyes through the dim light, I peered about me, convinced that the menacing outline of a figure would be standing just out of sight waiting to get at me. Images of witches, their black robes fluttering in the breeze, skittered across my mind as I tried to get a hold of myself. Systematically, now I trained my gaze along the length of the fence. Nothing. And then yes… a movement, swift and low. Too low. Too low for anything human.

I laboured hard to control my breathing and steeled myself for another look. It was a cat. Just a cat. A cat on some late-night mission, sashaying up and down along the asphalt and swinging her long black tail. It was her tail that must have brushed against me. I nearly laughed out loud. A hysterical laugh. The laugh of a person momentarily unhinged. At least, I hoped it was momentarily.

"Shoo," I whispered, once my heart had reverted to a steadier beat. The cat ignored me.

"Scram," I hissed, flicking my fingers and attempting to wave her away. But she was having none of it. Fighting down another giggle of hysteria, I began flailing my arms about, but it was clear she wasn't going anywhere because, with a sudden leap, she launched herself onto the window sill and began mewing piteously to be let in. So this was Zoe's cat. A black cat. A witch's cat. Is that dramatic enough for you? I asked myself crossly and was busy thinking of how I would describe this discovery to Flan when I realised that someone had come to the window and was fiddling with the latch. I melted back against the wall as the window casement slid up and a pair of arms scooped up the cat and brought her inside. It was definitely Zoe. I could see her long black hair spilling forward and the cream satin strap of a nightgown or camisole that had slipped over a bare shoulder.

"Tabitha," she said coaxingly, "you've been out late tonight."

Tabitha. Infant daughter of the famous TV witch that wrinkles her nose. A witchy in-joke, I supposed. How bloody hilarious.

Turning away from the window with the cat still in her arms, Zoe then said with a seductive curl to her voice, "Tabitha is a huntress. She knows what she wants."

"Come here," was the reply from the sofa.

Zoe hadn't bothered to reclose the window and the sounds of kissing and the rustle of clothing were distinctly audible. I was done here. I had discovered nothing. My haunches were aching from all the crouching and I had no intention of listening to any more. Zoe was obviously on a date night with her husband or boyfriend and voyeurism was most definitely not my thing. I scuttled away from the window and, taking a quick glance about me before straightening up, stepped around the side of the building and legged it back across the forecourt, over the road and into the car.

The clock on the dashboard showed it was nearly eleven o'clock and I thought longingly of the glass of wine I'd down before bed, in the comfort and safety of my own home. But, unbidden, Diana's last words on the phone that morning came back to me: *I am instructing you to find out all that you can* she had said. I sighed heavily and reached for the remainder of my sandwich. I'd give it until midnight.

*

The hour ticked slowly by and I was glad I'd brought the coffee. The couple I'd seen earlier returned from wherever they'd been and, moments after they'd entered the building, I saw a light shine out from a first-floor window. A young guy let himself into the right-hand block of flats but no one else entered or left the middle block.

Five past midnight. Finally, it was time for bed. I was just about to turn the keys in the ignition when the door to the middle block opened and someone walked out into the night. It was a man. From a distance, I couldn't make out much more than the fact that he was of medium height and quite well built. I sank down low in my seat and followed him with my eyes as he made his way across the road and headed to a car parked two down from the Renault. Through the wing mirror, I watched him pat down his pockets for his keys and open the door. I didn't get a glimpse of his face but, as he stepped into the car, I could see, picked up in the glow of a street lamp, that on his feet were a pair of black suede loafers.

I left it a minute or two before pulling out after him. He was driving a silver Jeep. And it was the car's height that helped me keep him in sight as he drove onto Coombe Lane and then took the exit for the A3 heading north. He kept to the middle lane and drove at a speed just below the legal limit. Something I was grateful for. If he'd been one of those aggressive, weaving-in-and-out drivers, I would probably have lost him. We came to the roundabout where there is a choice between heading into Wandsworth and Central London or taking the road that leads onto Putney Hill. He chose the latter. It was easier to track him now as the road had two lanes rather than three and there was less traffic about. I maintained a distance of three cars back as we proceeded down the hill and onto the High Street but was on the alert when he signalled left just before Putney Bridge.

We were now on the Lower Richmond Road, a long, meandering street that follows the riverbank. Once we were past the antique shops, restaurants and bars on the first stretch of the road, we entered residential territory, and it was into a series of side streets that I followed him as he finally pulled up and parked in the drive of a substantial double-fronted house.

There was a light glowing in the porch and a faint glimmer coming from a window on the upper storey. I had no option but to drive on past, doubling back at the first exit I came to, and anxious lest I lost myself in the maze of connecting streets. I drove back down the road very slowly and there was the Jeep. Alongside a Volvo. I drew the Renault into a space across from the house, killed the engine and peered through the windscreen. I could only pick out the final three letters of the car registration number and I couldn't see the house number at all. I wanted both.

Uncertain, I looked up and down the street. This was likely to be a neighbourhood watch area, as many of the houses were detached, some with private gates and intercoms. Trying not to think about CCTV cameras, I let myself out of the car, being careful not to clunk it closed behind me. I kept to the shadows and slipped across the street and then dropped to a crouch as if retying the lace of my trainers. All was quiet. I squinted and made out the number 114 on the heavy oak door. I took a step forward and, through a side gate, I could see into a back garden which, in the darkness, looked like it stretched on forever. Propped against the inside of the gate were four bicycles, two of which were of a size only suitable for children. I hastily memorised the registration numbers of both cars and then took a quick peek through the windows. The Jeep disclosed nothing except that its driver listened to old school rock music, but the Volvo was more revealing. In its footwell on the passenger side lay a small stuffed teddy bear with one mangled ear and both eyes missing. I'd seen enough. It didn't take a detective to work out what was going on.

CHAPTER SEVENTEEN

Working in a restaurant, I'm used to late nights, and so, by seven thirty the following morning, I was again parked opposite *Loafer's* house. With my baseball cap shielding most of my face, I sipped the double-shot latte I'd picked up at a drive-thru and tried to look like I had a legitimate reason for being there. I'd grabbed a couple of files and a notebook from home and spread them on the passenger seat beside me so that I could appear absorbed in paperwork if anyone noticed me. The fact that the files only contained old household bills was neither here nor there. It was the best I could come up with at this time of the day.

The street was already astir with activity and there were lights on in most of the houses. I'd already seen people in suits and with briefcases leaving for work, and a mum with three children on an early school run. At number 114, the Jeep was still there, but the curtains had been drawn back in the front bedroom. Flicking a dusting of almond croissant flakes from my knees, I wondered exactly what I was hoping to gain from being here. So what if Zoe had a married lover? It was hardly relevant, but I wanted to be thorough. I'd made a commitment to Diana and, more than that, I *felt* a commitment to Vanessa. Even if she didn't know it. And what was it Flan always said? "Background research, darling. Invaluable."

At eight fifteen, the front door opened, and *Loafers* made an appearance. He was dressed for the office in a suit and tie. The night before, I'd thought he was well built but now, in the full glare of daylight, I could see that his weight was top heavy and, at five foot eight or nine inches tall, it didn't suit him. He had the paunch of a man who had dined too often and too well. Probably on expenses.

Two little boys, one about eight years old and the other around five or six, came out behind him but remained on the front step, waving him goodbye. Both were wearing the uniform of a local private school. They talked over their shoulders to someone standing behind them within the house. I was too far away to make out anything other than the fact that she was female and quite tall. Taller than her husband. *Loafers* blew a kiss to the figure, then hugged the boys and got into the Jeep. The children disappeared back into the house and I was left wondering about the unseen woman. I pictured her as much like any other wife and mother, going about her normal daily life, occupied with her own concerns and those of her family. For, I could only presume that she was *Mrs. Loafers*. And despite the beautiful home, the smart car and the two lovely little boys, I couldn't help but feel a flash of pity for this unknown woman. Did she have any idea that her husband was cheating on her? When she found out, which inevitably she would at some point, a world of pain awaited her. But, I told myself, I could just as easily have it all wrong. Perhaps they have an open relationship or maybe she was having a passionate affair with a handsome Italian waiter from a local restaurant? One of those guys with soulful eyes and that easy flattering charm that can really work its magic after a bottle of Chianti. I certainly hoped so. For her sake.

Loafers had started the engine and I don't know whether it was the fact that he was cheating on his wife, but I decided then and there that I didn't like this guy. I didn't like the performance he'd just given of the perfect husband and father. I didn't like the way he oiled his thinning dark hair back from his forehead. I didn't like the way he backed his car too fast out of the drive, with the windows wound down and his old school rock music turned up high. And I didn't like his loafers.

It had been too early a start to do anything other than brush my teeth and throw my clothes on. Now, as I headed for home, I was looking forward to a hot shower.

*

Flan was on the phone as I was drying my hair.

"I have a lot to report," she announced by way of a greeting.

"Coffee in an hour?" I asked. "Right. I'll be with you then. Got to go now or my hair will dry all frizzy."

And I have a lot to tell her, I thought as I got dressed. Looking in the mirror, I realised that it was over six weeks since I'd had my highlights redone and I was looking a little faded. Slapping on some coral lip gloss to perk up my complexion, I trotted downstairs for a second breakfast.

Damn. There wasn't any. I'd used the last of the bread for last night's cheese sandwich.

*

Luckily for me, Flan had cake. An iced walnut cake. And I'd already had an almond croissant.

"Business isn't exactly booming," remarked Flan as she poured milk into a blue Spode jug. Flan had a collection of Spode ware from different decades and, antiques or not, she likes to use them every day.

"What business?" I mumbled through a large mouthful of cake.

"The Nook, of course. What's the matter with you this morning?"

She shot me a penetrating look. "We are going to need all our wits about us if we are going to go detecting."

"Detecting what?" I asked thickly. "And where precisely does the *we* come in?"

"Now, don't start that again," said Flan, opening her eyes very wide. "And don't splutter through your cake. You'll choke."

I swallowed hastily but a crumb went down the wrong way and I started to cough.

Through streaming eyes, and under Flan's satirical scrutiny, I thumped myself on the chest until my airways were clear.

"All better now?" asked Flan with assumed sweetness. "Good. Well, you told me that you would be researching this Sarah person and so, last night, Harold and I got to work."

Harold is the retired undertaker.

"We thought that we'd save you a job, so we fired up my computer." Flan had signed up for a class a few months ago to learn basic computer skills. "I feel so out of the loop, darling," she had said. "This net thingumy seems to have really caught on." She had therefore invested in a computer and had paid some IT company to set it up for her. Possibly the one who had celebrated their fifth anniversary at the restaurant. I wondered how many other pensioners they provided this service to. Maybe that was why they were doing so well? And there the computer had sat, in Flan's back sitting room, gathering dust ever since. I don't think she had even switched the thing on and, after attending two of the classes, I never heard her mention the matter again.

"Harold turns out to be a whizz at this computer stuff," she continued. "He had to be when he was running the family firm. How do you computerise dead bodies? I asked him. It's so dehumanising. It's as if when one dies, one simply ceases to exist."

"Isn't that how it works, Flan?" I asked.

"Well, I don't know about you, but I have no intention of being toe-tagged and splayed out on a slab like a plucked chicken," said Flan with feeling. "That's why I've decided to be placed in a wicker basket, set fire to, and floated out to sea. See to it for me, won't you, darling, when my time comes?"

"There's probably some by-law…" I protested, about to point out that her version of a Viking funeral on the River Thames wouldn't be allowed, but thought better of it. "Let's not worry about that now, shall we? After all, it'll be another couple of decades before…"

"My parents lived until they were well into their nineties," observed Flan with satisfaction. "And so you're probably right. Now, where was I? Ah yes. I was telling you how clever Harold was on the computer. It put him in an awfully good mood. Well, you know how pleased men are when they can teach you something."

She smirked and crossed one lilac cotton-trousered leg over the other.

"And did he?" I asked.

"Did he what?"

"Teach you something."

"That's hardly the point, darling. Now, do pay attention. Sarah Gaitskill, that's her name, opened the shop three years ago. She is the sole owner of the business and retains a hundred per cent of the shares. Although from what I understand, they are worth next to nothing."

Flan took a delicate sip of her coffee and then set her cup back down.

"Harold took a look at the accounts and, apparently, it did not make for happy reading. I had no idea that such things were open to scrutiny, but they are, apparently. He did try, at some length, to explain the process to me but…" She waved an airy hand. "…I felt it was enough that I appeared to be following all he said, when in actual fact, I was thinking of something altogether different, but the gist of it was that The Nook is hanging on by a thread."

"That doesn't really surprise me," I said, after a moment's thought. "I mean, you saw the place."

"Yes," remarked Flan. "There can't be much money in notelets."

"You're forgetting the fairy figurines," I said.

"If only I could," she replied. "Hideous creatures. Now. You haven't asked me what I was thinking about." Her eyes bored into mine. "Whilst Harold was busy explaining."

"That's because you are just about to tell me," I replied.

"I want to know what's behind that purple curtain," she said evenly.

"Why? What's so interesting about it?"

"Because it's where Sarah was taking all that money I saw her with. And with what you've told me about the donations those women make... well, *that's* what makes it interesting, Clarissa. Now my idea is this..."

I gave it up. I know from experience that whenever Flan calls me by my full name, resistance is futile.

*

My next stop was a dash around the supermarket. I think we've already established that I'm not a list person. And so yes, of course, sometimes I do forget the odd essential, milk or washing powder, for instance, but I like to buy on impulse. And, coming home with lots of little plastic bags containing interesting items bought from the deli counter, does keep the shopping experience fresh. I was just studying the suggested recipe on the back of a bag of wild rice, when my mobile rang. It was Ed. Finally.

"Hi," he said, "how are you?"

Great," I replied, a little too heartily and blindly dropping the bag of wild rice into my trolley.

"There's a lot of background noise," he observed. "I hope I'm not interrupting you in anything important? Like one of your cases?"

I laughed. "I did tell you that I'm an amateur, right? My life isn't all that exciting."

Although the last few nights have had their moments, I thought, as I continued down the aisles, blindly browsing the shelves.

"Actually, I'm in the supermarket stocking up. Even an amateur detective has to eat, you know."

"That's quite a coincidence," Ed said. "Because garden designers have to eat too. Very regularly. We need to keep our strength up. So, what do you think about joining forces and keeping our strength up together? How about tomorrow night? Do you think you might be hungry then?"

"Absolutely," I replied. "No question about it."

By the time we'd hung up, I was at the checkout wondering what on earth had possessed me to pick up a family-sized box of mini meringues, a jar of something called *zhoug* and three fresh artichokes; a vegetable I had no idea how to prepare.

CHAPTER EIGHTEEN

It was raining slightly as, at seven thirty that evening, Flan and I sat in the Renault parked on the opposite side of the street from The Nook. The shop was in the middle of three single-storeyed units. It was closed, as were its neighbours: a hardware store offering an assortment of torches, galvanised buckets and plastic storage boxes and an independent shoe shop that, if the chunky brogues on display in the window were anything to go by, specialised more in comfort than in style. The couple of bars in downtown Teddington were busy tonight, but this side road was quiet with very little footfall, except for the French bistro two doors down on the corner. That worried me. Like most shops, The Nook didn't have a porch or outer lobby. We would therefore be completely on view to the restaurant's customers as they came and went.

"George is mortified to be missing the adventure," said Flan.

George Huxton, Flan's seventy-two-year-old lover, was a retired joiner and locksmith. He had helped us a few weeks ago break into the house of a guy I'd been investigating. Helped might be understating it. Mr. H was the one that had got us into the property. He and his collection of pick-locks.

"So kind of him to lend them to us. But then he's like that," said Flan warmly. "Generous. Always has been. So different from Harold. Harold, as I think I may have told you, darling, can be a little close with his money."

Mr. H, who was in York visiting his daughter, had told Flan where the tools of his old trade were kept, and she had trawled through his attic to find them. She regularly watered his plants and collected his post whenever he went away and so she retained a set of his house keys. He was a lovely man and utterly besotted with Flan. He could also, on occasion, be relied upon to help keep her exuberance in check. It wasn't only for his locksmith skills that I was missing him this evening.

"I've been practising," Flan informed me, cradling in her lap the giant bunch of keys and collection of thin pointy implements which reminded me of the stainless steel compass from old school geometry sets.

"I tried them out on my own front door and, after a dozen or so attempts, I got in. It only took me twenty minutes. But then I've always been a quick learner."

"We've got to get in quicker than that!" I exclaimed. "People are going to be coming in and out of that restaurant, and they can't help but see us."

"Don't worry, darling. They will be too hungry on the way *in* and far too sloshed on the way *out* to notice much."

I hoped she was right.

"I rather like the look of the place," observed Flan. "I love French food, as you know. Perhaps I'll go there with George one evening. Mind you, he is somewhat conventional in his tastes. And not just about food. I think that's one of the reasons he likes to spend time with me; he says I educate him."

I bet you do, I thought.

We waited as the rain grew heavier and the shadows deepened around us. Thankfully, the street was poorly lit, the nearest lamppost being about six feet away.

"This weather may work in our favour," observed Flan. "People will be more interested in getting into the dry than wondering what we are up to."

Swivelling around to look on the back seat, she asked, "Do you have an umbrella?"

"This is no time to be worrying about your hair," I said, my eyes on the rear-view mirror, where I could see a couple making their way down the hill behind us and heading towards the High Street.

"I'm not. I just thought it would give us some cover if you stand beneath it and pretend to be waiting for somebody. You can shield me whilst I have a go at the locks."

"Actually, that's a good plan," I admitted. "But I should be the one to commit the actual breaking and entering, Flan. It's my investigation after all."

"But this was my idea," she objected. "I talked you into it."

That was true. And I still wasn't convinced. What did it matter what Sarah had in the back of the shop? What were we going to find? Bags of cocaine amongst the lavender soaps? Blood diamonds stashed beneath Polly's butterfly pendants? But Flan had been adamant. Something about the purple curtain intrigued her.

"We don't want to leave any stone unturned, Clarry."

"Look," I said patiently, "this is against the law. You know that. I don't want you getting into trouble because of me."

"Nonsense," she said crisply. "I'm the one that's been practising and so I'm the—"

"But what if we're caught?" I persisted. "What if someone calls the police?"

"They are not going to arrest an old woman."

"I've never heard you admit to being old before," I said, surprised.

"And you never will again," she replied. "Now, be sensible, darling, and leave this side of the operation to me."

I regarded her. The relish with which she said the word *operation* made me nervous. Flan has a tendency to be overconfident. Something, I fear, which may have rubbed off on me.

"Don't go getting too gung-ho about this, will you, Flan?" I said. "We go in. We take a quick look around. We get out. And that's it."

*

At eight fifteen, the rain had intensified and was beating an insistent tattoo on the roof of the car. There were fewer people about and we had seen no one enter or leave the bistro for quite a while. They'd all be sitting down to their steak and frites and red wine, I thought with a pang. Just the thought of that made my mouth water. "Right," I said abruptly, before the idea of a hot meal became too tempting and I weakened. "Let's do this."

We slipped out of the car and left it unlocked, having decided this earlier, in case of the need for a quick getaway. We were both wearing dark trousers and tops. I had on my baseball hat and Flan had wrapped her white hair in a long chocolate-coloured silk scarf.

We stood hesitantly peering in through the windows of the shop for any sign of life. The outsize pair of onyx hands that displayed rings and bracelets during business hours had been stripped for the night. Naked, the giant black fingers seemed to clutch at the air with menacing intent.

Our immediate worry was whether the shop had an alarm. If so, then the plan was to abandon ship. We hadn't spotted one when we'd surveyed the frontage from the safety of the car, but it was an anxious moment whilst we scanned the old brickwork, the door and the windows for signs of a tell-tale box.

"Doesn't mean there isn't one," I said warningly to Flan as she got out the pick-locks.

"Only one way to find out," she said, leaning into the doorway. "Now, quick. Cover me."

And so that's what I did. Whilst Flan tested key after key and kept up a running commentary on her progress, I maintained a pantomime of waiting. I looked at my watch, I checked my phone, I paced on the spot as if in irritation but, all the time, keeping my back to Flan and using my body and the umbrella as a screen.

It may not have taken twenty minutes but it certainly felt like it when Flan finally gave a grunt of satisfaction as the first of the two locks gave. Flushed with success, she grew cocky.

"You see, darling," she exclaimed. "I told you I could do it."

"We're not in yet," I reminded her. "Hurry up. I'm not sure how much longer I can keep up this pretence of being stood up."

"An artist should never be rushed," replied Flan, addressing herself to her task once more. And I had to hand it to her, an artist she proved herself to be. After only another five minutes of inserting and poking about with the pick-locks, the second lock yielded. "We're in!" crowed Flan, dancing up and down in excitement.

"Quick," I hissed, shoving up behind her. "Get in. Get in."

The peal of tinkling bells that rang out as we pushed open the door and crossed the threshold, had us both nearly jumping out of our skins in fright.

"*Bloody* wind chimes," I croaked, reaching up in the darkness and grabbing blindly at the metal cylinders, only to find that one of them came away in my hands.

"Crap!" I said, trying to shove it back into the supporting disc and making more noise than ever. Flan recovered her composure before I did. She shut the door behind us and locked only one of the two locks from the inside.

"Leave it on the mat, Clarry. It doesn't matter. It will just look like it has fallen off. Put the umbrella there as well so we don't forget it on the way out."

Breathing more easily now, I knelt and placed the chime and the umbrella on the floor. The scent of resin and flowers that I'd noticed on our previous visit, our perfectly legal visit carried out in broad daylight, was more discernible now. The perfumes of vanilla, orange oil and incense were overpowering in the airless room and I felt a little light-headed. The nerves that I'd desperately been trying to overcome made another assault and I felt my stomach lurch.

"Flan," I whispered, "you do know that this is crazy, right?"

She ignored me and passed across one of the torches we'd brought with us. Switching the torches into life, we shone them over the timber-beamed ceiling and old plastered walls. The light from Flan's picked up the stand near the window where Polly's owl earrings bobbed and glittered in the darkness, and then moved across to the table of stationery.

"I've quite enough notelets for the time being," Flan said.

I flashed mine around and found that the fairy figurines on the back shelf were looking right at me through the gloom. There was the Woodland Princess, *Serenity,* her gaze just as spiteful as I remembered it to be. In fact, the whole gang was still here: *Delphinium* with her gauzy wings and impossibly long flowing hair, *Serafina,* nauseatingly coy amongst her flower petals, and the three creepily entwined *Fairy Friends*. What a surprise they hadn't sold.

Wary that the light from our torches would be spotted from the street, we crossed to the counter and ducked behind it. Here, between the counter and the purple curtain, there was space enough for a chair and a set of shelves. On the back of the chair hung a knitted pale blue cardigan with one of those floppy corsage broaches pinned to it. Too small to be Sarah's, I thought, and much more Sheila's style.

Crouching, Flan examined the shelves and extracted a dark blue A4 lined accounts book.

"It's the sales ledger," she said, squinting. "Look. They sold four candles, a necklace, a notebook, two incense burners and a wand today. Not a lot, is it? It comes to…" She made a swift calculation. "Less than £100."

"*Wand?*" I queried. "They actually sell wands?"

But Flan wasn't listening. She was leafing back through the pages. "Harold was right about their finances. Their takings are rarely above £70-odd a day. Apart from the rent, maybe their outgoings aren't very high? I suppose that once the utilities and stock is covered, there can't be much else to pay out. I wonder how much that nice Sheila woman earns?"

"Enough to make a donation to the Cause," I observed. I was feeling less anxious now that we were out of sight of the street. This wouldn't take long, I told myself. Ten minutes tops and then we'd be on our way home.

Flan had put back the account book and was now rummaging through the shelves. Pulling out a sheaf of paperwork, she passed it to me and shifted uncomfortably on her haunches.

"Are you OK?" I asked, suddenly concerned about her.

"Yes. Yes. Just need to stretch a bit, that's all. And my clothes are damp. I feel a bit chilled."

"Two minutes," I promised and flicked through the papers.

"Nothing of interest," I said. "A couple of suppliers' invoices. One for two dozen goblets and one for a box of dream-catchers."

Flan raised an eyebrow.

"Don't ask me," I said and scanned the remaining paperwork.

"And the rest are just catalogues. I'll put them back."

I played the torch about, not wanting to miss anything. There was a calculator, some pens, an unlocked petty cash box containing £45 in notes and a handful of coins, a duplicate pad for handwriting receipts and some flowery paper and sticky tape for gift wrapping. Nothing at all of interest.

Flan uncurled herself to a standing position and rubbed at the small of her back. "Ready?" she asked, and even in torchlight, I could see her eyes gleaming.

"As I'm going to be," I said.

She turned to face the purple curtain, inclined her head with a theatrical bow, before drawing it aside and exclaiming "Ta-da!"

CHAPTER NINETEEN

"Oh," we said simultaneously, and I could hear the disappointment in Flan's voice. We were looking at a miniscule kitchen containing a sink with a water heater above it and a counter the size of a chopping board. On it stood a kettle, a jar of coffee, a bag of sugar, a couple of mugs and a neatly folded tea towel. A calendar hung from a drawing pin on the wall. That was it.

"Oh well," I said. "Never mind," and then spotting another door in the corner added, "got to be the loo."

Opening the door a crack, I poked my head around.

"All this effort for nothing, darling." Flan sounded deflated. "I am sorry."

"You've nothing to be sorry for," I reassured her. "We knew it was a long shot."

At least I'd known that. The chances of finding anything juicy or even remotely revealing had always been highly unlikely, but at least we had tried. And satisfied her curiosity. I was just about to close the loo door, when I spotted another door to the left of a towel rail.

"Hold on a sec," I called. "There's another door here. Probably just a cupboard."

I crossed over to it and turned the handle. I was fully

expecting a broom and a mop to come crashing down on me, but instead I found myself peering into blackness. I hesitated and then, without stepping forward, I shone my torch around.

"Flan. It's another room. Come and see."

She joined me, and we entered into a small circular room draped all around in the same silky purple curtains that we'd just come through. Here, they were not only full length but pinned up and over the ceiling in great looped swags, like a Bedouin tent. Or how I imagine a Bedouin tent to look. There wasn't a window, and no obvious source of artificial light. The only furniture in the room was a bare chipboard table with its flaps down, and two hard-backed chairs painted black but with their armrests and seats picked out in silver gilt.

On the table lay a rectangle of the purple fabric which I assumed was used as a cover, a pair of candle holders with their candles all but burnt down, and a pack of cards. I stepped across and drew out one of the cards. A jaunty-looking chap in green, with a feather in his cap, stretched out his arms to the sun.

"Tarot?" I asked, showing it to Flan.

"Ah. The Fool," she said, flashing her torch. "Face up. That's good, I think. Something about innocence and naivety, if I remember rightly. Suits you, darling."

"I didn't know you knew Tarot," I said in surprise.

"I don't. But a friend I had years ago, used to go and see a lady in a flat in Tooting. I went with her a couple of times and sat in."

She glanced at the candle holders. "Not a very good idea with all this fabric about. And having to make one's way through the lavatory is hardly inviting."

I was just agreeing with her and replacing the card, when my mobile rang. The noise was very loud and very shocking in that small enclosed space. I started and dropped the pack of cards.

"Shit." I fumbled in my jeans for the phone and then stabbed at the buttons to reject the call. It was Vanessa. I'd been wondering how she'd got on last night with Jonian but now was not the time for a chat. I breathed out noisily, feeling a twinge behind my eyes, the suggestion of a headache to come.

"Sorry," I said to Flan. "I never thought to turn it off." I closed my eyes for a moment, trying to imagine somewhere calm and serene and far away from the mental image I'd just had of myself wearing prison blues and locked up for a lifetime behind metal bars. Somewhere like a beach, maybe, with the waves rising and falling and seagulls overhead...

"Oh!" said Flan.

"What?" I demanded, instantly opening my eyes.

"Look," she said, pointing at the floor where a couple of the cards had spilled out from the pack. She bent down. "The Fool again. But this time reversed. Oh dear, I have a feeling that when it faces down, things don't bode so well. It represents impulsiveness, I believe. Ill-advised risks." She laughed nonchalantly and gazed about her. "There may be some truth in that."

"Hmm," I said and felt a prickling of sweat break out at my temples. "I don't believe in all that stuff."

But, as I picked up the other card, I couldn't stop myself from asking, "What does this one mean?"

On it was a picture of a white stone tower from which bodies fell, with forks of lightning zigzagging about them.

Flan shook her head and replaced it with the others back on the table.

"Can't remember that one, darling. Well, I think we've seen enough, don't you?"

She took one last look about her, playing her torch over the curtained walls.

"What an odd layout, but I suppose the building is old. Hold my torch a minute, would you?"

She handed it to me, and I shone both beams on her as she padded around the small space, lifting up bits of curtain to expose only the plastered walls behind. It was on raising the last panel of curtain, exactly opposite the door we'd come through, that she said, "Look here, Clarry."

I joined her, directing the torch beam over a small recessed area just wide enough for two people to stand in. I ducked under the curtain to take a look.

"Nothing," I said, having examined the empty space. I was just reversing myself out, when my foot struck something. I flashed my light down onto a small triangle of black rubber. I picked it up. It was a doorstop. That was odd. There wasn't another door here, so why should there be a doorstop?

"Hold on a minute," I said, and shone the light up and over the walls again. It was then that I spotted it. Another door set flush into the wall. A door without a handle. I pushed at it tentatively but it didn't give. I got down on my hands and knees and examined it minutely for signs of a lock or any means of entry but there was nothing. In frustration, I tapped and prodded but still it didn't budge.

"It must be blocked off," I said to Flan, who had now stuck her head through the curtains and was watching my efforts with interest.

"Let me try. It reminds me of the adventure stories I used to read as a girl. All about discovering mysterious tunnels running under the cliffs and down to the sea."

"We're nowhere near the sea," I grumbled, and then recalled the fact that we weren't that far from a river.

"And stone passages and secret doors," Flan continued. "I used to love them. I remember how my father would sit and read to me every night before I—"

"Flan," I said urgently, "can we please reminisce about this later? Like maybe when we are out of here and safely home with bloody big glasses of wine in our hands."

Flan nodded. "Let me just give it a try."

And, pushing in front of me, she pressed lightly on the upper part of the door, just where a lock would have been situated if there had been one. We heard a faint creak. Then another. And then another, louder this time. We exchanged a look and watched in wonder as the door started to swing slowly back on its hinges to reveal a narrow staircase winding its way up into total blackness.

"Flan, you really *are* an artist," I breathed.

Flan acknowledged the compliment but didn't move to start up the staircase. Neither did I. A moment passed. And in the silence, I felt a mounting reluctance to venture up those stairs.

"What do you think is up there?" I whispered eventually.

"Just what I was asking myself, darling." She gave her head a slight shake. "Well, shall we go and find out?" And, stooping, she picked up the doorstop and inserted it firmly beneath the bottom of the door, ensuring that it would remain open.

"Must we?" I asked. "No, you're right. We've come this far and so…" I swallowed and continued. "Right. OK." And then, because I felt that I really had to, added, "I'll go first."

Placing my foot on the bottom step, I shone my torch upwards. The bare brick walls were powdered with dirt and trailing cobwebs. The air felt cold and held a trace of damp, that old mildew smell of cellars long disused, but wasn't completely stale. I took another step and felt Flan behind me.

"I didn't see any sign of an upper floor from the street, did you, Clarry?"

"No," I agreed, taking another hesitant step. "It's weird. But then we are at the back of the building, aren't we?" I paced out the layout in my mind. "At least I think so. So, maybe we just couldn't see it."

We were both whispering now. The narrow space, the enveloping blackness, the strangeness of it all, repressed even Flan's habitual high spirits. We made our way cautiously upwards. Before taking each step, I shone my torch directly onto the next stone tread, fearful of finding the surface unstable and wrenching an ankle. The steps, although begrimed, were not blackened with the dust of years. Someone uses this staircase, I thought, and often enough to keep the dirt from having settled and solidified. As if to confirm this, my torch picked out a heel print. It wasn't possible to say if it was a man's or a woman's, but its outline was clearly discernible. I pointed it out to Flan.

We had crept up over a dozen steps now and still the flight stretched on up into the darkness. The reluctance I'd felt on first starting up them, intensified. Without Flan, I knew that I would never have dared to go on. The higher we climbed, the less close the atmosphere became and the more the smell of damp was left behind, but this did nothing to abate my unwillingness to keep going. I hadn't thought myself claustrophobic, but the feeling that the walls were pressing in was a difficult one to shake off.

Flan counted the steps as we continued our groping way upwards.

"That's twenty-five. My legs are beginning to ache," she said. "How much higher can this go?"

I felt a faint waft of air shift about me and said, "We're nearly at the top, I think," and then noticed that, from this point on, there was, on either side of the wall, after every three treads, a rusted ring of metal fixed into the brickwork.

"They aren't large enough to be handrails," said Flan. "Footholds, I think. Perhaps there weren't always stairs here…"

She broke off. "Ah, of course. We're in the original chimney."

I stopped abruptly and swivelled around to face her.

"I think you're right," I said. "And that means there's no need to go any further."

I laughed in relief. The sound echoed eerily in the narrow chamber. But Flan shook her head.

"Let's not give up now. Keep going."

"What on earth are we going to find up a freaking chimney?" I hissed. "Come on, Flan. This is pointless. I've had enough. Let's go back down."

In the beam from the torch, her eyes glittered. With the scarf wound about her hair, she looked rather like a pirate, I thought. All she needed was a cutlass and a hoop earring. Sighing, I turned back around and pushed on.

Another six steps and we were at the top. I poked my head up and peered into an area about eight foot wide with a brickwork floor and walls partially built out of the same brick. Timber formed the upper part of the walls and the curved ceiling, rather like someone had stuck a lid on. It made me think of an old-fashioned tugboat turned upside down and shoved on top of a chimney. And the boat appeared to be leaking. Water dripped through the gaps where the wood was starting to disintegrate. I could hear the rain pelting down around me and the wind whistling and sighing through the rafters. I shivered. Glancing at my watch, I realised that it was only twenty to nine. We'd been in the shop less than half an hour, but in that time the rain and wind had fretted and whipped themselves up into a storm.

I shone the torch over the floor and then stepped up and into the space and crossed to a small antique desk. Its top had once been fine leather, but damp and dirt had pitted and scarred the surface. A plastic folding chair was placed before it, and a lantern, of the type that are sold in garden centres to hold tealights, sat upon the floor. There was nothing else in the room.

Flan heaved herself up through the opening. She was breathing a little heavily and I felt a stab of alarm for her. She's so intensely alive and with such an indomitable spirit, that I sometimes forget she is seventy years old.

"Sit down and catch your breath," I said gently and indicated the chair.

She sank gratefully into it and looked about her. "It's rather like the top of a lighthouse, darling. Except without the windows. I can practically feel the floor swaying beneath us."

I didn't like that thought at all. Was the floor moving? What was beneath us? The room was much broader than the width of the staircase and so what supported it? The idea of being suspended in mid-air made my legs feel wobbly. I was scanning the ceiling and walls again, more carefully this time, when the beam from my torch picked out a small hatch that presumably led out onto a roof. I turned back to the desk. Flan had been lightly running her hands over a pair of drawers, both of which were locked. She placed her torch down, directing its beam over the edge, and fished out her giant bunch of keys.

"Time for a touch of artistry again."

She sounded back to her usual self and I felt instantly cheered.

"Over to you," I said.

"I hope there's a map," she whispered.

"A map? Of what?"

"Treasure, of course."

"Flan," I said sternly, "this is *not* an adventure novel. And you are not a pirate. Even though you do look a bit like one at the moment. It is highly unlikely that we will find any kind of map. In fact, ten to one, the drawers are empty."

"Then why would they be locked?" retorted Flan as she got down to work with the pick-locks. "I'm sure we'll find something highly suspicious. I feel it in my water."

She had the left-hand drawer open within a few minutes. We peered expectantly inside to find it contained only a clear flexi-file of papers and a large brown envelope.

"In your water, huh?" I grinned at Flan as I lifted them both out. Loosening the envelope's gummed-down flap, I gingerly drew out a set of photographs. The first was an exterior shot. A street at dusk, cars parked, people walking by. And, clearly lit by the glare of a neon sign, was the image of Zoe hand in hand with a middle-aged man with dark, thinning hair gelled back from his forehead. It was *Loafers*. And there were more photos. One of the couple in his Jeep, in what looked to be a pub car park. His arms were about Zoe's shoulders; their lips were locked together in a passionate embrace.

"Wow. Look at this, Flan. It's Zoe and the guy I told you about."

"Darling, I'll look at them later. I want to get this other drawer open. This has to be where the money is kept. Ah." She gave a satisfied grunt as the lock gave. "I'm getting so good at this. Now, let's see what we've got."

She drew out two maroon-coloured passports, opened one and handed the other to me saying, "Yes, that's her. *Name: Sarah Gaitskill* but, oh dear, not a very flattering photograph."

"They never are," I replied. "Hold on, this is also hers. It's a different photo because her hair's slightly longer but it looks current."

I studied the printed information. "*Surname: Perry*. Well, that's weird."

"Maybe it's her maiden name?" suggested Flan.

"I suppose so," I agreed, and took another squint at the printed boxes besides the photo: "*Place of Birth: London. Date of birth: 11th September 1975.*"

"Yes, London for place of birth," said Flan, playing her torch over the small print. "But *Date of birth: 15th October 1974.* What did I tell you? Something suspicious!"

It certainly was. "Is there anything else in there?" I asked.

Flan slipped her hand in the drawer again. "Yes, there's something at the back. Wait a sec."

Suddenly I froze. What was that? I'd heard something. I was sure that I had. There had been a noise, a faint sound from a long way off. The strain of something high-pitched and vibrating. My heart thumped painfully in my chest and I glanced warningly at Flan. She'd heard it too. Sitting tense and upright in the chair, her face looked drawn and white in the torchlight. A second later and the sound came again. A melodious tinkling of bells, clear and unmistakable. Flan and I stared at each other in stricken panic. I held my breath, paralysed. I knew that sound. We both did. It was the distant peal of wind chimes.

CHAPTER TWENTY

Everything that I was going to lose danced before my eyes. My house, my job, my parents, my friends, my date with Ed tomorrow night. Everything gone. Nothing would ever be the same. That vision I'd had earlier, of prison blues and metal bars, would be real soon enough. We were going to be caught. The police would be called, we'd be arrested and go to prison or, at the very least, get a criminal record. But I'm *not* a criminal, I wanted to yell at the top of my voice. I was just larking about. Playing at being a detective. Daring myself to be brave and fearless. This wasn't meant to happen.

Self-pity threatened to overcome me, and I could feel tears starting in my eyes. I blinked them away, turning to Flan, and then felt immediately ashamed. Flan. I could see the deep lines of worry etched about her mouth and she was trembling. Her face looked naked in spite of the make-up that she wore. She was afraid. I'd never seen that in her before. And it was entirely my fault. Wonderful, warm, life-enhancing Flan; she'd been there for me all my life, I loved her, and I'd got her into this terrible situation. That thought hit me like a draught of cold air and my mind cleared. Regret and self-pity were not going to get us anywhere, I realised.

Now was the time for action. I'd got her into this and I was bloody well going to get her out of it again.

"The door!" I whispered. "I'm going back down."

Flan put out a hand to stop me but I shook it off. The door to the concealed staircase was wedged open and the minute whoever it was downstairs realised that fact, they'd be up after us. We'd be cornered, trapped. But, my brain protested, won't you then be trapped in this little secret room in the chimney? Would we ever be able to get out? Was there a handle on the inside of the door? We hadn't thought to check. And what if the person, Sarah, I assumed, was planning to come up here? We'd be caught then, either way. But I couldn't think about that now. There was no time to lose. I had to reach that door and close it noiselessly behind me. Locked in we might be, but it was our only chance.

In complete darkness, I began to grope my way down the stairs. Each careful footfall felt like I was walking nearer and nearer to disaster. I daren't rush or I'd slip and might be heard. I crept on, counting each step as I went. Nine steps. Ten steps, eleven, twelve. My hands grazed the brick walls as I tried to speed up and take two at a time. Something caught and tugged at my hair and I nearly shrieked aloud. Cobwebs, I told myself, just cobwebs. They can't hurt you. I flapped them away, dislodging my baseball cap which fell from my head. Seventeen steps. Eighteen. The air grew mustier the lower I went, and I thought that I could hear something. I strained to make out what it was. I didn't think it was voices. Was Sarah alone then? And what was she doing here at this time of night? The thought of coming face-to-face with her filled me with dread. Of finding her at the bottom of the stairs waiting for me. Staring up at me. My legs felt weak and I nearly missed my footing, but I had to keep going.

Twenty-five steps now. Twenty-six. Twenty-seven. There were only nine or ten left to go. The sound I'd heard was becoming more audible. The slight whirring hum of something mechanical. I hadn't seen a photocopier or a computer downstairs, but maybe I'd missed it. I stealthily made my way down another step. And then another, expecting at any second to see the outline of a figure framed in light at the bottom of the staircase. But it was still pitch-black. Only another four steps to go. That was all I needed to get to the door and release the wedge. But my legs refused to obey me. My body felt numb. I was seizing up. Come *on,* I silently screamed. *Move.* At last, my legs responded, and pitching myself forward as quietly as I could, I tip-toed down the last few steps. Thirty-three. Thirty-four. Nearly there. Nearly there. Thirty-five, thirty-six. I'd reached the bottom.

There was the curtained room just a few feet away from me, and I could hear the whirring hum, then there was a sharp click and the whirring stopped. It was the kettle. Sarah was making herself a cup of coffee or tea. She wasn't just dropping in to collect something she'd perhaps forgotten. She might be making her way up to the secret room at any moment. I dropped to my knees and fumbled in the darkness for the black rubber doorstop. My fingers felt thick and heavy as I grasped hold of it and tugged, but it was wedged in tight. I shifted my weight, tugged again and it sprang out with such a force that it propelled me backwards into the curtains. Flailing as they billowed and ballooned about me, I pulled myself to my feet and then watched aghast as the door slowly edged itself towards the closed position. And I was on the wrong side of it. My arm shot out and I caught it just in time. I wrenched it back and squeezed myself through, hearing it creak ominously and then swing firmly shut behind me. I didn't stop to grope about in the darkness in the hope of finding a handle on the inside of the door. I wasn't stopping for anything. I simply charged up the stairs, fleeing to the secret room and to Flan.

CHAPTER TWENTY-ONE

She was waiting for me with her torch beam trained on the top step as I plunged panting into the room. The light dazzled me for a moment and dust motes swam in front of my eyes. I put out a hand to steady myself and felt Flan's firm grip on my shoulder.

"Quick, Clarry," she hissed. "There's a way out. Onto the roof, I think. Come on."

She crossed swiftly to the wooden hatch I'd noticed earlier. Set in the upper portion of the wall, in the timber section, it was roughly three times the size of a cat flap but should just be broad enough to allow us to wriggle through. Flan wouldn't have a problem as she was slimmer than me and with much narrower hips. She had already moved the folding chair into position beneath it and I could see that she had managed to force open one side of the hatch. Great gusts of wind were tearing at the loose timber and rain pelted down through the opening.

"I couldn't get the other side free. It seems to be stuck," said Flan, steadying the chair as I climbed up. Locking my knees, I then shoved hard with the flat of both hands against the hatch and it gave a satisfying crack. I shoved again and this time it splintered and fell away outwards. I yanked off my sweatshirt and, using it to protect my hands, I knocked away the splinters and fragments of wood from the frame.

"OK," I said, stepping off the chair and pulling my sweatshirt back on, "let's do this." I saw a look of resistance cross Flan's face. "Come on. Put your torch in your pocket and let's get you through."

I helped her up onto the chair and then clambered up behind her and put my arms about her waist, ready to shunt her through the opening.

"We don't know what's out there, Clarry," she said in a low voice, as rain spattered down onto her head, soaking the silk scarf.

"What if there's nothing on the other side?"

I squeezed my eyes shut, trying to think. She could well be right. What if this wasn't a way out after all? But what choice did we have? The only other option was to stay penned up here and hope that Sarah didn't discover us. I exhaled and said into her ear, "The hatch must be there for a reason. I think we should try it, Flan. But if you don't want to, that's OK, because whatever happens, I'm not leaving you."

I heard her give a little strangled sound which could have been half sob and half chuckle, before saying with forced brightness,

"Right you are then, darling. Here we go. Chocks away!"

She stretched forward and, with a short jump, caught hold of the frame, heaving her shoulders through the opening, whilst I pushed at her bottom and legs.

"Can you see anything?" I called, but it was difficult to make out what she said against the sound of the gale. I could only presume that it was all right, because she continued to thrust herself forward until she at last managed to draw her left leg over the edge of the frame. She was now sitting astride it with her right leg dangling inside but the rest of her body outside. For several moments, she didn't move but then slowly pulled her leg up and out until she had completely disappeared from view. I prayed that she had landed safely on the other side. Flexing my shoulders, I was preparing myself to follow her when, between the fluting cries of the wind, I heard a noise from behind me. A groan. A creaking groan. The door! The door to the staircase creaked like that when it opened. And that meant only one thing: Sarah, or whoever it was, must be on their way up here. Well, bloody good for her, I thought, my adrenalin levels rocketing, because I sure as hell wouldn't be forming a welcoming committee.

Taking a jumping leaping lunge at the opening, I kicked out with my legs, knocking over the chair in the process. Using my hands to take my weight, I propelled my head and shoulders up and out through the hatch. Instantly I was soaked. My hair flew into my eyes and, for a moment, I was blinded as I lay flat half-in and half-out of the room. Buffeted by the squalling wind and the rain, I was like a prone surfer on her board, preparing to rise and ride the waves. As I blinked, trying to make out what was in front and beneath me, I could feel the edge of the timber frame pressing hard into my waistband, and the torch, which I'd thrust into the pocket of my jeans, digging painfully into my thigh. Then, I felt a protective pair of arms cradle my head and heard Flan's voice urgent in my ear. "It's all right," she shouted against the howl of the gale. "It's safe."

She pulled and I wriggled forward in a diving motion with my hands braced, and came down on something solid, my legs slithering out behind me. With Flan supporting me, I was able to drop down into a crouch before heaving myself upright.

"There's someone coming up the stairs," I yelled, and then looked anxiously about me. We were standing on a narrow platform edged by a waist-high brick wall. I glanced down and immediately felt my head swim. Far below, the headlights of cars winked like fireflies in the darkness. Thunder bellowed not far off to the west of us in great muffled claps as if someone had thrown a duvet over a pair of giant crashing cymbals. Jagged forks of lightning flashed and fizzed in the distance.

I turned to Flan. Her scarf had slipped down around her neck and her hair blew back from her fine-boned face. She no longer resembled a pirate. With her high cheekbones and regal nose, she looked like an eagle. An eagle in a nest. That was it. We were in a nest from which we couldn't fly down.

I clutched at the wall, finding in its rough surface something both tangible and symbolic to hold onto, whilst dimly recognising that we couldn't fall if we kept within its protective boundary. This thought steadied me and I started to think clearly again. Was there any way down from here or would we, after all, have to face Sarah or whoever it was that was so close on our heels? Wiping my streaming face, I took another look downwards, this time trying to orientate myself. The platform where we stood overlooked the entrance to the shop but, being at the back of the building, hadn't, in the dark, been visible from the road.

It was a sheer drop down to a flat roof that encompassed the front of The Nook, the hardware and the shoe shop, so that was no good, and, equally impossible as an exit, to the left of us, were the pitched roofs of houses. The only option we had was to work our way around the platform and see if there was any means of descent.

I grabbed at Flan's arm and slowly we started to inch our way within the curve of the wall, tracing a semi-circle around the secret room. Please don't let it form a full circle, I silently begged, or we'd be back to where we'd started.

The storm was overhead now. The duvet had been shrugged off and the cymbals clapped together in deep booming rolls. The lightning flashes were coming closer together and intensifying every moment. Could we be struck? I was thinking about the metal zipper on my sweatshirt, wondering if it could be a conductor, when the image from the Tarot card came back to me and I experienced such an inner shudder that my legs trembled. *The Tower.* I had always dismissed palm and Tarot readings as exploitative. A con trick practised by the unscrupulous to take advantage of the vulnerability and need for reassurance that some of us look for when feeling lost. But could there be some truth in it after all? *No!* my rational mind repeated over and over again. But we *were* on a tower and there *was* lightning zigzagging around us. And what about the bodies tumbling, falling like blown leaves to the ground? Was that to be our fate?

We edged our way forward until we found ourselves overlooking the inky black ribbon of the river. Twisting away on its endless course, it was indifferent to our plight and to the raging storm.

We crept on. I had all but given up hope, feeling certain that we had nearly doubled back on ourselves, when abruptly the height of the outer wall dropped. I looked down and there, set into the wall of the adjoining building, which looked to be a warehouse, was a narrow set of steps twisting downwards. A stump of rusting metal balustrade suggested that there had once, long ago, been a handrail, but now the outer edge of the stair run was completely exposed. I couldn't see how far or where the staircase led, and it would be all too easy to slip as there was nothing at all to stop us from falling off the edge, but it was a chance.

"Flan, we'll have to bump ourselves down on our bottoms. Can you do that if I go behind you?"

She nodded, her face set. Holding tight onto her shoulders, I stood behind her as, gingerly, she lowered herself onto the top step.

"Try not to look down," I instructed and then, not knowing if I was talking more to myself than to her, added, "Just focus on one step at a time."

With one hand on the wall and the other gripping the outer edge of the tread, Flan inched herself down onto the next step and I followed suit. So began a terrifying descent. Slowly and laboriously, lashed by rain and buffeted by wind, we negotiated our way down, aware that the slightest wrong move would mean a fall of thirty or forty feet to certain death. Every six steps or so, the staircase twisted and turned until I had no idea whether we were still facing the river or directly under the hatch through which we'd just escaped. Was Sarah looking down on us from within the secret room? The thought made my skin crawl but I didn't look up.

Resolutely, I took my own advice and focussed only on the next step down, locking myself in a bubble of concentration. It doesn't matter how long this takes us, I told myself. Or how wet and uncomfortable we are; we're heading in the right direction. Away from Sarah. Away, I fervently hoped, from pursuit. The Tarot card meant nothing, and we were going to make it. Luck was now on our side and all we had to do was press on. I kept repeating *we are not going to fall*, over and over in my head like a mantra. *We are not going to fall. We are not going to fall.*

CHAPTER TWENTY-TWO

About twenty-five steps down, luck deserted us. Flan stopped abruptly as we rounded yet another curve in the staircase and found ourselves discharged onto a flat corrugated roof. Flan heaved herself up and leant against the wall, pushing back her soaking hair from her face.

"Don't move," I said, fishing out my torch and directing its beam at our feet. "You rest and I'll check it out."

"Be careful, darling." Her voice held a slight tremor and I could see from the set of her shoulders how tired she was. Tired and cold. We were both wet through to the skin. I stripped off my sweatshirt and wrapped it around her.

"We're nearly there," I said, sounding infinitely more confident than I felt. "This is the last hurdle."

"I hope so," she replied and then, flashing me one of her brilliant smiles, added, "I've always found a storm rather exhilarating. But I think that perhaps we've both had enough excitement for one day."

The roof we were standing on was about forty foot wide and fifty foot deep. On either side of us, walls divided the building from its neighbours, both of which were much taller than this one, some three or four storeys high. Late eighteenth or early nineteenth century warehouses, they had been refurbished but retained their original wall-to-ceiling windows. The windows were all in darkness and so they hadn't been converted into apartments, I thought, but it was more likely they were used as office space. Either way, there was no chance of us getting out that way. Leaning down, I gave the metal corrugated roof surface a good hard push. Would it withstand our weight? It was difficult in the dark and the heavy rain to see what condition it was in, but it felt sturdy although slippery. I sank onto my bottom and scooted my way cautiously forward along the middle of the roof, feeling the metal beneath me shift and sag a little. I made it to the edge and peered down.

We were right on the river, its waters dull and lustreless only six feet away. I lay flat on my stomach and shone my torch along the facia of the building, hoping against hope for some sort of ladder or footholds set into the front of the brickwork, but there was nothing except a rusted winch with a short length of corroded chain, swinging backwards and forwards in the wind. It wasn't long enough to allow us to use it to drop to the ground. And not that Flan would have the strength to do that anyway, I thought with a pang.

The building was single storey but taller than a bungalow or one-level residential property. Whilst much smaller than its neighbours, it had, I guessed, also been a warehouse. The winch would have been used to transport whatever it was that was made here, out through the front of the building, onto a palette and then onto a barge for transportation. There were two arched windows on either side of the door and from one of them a rectangle of metal cladding had come away and hung only by one hinge. One section of brickwork at ground level looked blackened and smoke damaged. The building was obviously derelict. I flashed the torch over cracked paving slabs choked with weeds and litter, to the river. I studied the drop. Could I, even without the chain, swing myself down somehow and then get help and come back for Flan? No, it was too high. And I might land in the river or smash down onto the towpath. I'd have to phone someone to come and rescue us. But who? I looked at my watch and couldn't believe that it was only nine thirty. I felt like we'd been through two lifetimes since I'd last checked it in the secret room. I sat up and wrung some of the water out of my ponytail. My skin was clammy but I felt cold. There were friends I could phone. My best friend, Laura, for instance, or one of the guys from Abbe's, but for some reason I felt reluctant to do so. Maybe it was something about admitting failure to others, when I hadn't yet come to terms with it myself. But it looked like we hadn't any other choice. Depression threatened to engulf me and my eyes swam. My inner battery was running low and exhaustion was setting in. I glanced over my shoulder and across to Flan, who waved. She was still leaning against the wall, but her head was held high, and I could practically feel her smiling encouragement at me. Her silhouette, in the darkness, looked forlornly brave. I waved back and then shone my torch over the roof for one final look. Playing the beam back and forth, I focussed on an area at the front of the roof on the far left. That's odd, I thought, the corner directly above the winch appeared slightly raised and didn't reflect a metallic gleam like the rest of the surface. Gingerly, I bottom-walked my way along the outer edge until I reached it and found that this section wasn't metal at all but timber. It was about three foot square and must have been fabricated maybe a hundred years ago to allow for the installation of the winch. It was now completely rotten and had all but disintegrated. I put down my torch and stomped down hard with my right foot. Instantly, the timber gave way and I found myself looking down into blackness. I grabbed the torch again and flashed its light through the hole into a long galley-shaped room, its floor strewn with rubbish in which I caught the glint of broken glass.

Along both lengths of the room was built-in benching or worktops, most of which were broken and splintered. I felt a surge of energy and purpose. Although not directly beneath the opening, the benching was near enough that if I could just wriggle through and swing myself down, I should be able to drop onto it. I hesitated. Would it collapse beneath me as I landed on it? And what about Flan? It would be too much for her.

I made my way back to her and explained what I'd found. "It's worth a try, darling," she said. "If you think you can do it? And look, the storm's just about over."

So absorbed had I been, that I hadn't noticed that the rain had all but stopped. The thunder and lightning, having got bored of us, had chased each other away to beset another part of the city.

"You see. Things are looking up," said Flan.

They were? Here we were, soaking wet, filthy, stranded, with the possibility of Sarah hot on our heels, and things were looking up. I started to laugh. I couldn't help it. We'd just made a terrifying descent down the side of a building and yet Flan was all cheerful optimism. Or at least she was giving a bloody good impression of it. What a woman she was. I hugged her. "Come on then," I said. She kept close behind me as we made our way across the roof and then held the torches, directing both beams into the room as I lowered my body through the hole.

"Just to the left of you," she called, as my legs flailed about trying to get a purchase on the benching.

"No. Further back. Make a wider swing."

My arms, taking all my weight, strained in protest as I dangled inches above the worktops and kicked out again.

"You nearly had it then." Flan peered down at me. "Yes. That's it. You've got it."

I felt something solid beneath my right foot and, in a scissoring movement, managed to manoeuvre myself backwards until both feet were firmly set down. There followed an agonising moment when, like a trapeze artist reluctant to let go of her swing, I couldn't bring myself to release my arms and trust myself to the stability of the benching.

"It looks pretty solid," called Flan.

I closed my eyes for an instant then let my arms drop. Bending my knees in expectation that at any moment the timber would give way, I adopted the stance of a skier about to tackle a grand slalom. The timber buckled but held and hastily I jumped down. It felt so good to be back on the ground. Now all I had to do was work out a way to get Flan down here to join me.

"Well done, Clarry." Flan clapped her hands together. "That was most impressive. Oh, how frustrating it is to be old. I wish I could just drop down after you. But I can't. Now catch."

I caught one of the torches and swept the room with its beam. The benching had, I thought, been originally designed to create individual work stations or alcoves. Mouldering partitions separated one from the other to head height. I wondered what had been produced here. It couldn't have been anything very large as the workstations were only a couple of feet wide. Or very heavy.

But then I thought of the winch. That could only have been installed for the purpose of bringing something heavy in or out of the building. Oh, what did it matter what was made here? I thought crossly. Who cares? You aren't touring the derelict buildings of London for the benefit of your education. This isn't *Mastermind*. Nobody's going to test you or award you points for your knowledge of riverside industrialisation in the nineteenth century. Focus, for God's sake.

Right. Was there anything here I could use to create a platform for Flan to lower herself onto? I looked about me. There was only the benching and nothing amongst the dirt and rubbish on the floor except a few old bricks. Watching my feet, wary of stepping on broken glass, I made my way to the front of the room where it faced the river. One of the arched windows I'd seen from above was partially boarded up from within, but I could see moonlight through the timber slats. I could probably kick through the wood if the entrance door proved to be impenetrable. And where was the door in relation to where I stood? This room was narrow and would only take up a section of the frontage of the building, which meant there were other areas to explore.

I flashed my torch along the walls until I spotted a door on the internal wall. It had once been a pale green with ornate mouldings at its head. Now, what little paint remained was marred with mildew. I pulled at its handle and was surprised to find that it opened easily. I peered into blackness and played the torch beam along a hallway from which two other doors led off. And further down at the front end was the main entrance door.

"I'm going to see if I can find anything," I called up to Flan. "I won't be long. Are you all right?"

"A little chilled and achy, darling, to be honest, but nothing a warm bath and a large drink won't sort out."

The thought of lying in hot scented water with a glass of wine in my hand spurred me on, and I set off down the corridor, heading towards the main door. The air smelt of damp, and the walls, also painted in the same faded shade of green, were cold to the touch. On reaching it, I found that the door was completely encased in metal sheeting and so there would be no way out for us this way. There was less rubbish underfoot, but thick brambles and strands of ivy had snaked their way through the front brickwork and were creeping stealthily up the walls. Nature was slowly, inexorably, reclaiming the building.

I turned back. The silence was beginning to oppress me and I felt a resurgence of the same nervous dread I'd experienced in the secret staircase. When would this nightmare be over?

I came to the first of the two doors and tried the handle. Again, it opened easily and, after first anxiously spraying the room with the beam from my torch, I walked cautiously into a large open space. The room proved to be completely empty except for a stack of wooden crates all bearing the same faded insignia: *Johnsons' Pianos and Musical Instruments of Quality.* That explained the winch. This must have been the workshop where they made the pianos. What a sight that must have been. A shiny black piano, maybe even a baby grand, being lifted on pulleys and then slowly winched over the water onto a waiting craft. I wondered if one had ever slipped and gone crashing down into the depths. I could almost see it. Like a glossy black beetle on its back, its lid open to reveal a gaping mouth, the white keys grinning toothily, before being subsumed in the slime of the Thames.

I examined the crates. Could I stack them on top of each other to create a makeshift support? It might work.

I took another look around. Here was the other window overlooking the river, but this one's boarding looked more solid. I hurried back out into the corridor, tried the remaining door and found myself in what had once been an office. Along one entire wall was a partitioned pigeon-hole structure like a series of open post boxes, all thick with dust. Above each recess was a tarnished brass plaque. I rubbed at a couple with my finger and read *Piccolo. Flute. Banjo.* There weren't any chairs or anything to sit down on, but there was a narrow oblong wooden table. A refectory table which appeared to have withstood the corrosive effect of years of damp far better than the benching in the gallery. I put that down to the fact that windowless, the office had less air circulation. The table felt solid. Could I drag it through to Flan? Would it even fit through the doors?

I could. And it did. By alternately pulling and pushing, I managed to manoeuvre it into the gallery and position it below the roof opening.

"It's still a bit of a drop," I called up to Flan. "Hold on a minute."

Racing back to the workshop, I tested a few of the wooden crates for soundness before bringing three of them back to the gallery. I clambered up onto the table.

"I think two should do it," I said, hoisting up the crates. "I'll hold them firm and all you have to do is step down."

"*All* I have to do?" queried Flan with a slight intake of breath. "Right then. Here I come."

Without hesitation, she stepped lightly down onto the top crate, took hold of my hand as she sank down onto her bottom and then landed neatly onto the table. Jumping off, I pulled out the spare crate to make a step and, seconds later, Flan was on solid ground. She gave a little cheer. "What a relief, darling."

Dusting her hands down the legs of her filthy black trousers, she said crisply, "Now. How exactly do you propose we get out of here?"

"Flan," I said, choking back a snort of laughter that verged on the hysterical. "Flan… I have a plan."

I approached the window and, with a kick-box move I remembered seeing someone once demonstrate at a gym, I aimed my right foot at the rotten timber slats. Four hard kicks were all it took before I had it open wide enough for us to climb through.

The smell of the river hit us in fresh woody draughts as we stepped over the low ledge, across the cracked paving stones and onto the towpath. For a moment we said nothing but just stood looking down at the water and then, simultaneously, we turned to gaze up at the buildings behind us. I took a long breath out, hardly believing that we'd made it, and looked at Flan, my eyes smarting with tears. We'd been so very high up. Up in a nest. But we'd done it; we were safely down. The eagle had landed.

CHAPTER TWENTY-THREE

We didn't go back for the car. Stumbling along the towpath, we rounded the corner and spotted a black cab trundling along with its yellow light on. I flagged it down and, within half an hour, when Flan, fresh from her bath and in her robe and slippers was rummaging around in the fridge looking for something for us to eat, I had stripped off my clothes in her guest bathroom and levered myself down into the foaming water. My body felt stiff and aching. At some point during the night's doings, I'd managed to cut my arm. Blood encrusted a long, thin line that went from inside the elbow joint all the way down to my wrist. Closing my eyes and breathing in the steam and the scent of rose from the bath essence, I ignored the question of exactly when it was that I'd had my last tetanus shot and instead offered a silent prayer to whomever or whatever had been watching over us that night. We'd been incredibly fortunate. It could all have gone so terribly wrong.

"Clarry," called Flan, "I've left one of my nighties and a dressing gown out for you."

When I joined her in the kitchen, Flan was uncorking a bottle of Champagne.

"It's good for shock," she said, pouring some into a flute glass and offering it to me.

"I thought that was brandy," I said, accepting it.

"That too," she said, filling her own glass. "But Champagne, in my opinion, not only calms the nerves but instantly cheers the spirits."

"It certainly does," I agreed as the cold liquid fizzed down my throat and we clinked glasses.

"Do you know?" I said, sinking down on a chair, "I don't think I've ever tasted anything quite as good as this in all my life."

"We're celebrating being alive, darling," said Flan solemnly, before taking her first sip. "That's really what you're tasting."

*

I was awoken the next morning in Flan's guest room by sunshine streaming in through the white voile curtains. It was seven o'clock. The Champagne must have worked its magic because, untroubled by bad dreams, I had slept soundly. Perhaps we are only plagued by visions of pursuit along ghostly passages or down endless flights of steps when, in the real world, there is little or no chance of those things taking place. My nightmares had invaded my waking world. I'd lived them. And that, it seemed, was enough for even my unconscious mind to get a handle on.

I had no alternative but to pull on my filthy clothes of the night before and so, looking like a tramp that had spent the night in a ditch, I padded into the kitchen. Flan was still in bed, but on the table, I found a message written on one of the notelets she'd bought at The Nook, which was a nice, if ironic, touch.

Thank you for a thrilling adventure, darling.
Most of my contemporaries spend their days playing bridge and pottering about the garden. You can't imagine how much colour you add to my life!

Happy to oblige, I thought.

Oh, by the way – Flan had added a postscript – *I think you might be interested in these.*

And there, beneath the card, was the A4 brown envelope containing the photographs, slightly stained along its top, and the clear plastic flexi-file of papers. Flan must have shoved them down her jumper or into her pocket and I hadn't noticed. She'd have been delighted at her own cleverness and would have thoroughly enjoyed surprising me with them in this way. Scooping them up, I let myself quietly out the front door.

Last night's storm had left in its wake a fresh and vividly lovely morning. As I walked the short distance home along The Ridgeway, I found myself appreciating the song of the blackbird and the trill of the robin as never before. A brush with death will do that, I guess.

Once back, I phoned for a minicab, and whilst I waited for it to arrive, I hastily showered, put on fresh jeans, a faded blue shirt and sneakers and dug out a cotton scarf to completely cover my hair. I needed to retrieve the Renault and, although I didn't think that The Nook would be open yet, I didn't want to run the risk of being recognised by Sarah or Sheila.

As we pulled up on the corner outside the French bistro, I paid the driver and slipped on a pair of dark glasses, feeling like some minor celebrity trying to hide from the paparazzi after a night with an illicit lover. If only.

Walking as casually as I could, I didn't even glance at the shop as I let myself into the car and started the engine. It was highly likely that Sarah had called the police last night. Would they have taken details of cars parked outside the shop, I wondered, or was that only on TV? But they'd be bound to dust for fingerprints. I felt a fluttering of panic before realising that neither Flan's prints nor mine were on record. I hoped that the assumption would be that it had been a chance break-in. But the money in the petty cash box hadn't been touched. That didn't fit the theory. Calm down, I told myself. There is nothing to trace us to the scene and no possible way of linking Flan and I to the crime. *Crime.* The word made my stomach flip-flop and I hit the accelerator.

I'd been up for nearly two hours now and, so far, I'd managed to keep all thoughts of last night and the feelings of fear, guilt and utter helplessness I'd experienced, at bay. I wasn't ready to examine them. Not yet at least. If I wanted to continue to function clearly and pursue the case, then I mustn't burden myself with self-doubt or it might cripple me completely. I needed to trust myself. It was enough to accept that last night had been a low point. A very low point indeed. That, for now, was as much as I was prepared to acknowledge.

After a bowl of porridge and a cup of tea, I felt ready to go through Sarah's papers. I looked again at the photographs of Zoe and *Loafers*. There were half a dozen of them and all clearly showing a couple engaged in a clandestine affair. Why did Sarah have them? I wondered. Evidence of some sort? Blackmail? That's what compromising photos usually meant in detective stories. But if Sarah planned to extort money from *Loafers*, were she and Zoe in on it together? Were they partners? Whatever the reason, it certainly looked ugly. I sat back in my chair puzzling over different theories but not getting anywhere. And something else bothered me. I would have thought that, nowadays, photographs were mostly taken on a mobile phone, and so why would Sarah keep actual physical copies locked away at the top of a tower, when she could access them at any time on her phone or computer?

I turned to the file of papers. There were over a dozen handwritten pages of figures with each page containing three columns. The first column was of dates in chronological order, going back nearly two years. They didn't seem to follow any pattern, some being a week or a fortnight apart. Sometimes three days would follow in succession and then there might be a gap of nearly a month. I looked at the second column. A single capital letter. Either an *R*, a *W* or an *E*. I had no way of guessing what the abbreviations could mean. The third column was easy. Pound signs. Figures ranging from £150 to £900 with an average of about £450. Except for one entry that was for £250,000, and beside this figure, in the second column, were the letters *HW*. The only abbreviation to have two letters.

I checked the total in column three twice. The smaller individual amounts added up to £170,205, and that with the £250,000 made £420,205. A hell of a lot of money. I made more tea and looked at the pages again. The last entry was this Tuesday. The figure was £390, and the letter was *W*.

I banged down my mug of tea, slopping it over the papers. I must be more jaded than I thought not to have worked it out before. Tuesday had been the meeting at Helen's house. Helen lived in Wandsworth, hence the *W*. And, that night, I'd guessed the donations collected had been several hundred pounds. I thought back to my late-night drinking session with Polly at Kendall's. What was it she'd said? That there were other groups donating to the Wellness Centre. One in Richmond. That had to account for the *R*, and one somewhere in Surrey. So, places beginning with *E* in Surrey. Egham? Was that in Surrey? It could be Epsom or Esher. They were in Surrey, just a few miles away from where I'd been brought up, in Dorking, and where my parents still lived. So, whatever town the *E* represented, it looked like this was a record of donations collected by three covens of white witches. But what about the two hundred and fifty thousand and the letters *HW*?

Was *HW* a place? I racked my brains trying to think of somewhere that fitted but couldn't come up with anything. And surely the amount was too vast to be from a meeting. Perhaps the letters were the initials of someone's name? I replayed my conversation with Polly. Everyone had donated, she'd said, but Helen had given the most. Helen. *H*.

*

If Polly was surprised that I was phoning so early, she didn't say so.

"Hi," I said breezily. "I'd like to send Helen a note to say thank you for the other night. She hadn't expected me, and she was very kind."

"Oh, Clarry, that's sweet of you. She'd appreciate that."

Polly sounded genuinely touched and I decided that I would, indeed, send the note.

"I remember her address. It's her second name I don't know."

"It's Warwick. Helen Warwick," said Polly.

HW. Well, that explained that. But what I couldn't understand was why Sarah's notes were handwritten and not on computer and, like the photos, why they had been locked in the tower? Polly had said that Sarah kept the women updated with the amount collected and that they had paid a deposit on a property. Surely then, there would be a bank account with either paper or digital statements? Presumably, these were kept somewhere else. At her home probably; but why would the statements be kept separately from the list of donations? I sighed, wishing we'd had time for Flan to break into the other desk drawer. The statements might have been in there.

I had a lot of unanswered questions and no idea of how to go about securing answers. It was only as I was carefully blotting the spilt tea with some kitchen towel that a thought struck me. Maybe there weren't any bank statements; paper or otherwise? Maybe there wasn't a bank account at all? In which case, where was the money?

I tried to think it through. Flan had seen Sarah with a lot of cash, which could mean that there wasn't an account, but then Helen wouldn't have donated £250,000 in cash. No one in their right mind would do that.

I looked at my watch. It was nearly ten o'clock. Flan was normally an early riser but, after what we'd been through last night, she might still be in bed. I phoned her from my landline, and she answered on the third ring.

"Ah, Clarry." She sounded bright and her usual self. "I have just had breakfast in the garden. Such a beautiful morning after that terrible storm. But isn't that so like life? We fight our battles and then are given the blessing of restoring ourselves so as to be ready to fight the next one."

"How are you feeling?" I asked, all of last night's guilt returning. "You must still be exhausted. And physically, are you OK?"

"Darling, I'm absolutely fine. Now, tell me what's in those papers. I was simply too tired last night to even glance at them, but I've been burning with curiosity ever since I got up. I was about to phone you."

I filled her in on the details and on my suspicions. She sighed. "I'm just sorry that I didn't think to grab the passports too."

"You did brilliantly, Flan. Oh, did Mr. Babcock, when he was looking up the shop, come across Sarah's home address? I thought I might check it out."

"I'll ask him," she said. "But I'm not sure staking out her house is a very good idea, Clarry. At least, not in your car."

Damn. I hadn't thought of that. If Sarah or the police had taken note of cars parked outside or near to the shop, then my old Renault couldn't be seen anywhere near her home. I was just wondering if I could phone Ian or Steph and maybe borrow one of their cars for a couple of hours, when Flan said, "I have an idea. Give me ten minutes and I'll call you back."

We'd just hung up when my mobile rang and Vanessa's name flashed up. I had completely forgotten the shock it had given me last night in the Bedouin room, when she'd phoned and I'd rejected the call.

"Hi, Vanessa," I said. "Sorry about last night. I was… I was a bit tied up."

"No problem. I just wanted to tell you about Jonian."

She sounded happy and excited.

"After you left the other night, we had another drink and then we went for a pizza. He's great, Clarry. Different from anyone I've ever met. And so interesting. Before I met him, I knew absolutely nothing about Albania but, from the way he describes it, I feel like I know the country."

"Hmm," I interrupted dryly, "and that has nothing to do with his lovely long eyelashes?"

She laughed before admitting, "Well, yes, maybe just a bit. But he's *so* gorgeous."

"He is," I agreed. "Are you seeing him again?"

"Yes, that's the other thing I was going to tell you. We are going on a date. Tonight!"

And you're not the only one, I thought, with a flash of anticipation. After all the drama of last night, I hadn't had a moment to think about my dinner date with Ed.

"That's great," I said, and meant it. "Where are you going?"

"We're meeting at the Dog & Fox and then probably going to one of the Thai restaurants."

I made a mental note to avoid them. I liked Vanessa but she'd interfered in my last date with Ed and I didn't want that happening again.

"Thanks, Clarry, for setting me up with Jonian. I know that's what you did and it was good of you. I'm grateful. I might never have met him again without you."

"I just live to help others," I said airily, and she laughed.

"And you rescued me at Mum and Dad's party. I never thanked you properly for that. And again, when I crashed and burned at your restaurant and now this. I really do owe you."

"Don't be silly," and then, taking advantage of the moment to change the subject, I said, "so the other night at Helen's? Pretty weird stuff, right?"

As I uttered this, I realised that, by anyone's standards, every night this last week for me had been not merely weird but totally bloody insane.

"Not what you expected?" There was an edge to her voice.

"No," I replied, nettled at her response. "Why would it be? The idea of a bunch of white witches casting spells at a house in Wandsworth was the last thing I'd imagined."

There was a loaded pause before, sounding every inch her mother's daughter, she said, "You are under no obligation to join us again."

God, the girl was prickly. One minute she was full of gratitude, enthusing down the phone, eager to confide the details of her love life, and the next, she was getting all lady of the manor on me. Hastily, I backtracked.

"I'm not saying that I didn't find it... um... interesting... it's just that it was a lot to take in. Especially when unprepared."

"You're right," she agreed, sounding mollified. "It is. But if you really did enjoy it, then just give it a chance. It can be so enlightening. So freeing."

My mind snagged on the image of Sarah and Zoe escorting her away from the meeting. Free? Was Vanessa free? I wondered. Or had she, in shrugging off the conventions of her background and the restraint of her mother's approval, simply found new fetters? Not the time to ask her.

"Have a great night," I said. "I'll want to hear all about it. I've got my matchmaking reputation at stake."

The landline then rang. Flan was brisk.

"Harold has got the address and we're on our way to pick you up."

CHAPTER TWENTY-FOUR

Twenty minutes later, I heard the toot of a car horn and, grabbing my bag, I locked up and made my way down the path and out through the front gate. There, I stopped in astonishment. A hearse was parked outside my house. A hearse with a coffin in it.

In the driving seat was Mr. Babcock. He looked like an elderly tortoise, with his short wrinkly neck thrust forward above a stiff white collar and wearing a top hat. Flan, also wearing a top hat, was perched beside him. She stretched and opened the passenger door.

"Hop in, darling, and we'll be off."

"In *this*?" I exclaimed, gaping.

"I agree that it's not ideal for a stake-out," she said regretfully, "but it's the best we could come up with on the spot. Harold's other car has developed crotch problems, I'm afraid."

"*Clutch* problems," corrected Harold with a sniff. "Clutch problems."

"But I thought you were retired," I said irrelevantly as I became aware of the curious glances of a couple passing by on the other side of the street.

"I like to keep my hand in," he replied.

Keep his hand in *what?* My mind skittered away from the image of cadavers on a slab.

"And does one ever really retire?" asked Flan thoughtfully. "If it's something one has done all one's life then one can't help but retain an interest. Undertaking is in Harold's blood, you see, even if now, his nephew does run the company."

"It's funeral directors," said Harold with another sniff. "We don't use the term undertakers anymore."

"Well, whatever it is you're called and whoever it is that's in *there*" – I gestured towards the coffin, which was topped with a simple sheaf of white lilies and encircled by individual flower arrangements in baskets and bouquets – "I'm not going anywhere with you in *this*."

"But I've got you a top hat," protested Flan, pointing down at one she held in her lap. "They're surprisingly comfortable. It's the soft brim, apparently. Now, do get in, darling. We've just got to make a quick drop-off and we'll be on our way."

I felt my eyes cross as she pulled me unresistingly into the hearse beside her.

"You will have to stay in the car," instructed Flan, as we made our way out of the Village and onto the A3 heading south. "It's the jeans, Clarry; it wouldn't be respectful. And, as you'll be visible through the window, you'll need to put on the hat. How lucky that Harold always carries spares."

She looked down complacently at her own black flared trousers and cream silk tunic.

"I nearly put on my rose cable-knit sweater this morning, but I was feeling more Lauren Bacall than Katherine Hepburn today. It's almost as if I'd known."

She turned, craning her neck.

"You don't happen to have one of those long coats or waistcoats in the back, do you? There's plenty of room available to store a few necessaries."

What was she expecting to find back there, apart from a body in a coffin and the flower arrangements? I thought. A couple of beach towels and a picnic basket?

"No, Flan," said Harold warningly, with his eyes on the speedometer. We were maintaining a strict thirty miles per hour.

"And you're to stay in the car. I don't want you mingling with the bereaved. I've got a job to do and you'll only—"

"Nonsense," she retorted. "I know perfectly well how to behave. And I think you'll find I have a very sympathetic way about me. I'll be an asset. People regularly come up to me in the street asking for directions. I have that kind of face. Confidence-inspiring." She turned and favoured me with what she presumably considered to be a deeply reassuring smile. "See what I mean, darling?"

I covered my face with my hands, and we drove on.

"So, who's in the box?" I finally asked, unable to stop myself.

"That's Mrs. Florence Paige," answered Flan, pulling a clipboard from the glove compartment. "Harold has the paperwork here."

She read, "Eighty-nine years old. A widow. Died in her bed. Marvellous way to go. I hope that happens to me. By the way, Harold, I don't much care for the shade of wood. Too orange. If one has to face eternity in it, one might as well choose a colour flattering to the skin."

"The skin changes colour as the decomposition process develops," observed Mr. Babcock in a matter-of-fact tone.

"It starts out yellow and then turns a rather deep shade of—"

"Stop!" I begged. "Please. Enough."

"Squeamish?" asked Flan.

"*Duh!*"

"I take it by that, you mean, yes," Flan said reprovingly as Mr. Babcock swung the hearse through the high iron gates of Putney Crematorium.

"Time to put on your hat, young lady," he instructed, as we clunked slowly over a metal grid and onto a driveway bordered with purple and white bougainvillea.

We parked outside the chapel beside two other funeral cars. There were only a handful of mourners, most of whom looked to be well over the age of retirement. When you get to the age of eighty-nine, and unless you have a large family, I supposed, then most of your friends would already have died. I felt a stab of sadness for the lady in the coffin. When Grandma P. had died, there had been a much better turnout.

Mr. Babcock clambered creakily out of the car, but as Flan made to follow him, he shook his head discouragingly. She, of course, completely ignored the gesture and stepped lightly out onto the gravelled path to stand beside him.

"Just try and look quietly dignified," she hissed at me as the door closed behind her.

I pulled the brim of my hat down low over my eyes and tried to concentrate on doing just that because, after all, I was now alone with a corpse. Alone with Mrs. Florence Paige. Deceased. I shuffled in my seat, finding the experience bizarrely awkward but oddly intimate. I hadn't known the lady and yet here I was, just inches away from her earthly remains.

"So, here we are then, Mrs. Paige... or... or... may I call you Florence?"

My words hung heavily in the silence.

"Well, to be accurate, here *I* am," I explained, swivelling around in my seat and addressing the upper section of the spray of lilies, which I assumed would be roughly in line with where her head was laid. But maybe I'd got the foot end? I thought. How could you possibly tell? It appeared coffins didn't come with a sign stating *This Way Up*.

"Because, Mrs. Paige... Florence... I'm not actually sure *where* you are. I do understand that you are here physically, but it's just that I've no idea where the rest of you might be. If, in fact, you are anywhere at all. No, I'm sorry, that came out wrong. I'm sure you are somewhere or other, but what I mean is..."

A shadow crossed the rear window as someone approached the car, and I turned hastily back around in my seat. What the hell was wrong with me? I'd just been talking to a dead person.

The back door opened. Mr. Babcock stretched in an arm and began carrying out the flower arrangements. Then he clicked something that released the coffin from its retaining clips and allowed it to slide forward on silent runners. Three pallbearers in striped trousers and grey waistcoats then drew it out and, with one practised movement, raised it up onto their shoulders. Mr. Babcock made up the fourth, as, in sync, they stepped slowly off to then disappear around the back of the building.

Flan, smiling benignly, was standing close to a lady vicar who, in cassock and white surplice, was greeting the mourners as they entered the chapel. A woman in her late fifties in a smart black suit and a black feathered hat, dabbed at her eyes with a tissue, and I watched as Flan patted her gently on the arm and murmured something. I could only hope that the something was soothing.

Once everyone was accounted for, the vicar turned and entered the chapel, the doors closing behind her.

Flan had moved over to the Garden of Remembrance and could be seen stooping amongst the rose bushes to examine the commemorative urns and plaques.

"Some lovely flowers," she said as she climbed back into the hearse, "and I had a nice little sit-down on a memorial bench. By the way, that was Florence's daughter, Patricia, in the feathered hat, I was talking to. Only child and unmarried. Sad not to be able to share her loss."

We could hear the strains of organ music starting up as Mr. Babcock and his team appeared from behind the chapel. The ceremony had begun, and it wouldn't be long now before a curtain glided noiselessly around the coffin and Mrs. Paige would be lowered into the flames. Goodbye, Florence, I thought sadly. Sorry we never got to meet. In the conventional way, that is.

Mr. Babcock appeared to be giving the pallbearers some final instructions before leaving them to it, and I kept my eye on the three men as he headed towards the hearse. Now Mrs. Paige had been offloaded and they were no longer in view of an audience, they had shrugged off their solemn bearing and were lounging against one of the funeral cars and lighting up cigarettes and chatting. What an odd way to make a living. Every day, they took part in the ritual of death, witnessing the inevitable end of man's brief time on this planet and then they went home to their families, their dogs and their gardens, just like everybody else. No wonder they smoked their fags and shared their jokes. How else would they be able to deal with so much unrelenting reality?

Mr. Babcock was back in the driving seat. "Now," said Flan, "Epsom, I think you said?"

I'd thought Epsom might have been location E on the list.

"Sarah lives in Epsom?"

"Yes," said Mr. Babcock as he started up the engine. "It won't take us long from here."

As we crossed over the metal grid and headed out through the heavy iron gates, I asked, "Now, can I take off my hat?"

CHAPTER TWENTY-FiVE

Even though we were no longer transporting a coffin, we stuck to a speed limit of thirty miles an hour. I didn't know if this was a hearse thing or an elderly man thing.

Flan kept up an animated conversation regaling Mr. Babcock with a highly sanitised version of the previous night's events. From her description, you'd think we'd just been on a bit of a jaunt.

"Such a shame you missed it, Harold," she said with a regretful smile. "But I'm not sure, with your knees, you would have been up to it."

"Sounds a completely hare-brained scheme, if you ask me," he said disapprovingly. "You shouldn't have been there at all." He sniffed. "Either of you."

He was probably right. No, he was definitely right. I knew that, but I still didn't like being told off. I glanced at Flan, who winked slyly back at me. Mr. Babcock was seventy-three to Flan's seventy, but he seemed a decade older. Whilst George Huxton, Flan's other gent, still retained much of the vigour of his prime, Harold Babcock was decidedly an old man. And rather a miserable one at that. I'd never understood what it was that Flan saw in him. I'd asked her about it once. "Oh, darling," she'd said, "he has simply the most *enormous*…"

I'd clapped my hands over my ears to drown out the rest of the sentence.

We had now reached Epsom. An old market town made famous by The Derby, it still has a strong racing community. Sarah Gaitskill's address was up on The Downs, where many of the rich stud farm owners and trainers lived, at the affluent end of town. Huge detached properties, down shady tree-lined lanes, bore signs for private stables, equine spas, grass and all-weather gallops. We passed rolling fields with training jumps set out at varying heights and watched as a colt, whose coat of beautiful deep russet burnished brilliantly in the sunshine, was put through its paces.

"It's the next road on the right," said Mr. Babcock. "Am I to pull up outside of the house?"

I gulped. Why hadn't I used the journey and the waiting time in the car with Mrs. Paige, to come up with a plan? My mind struggled impotently as I rejected one idea after another. It was hopeless. We were in a bloody hearse and so there could be no question of laying low and discreetly observing the comings and goings. We'd have the entire street peeping around their designer curtains, wondering which of their neighbours was being carted off to the Great Paddock in the sky.

My gaze fell upon Mr. Babcock's clipboard and I picked it up.

"Can we just stop here for a moment?" I asked, and he slowed to a halt outside a vintage-style newsagent with a white painted façade and big glass jars of sweets in the window. I dragged my eyes away from the toffee bon bons and stripy humbugs, flicked over Mrs. Paige's details and then considered the half-dozen sheets of notepaper beneath. They were blank except for the header *Babcock Funeral Directors* and the contact details for their premises in Kingston. I thought hard for a moment. As there was no way we could avoid drawing attention to ourselves, then shouldn't we make the hearse a feature and use it to our advantage? Not a question I ever thought I'd ask myself. But how to use it? How to see it as a benefit rather than a bloody big white elephant? I closed my eyes, the better to concentrate, until Flan nudged me in the ribs.

"Are you thinking what I'm thinking?" she asked in an excited whisper.

"Probably not," I replied with a sigh and opening my eyes. "Why, what *are* you thinking?"

"How about this? We're canvassing the area looking to drum up business. Door-to-door sales calls. Like they used to do with vacuum cleaners and encyclopaedias. You know the kind of thing."

"We can't tout for business in a hearse!" I cried. "It's macabre."

"Why ever not?" she demanded. "I think it lends an air of distinction. And it's a free market, isn't it? I bet there are a lot of elderly people in a smart area like this who'd like to get all their arrangements made before they become infirm or can no longer make those kinds of decisions for themselves. I should think they'll be very glad to see us. I'm sure I would."

I shot her a look. "What about the willow basket and your idea of being set fire to and chucked into the Thames?"

"I haven't come to any firm decision one way or another about that," she said, pressing her lips together as Mr. B looked on askance.

"I'm just saying, that planning the details of one's *final journey…*" she continued with solemn emphasis "…might actually be a comfort. What do you think, Harold?"

"It is a bit irregular," he said. "We usually rely upon word of mouth or passing trade. And sometimes we—"

"*Irregular?*" I interrupted. I seemed to have been exclaiming a lot in the past few hours. "It's the craziest idea I've ever heard. I was thinking more along the lines of pretending we are conducting some kind of survey. Something about the modern attitude to death or… or… oh, I don't know."

"That's nowhere near as interesting, darling," Flan said. "My idea would be much more fun."

"What's fun got to do with anything?" I cried. "This is death we're talking about here."

"Well, that I grant you," she conceded, "but there's something else to consider. Harold has kindly gone out of his way to chauffer us, and so why shouldn't he get something out of the proceedings? Even if we sign just one person up, it will have been worthwhile. How does that TV advertisement go where they tap the back pocket of their trousers? *Every Little Helps.*"

"That's for a supermarket, Flan," I protested. "It's not the same thing at all."

But I could see by the way that Mr. Babcock was thoughtfully running his finger around the inside of his stiff collar that he was considering the idea.

"We never turn away new business," he said. "Not if we can help it."

"I bet there's stiff competition out there," Flan persisted. "If you'll forgive the pun. And what with the recession and everything, business must be slower."

"People still die in a recession," I pointed out. "How can business be slow? You have a never-ending supply of customers. And it's not like anyone ever changes their mind, is it? This must be the one business in the world where, once a job is booked, there can be no chance whatsoever of a cancellation. Undertakers are always in demand."

"Funeral directors," corrected Mr. Babcock and then nodded sagely. "But you do have a point about cancellations. That practically never happens."

I let that one pass.

CHAPTER TWENTY-SIX

After debating various options, all of which grew increasingly fanciful, we settled on a combination of both mine and Flan's original plans and drove into Wilmerhatch Lane, where we cruised slowly along until we spotted Sarah's house halfway down on the left-hand side. I was to stay safely in the car until it was established whether or not Sarah was at home. There wasn't a car parked on the drive, but that didn't necessarily mean that no one was in.

I donned my top hat again and hunkered down in my seat, watching Mr. Babcock and Flan open a low gate and make their way down the path to Sarah's door. The house was a large yellow-brick semi-detached late Victorian property, fronted by black metal railings. The front garden was paved in slabs of a lighter yellow shade to the brickwork, and the only other patches of colour were a few dismal evergreen shrubs in two narrow planted borders. A pair of miniature bonsai trees in need of a trim stood to attention on either side of the front door. On the detached side of the house there was a tall black-painted side gate leading to the rear garden. The windows were the original sash and, whilst the upper ones had the curtains fully drawn back, the lower ones were partially closed.

I waited as Flan, clipboard in hand, lifted a lion's head brass knocker and rapped smartly on the front door. A minute or two passed and she knocked again. I saw her and Mr. Babcock exchange glances as she tried once more and then gave up. I climbed out of the hearse.

"It's a big house," observed Flan, shutting the gate behind them. "I assume she must have a family to need so much space. Odd. Normally, there's some evidence of children. Wellington boots in the porch, that sort of thing."

I thought of the kids' bikes at the home of Mr. and Mrs. *Loafers* and nodded. I didn't know if Sarah had a family or not. I turned about, scanning the neighbouring properties. In the ancient oak tree of the house opposite, I spotted a rope swing, and in another, a child-sized wheelbarrow lay on its side in the gravel.

All the other front gardens were bright with flowers. Roses grew up and over stone walls, and window boxes were a riot with geraniums and lobelia, but Sarah's front garden was untended and her house featureless. Solid, elegant in its way, but it revealed nothing about the personality of the owner.

Mr. Babcock, who had been looking from one to the other of us, asked "What happens now?"

"Now," said Flan, starting purposefully off down the street, "we talk to the neighbours."

"What is it that you're looking for?" puffed Mr. Babcock, trotting behind her. "I'm not sure that I understand exactly what it is you are trying to find out."

"We don't know either," said Flan, tilting her topper at a more rakish angle. "And that's the fun of it. The not knowing. This is a fact-finding mission. We're merely gathering…"

She broke off and nodded to me to take over.

"Background information," I finished for her. "Now we know Sarah's not in, we can talk to her neighbours. We'll break the ice with this undertaker stuff and then—"

Mr. Babcock automatically cut in with "funeral directors," but I wasn't listening to him.

"And then, we try and get them to spill the gen about Sarah. Simple."

"Isn't it?" agreed Flan with a brilliant smile.

"Spill the gen?" asked Mr. Babcock, fishing in his waistcoat pocket and drawing out a packet of mints. "I didn't understand half of what you just said. The way I see it, is that the both of you are a bit touched and we'll probably get all manner of complaints for disturbing people but, come on then, if we must. Let's see if we can rustle up my next customer."

"You see," hissed Flan as we started up the drive of the neighbouring house, "he does have a sense of humour."

I rolled my eyes but forbore to comment.

The door to the house on the semi-detached side of Sarah's was opened by a harassed-looking dark-haired girl in her early twenties. She, quite understandably, looked rather taken aback at the sight of the three of us in top hats, but our appearance did have the effect of making the grizzling toddler clinging to her right leg stop crying, which could only be considered a positive, I thought. The infant she cradled – and I couldn't tell if it was a boy or a girl – merely stared at us with round blue eyes and continued to suck gummily on its fingers.

"Hi," I said, "we're from Babcock's Undertakers."

"Funeral Directors," corrected Mr. Babcock, crunching noisily down on a mint.

"Funeral Directors," I repeated dutifully. "And we are in the area today to canvass opinion as to whether or not the more traditional form of dress worn by my colleague here…" I indicated Mr. Babcock, who bowed stiffly. "Is still suitable for the modern age *or* if a less formal look…" I gestured to Flan, who fluttered her fingers up and down her tunic and trousers as if modelling an outfit for a shopping channel. "If a less formal look," I repeated, frowning at Flan, "better reflects the changes undergone in wider society." That sounded rather good, I thought. And I found myself genuinely interested in the woman's answer. I didn't get one. She and the two children continued to regard us blankly.

I tried again.

"So, what would your preference be, I wonder, if, in the unfortunate occurrence of a death in your family, you had to decide…?"

"*Muerto?*" the woman exclaimed in a heavy South American accent, fervently crossing herself.

"Dead? *Ay Dios Mio!* Who died? No! Tell me it's not Meester and Miiissis Scarborough?"

She crossed herself again and clutched the baby so tightly to her breast that it immediately started screaming, which set off the toddler, a flaxen-haired boy in Spiderman pyjamas, to grizzling again.

"*Pobre nino sin madre.*"

"No!" I cried in urgent apology, not having a clue what her words meant but recognising that she'd clearly got the wrong end of the stick. "I'm sorry. It's nothing like that.

Really. No one's dead. I promise you. We are just asking people their…"

"Tell me what happened." She hadn't understood me and had raised her voice to a wail in competition with the racket the children were making.

"Was it in that fancy car of theirs? *Ay Dios Mio*. I told the Meester that he drives too fast…but he don't listen to me. I'm just the nanny…why should he listen to…?"

It took a while to straighten things out. Following the nanny's frantic phone calls to both Mr. and Mrs. Scarborough, and their repeated bewildered reassurances that they were, in fact, very much alive, we were finally able to back hastily down the path and out onto the street.

"We'll definitely be getting complaints," breathed Mr. Babcock. "I think, young lady…" He turned to me, his neck pink with agitation and swollen over his tight collar. "…That we should give up this foolishness. Don't you?"

"Certainly not," Flan answered for me. "There's no reason at all to give up, Harold. Whilst our first attempt may not have gone quite as we would have liked, we'll do better the next time. Won't we, Clarry?"

I nodded and Mr. Babcock sniffed but didn't look convinced.

Sarah's other immediate neighbour, on the detached side, was a crotchety old fellow in bedroom slippers, wearing a stained brown cardigan over an ancient suit, shirt and tie.

He looked us up and down interrogatively and then, before I had chance to start with my spiel, snapped, "You're ten years too late for my wife and at least five years too early for me. You've got the wrong house," and he slammed the door in our faces.

"Very disappointing," clucked Flan. "On the television it's always a pensioner with nothing better to do than look out of his windows observing the doings of his neighbours, who provides a vital clue that solves the case. That chap doesn't look like he gets out much. And at his age, you'd think he could have been a bit more civil and invited us in. I mean, what else can he possibly be doing with his time?"

"*You* don't spend all day looking out of *your* window," Mr. Babcock pointed out reasonably.

"That is because…" said Flan, flashing him a withering look with which I was only too familiar, "…*I'm* not elderly."

"Well," Mr. Babcock persisted, "technically, you *are* a pensioner and…"

I decided to come to his rescue as he had really been very good about the hearse.

"I don't think he meant it quite like that, Flan," I said soothingly. "Look. Time's getting on. Why don't we split up? Mr. B. and I will try across the street and you, Flan, give a few more houses on this side a shot."

Mr. Babcock and I spoke to five of Sarah's neighbours in total, learning that they all preferred the formal dignity of traditional undertakers' attire, I mean funeral directors', and that Sarah Gaitskill kept herself very much to herself. She wasn't involved in the neighbourhood watch scheme, hadn't contributed to, or even attended the royal wedding street party, didn't put up lights or a tree at Christmas and didn't have children. She'd lived in the lane for about twelve years. For the first couple of those, she'd occupied the house with a man thought to be her husband. She was now presumed to be divorced. She spent a couple of nights a week away from home, but no one knew where and, as she didn't let off fireworks or throw wild parties, none of the habits that habitually incense near neighbours, no one took much notice of her. That was it.

We got back in the hearse and waited for Flan, who we'd last seen going into a mock Tudor property, two doors down from Sarah, on a corner plot with steps up to a storm porch. Twenty minutes and two extra strong mints later, we spotted her exiting the house. I could tell at once, by her swift confident stride, that she was feeling pleased with herself.

"Uh-oh," I muttered to Mr. Babcock. "She's been up to something."

He gave a deep sigh and said, "I can only hope that she's maintained the dignity of the profession and of the firm."

"I wouldn't count on it."

CHAPTER TWENTY-SEVEN

"Didn't I tell you that I inspire confidence?" demanded Flan, before she had even got the car door fully open. "The Cunninghams. He's seventy-six and she's seventy-one. They've lived in that house for over forty years. Such an agreeable couple. I really took to them."

She buckled up and Mr. Babcock started the engine. "They want matching top-quality coffins, Harold. I told them about Mrs. Paige's being too orange and they quite agreed with me that a paler colour would look more distinguished. And they don't want any of that faux brass. It has to be the real stuff. They're coming over to your showroom on Monday morning at eleven o'clock to go through the brochures."

"We don't call it a showroom; it's a—" said Mr. Babcock, but Flan rode over him impatiently.

"Don't quibble, Harold. How am I supposed to know what you call the place? The point is that they're coming. I was worried that Kingston might be too far for them to travel, but Mr. Cunningham drives and they know the area. They plan to make a bit of a day of it, I gather. Arrange their last rites in the morning and then have a spot of lunch afterwards. Ah…" she broke off and then turned to me.

"Lunch sounds rather a good idea, doesn't it? Drive on, please, Harold, and I'll tell you all they had to say about this Sarah Gaitskill character."

*

"Parking a hearse in a pub car park is a little irregular," said Mr. Babcock to Flan's suggestion that we lunch in a lovely-looking pub-restaurant, The Derby Arms, near to the racetrack. However, so pleased was he with her news about the Cunninghams, that he gave in without protest and even insisted on paying for our sandwiches.

"What a red-letter day," remarked Flan as we settled ourselves around a table by the window. "Harold hardly ever takes his wallet out. Make sure that you have a pudding."

Once we'd got our drinks, Flan was ready to share what she'd learnt.

"Well," she breathed, giving a quick glance about the room as if worried that Sarah might be hiding beneath one of the tables. "They don't like her one little bit. They had quite a to-do with her six months or so back." She took a sip of her white wine before continuing. "It was Freddie, their cat, that started it. He likes to explore the neighbouring gardens. Well, cats do, don't they? And so, one evening, Mr. Cunningham – he asked me to call him Ron and she's Mary – anyway, Ron was taking a stroll up and down the lane before bed, calling for Freddie, when he saw Sarah at her front door pick up a stone and throw it at the cat to drive it from her garden. And the stone hit poor old Freddie on his back. Bled a lot, they said. So, you can imagine how they felt. They dote on that cat. He was there in the sitting room on a special cushion. Lovely old thing he is. Relations between them and Sarah have been very poor ever since. Sarah wouldn't apologise when they confronted her about it. Said the cat was trespassing."

She took a bite of her sandwich.

"That's great, Flan. It really is," I said, "but how does that help us? I mean what does that tell—?"

"Don't rush me, Clarry. You know how I don't like to leave anything out."

I did.

"And so, the Cunninghams have been keeping an eye on her ever since. It's a friendly road where everyone gets on well with everyone else. As they've lived there so long, I think the Cunninghams feel proprietorial about the street. They'd hoped, when it appeared that her husband had left, that she'd sell up and they thought that might be the case when... wait, I haven't told you about the husband."

Mr. Babcock and I explained what we'd heard from the other neighbours; that a man, presumed to be Sarah's husband, had once lived with her.

"Mary saw an estate agent go in two or three months ago," Flan continued. "An Epsom firm, according to the sign on the car, but the house doesn't have a For Sale board and they haven't seen anyone looking like potential purchasers."

"I can check online and ring around the local agents," I said. "And so did they say anything about the husband?"

"Pleasant enough chap, they said. He used to leave at the same time every morning to catch the train into town.

Worked in London, they thought. But they haven't seen him for nine or ten years. I wonder what happened to him."

"Probably under the patio," I joked.

Mr. Babcock, ears pricking up at the thought of a body, looked as if he was about to say something, but Flan said, "One other thing they mentioned – and it would tie in with a house move – Sarah has moved a lot of her belongings, apparently. They saw her carrying boxes and crates into a van last week. One of those self-drive jobs. Maybe she was putting it into storage? I don't know. But what I can tell you is that the Cunninghams have my telephone number and yours, Clarry. And they are going to call us if they notice anything odd or suspicious. They are going to keep a special lookout. Ron's a keen bird-watcher so he's got a pair of binoculars. From now on, they will be carrying out a full surveillance."

She caught my look of concern. "Don't worry, darling. I didn't give them the full story, but I had to tell them something. I explained that when we're not busy with the funeral business, we moonlight as investigators. They were both very impressed and excited at that. So, we can rely upon them to help us. Which means, darling, that with me, Harold, George and the Cunninghams, you now have five additional investigators."

Yes, I thought, and all of them septuagenarians. Flan beamed at the two of us before asking, "*Didn't* I do well?"

CHAPTER TWENTY-EIGHT

It was four o'clock before I got home. I wanted to give myself at least an hour and a half to prepare for dinner with Ed, which meant that I had enough time to make some notes about the case. There was a lot of information buzzing about my head and I hoped, that by writing up everything I'd seen and done, I might be struck with a flash of inspiration or, if nothing else, bring a level of clarity to my mind. Sitting at my computer in my spare room and laboriously going over the events of the last week was harder than I imagined. Impressions are fleeting and I wasn't sure that I'd retained them all. Was it really only a week since I'd sat having tea in the Maitland house and agreed to take on the investigation? So much had happened over the last seven days. From now on, I would keep a record of what I'd learnt as I went along.

It has already been established that I'm not a list person, but now I made two of them. The first was short and detailed the few facts I knew. The second, comprising a series of questions, was much longer. I then made a note of how many hours I'd spent on the case so far, trotted downstairs and picked up the phone to ring out.

I hoped that it wouldn't be Vanessa that answered and

was ready to put down the receiver if she did, but Diana Maitland herself picked up.

"Hi, it's Clarry. Can we meet tomorrow morning?"

*

Dressing for a second date is even more of a challenge than dressing for a first. I didn't want to look like I was trying too hard; but on the other hand, I didn't want to appear too casual. Whilst shaving my legs in the bath, I'd found some nasty bruises mid-thigh, courtesy of last night's adventure, and so that ruled out wearing anything short.

In the end, after trying on practically everything in my wardrobe, I settled on a white broderie anglaise dress flaring just above the knee, with a square neck and three-quarter sleeves. It's more of a demure look than I normally go for, but with heels and my pale pink clutch bag, it looked good. Or at least I hoped it did.

I followed my usual make-up routine but applied extra layers of mascara and a glossy bright lipstick which I then blotted off, having read an article recently claiming that men don't like kissing too sticky a mouth. It puts them off, apparently. So, I did want him to kiss me then? The thought made me nervous. Not the kiss itself, but the idea that I wanted him to. Because what if he didn't? The fact that, after our first date, he'd not immediately followed up with the request for a second, had only increased my interest. The thought then occurred to me that perhaps *he* was playing *The Rules* on *me*. Damn. But if that was the case, it only goes to prove that they work.

I gave myself a final once-over in the hall mirror. My dress was a bit plain. Maybe I should put on some bangles? They would also cover the cut on the inside of my arm that I'd sustained during the flight from The Nook. I nipped back upstairs. On my dressing table was the silver leaf bracelet that Polly had made for me. I slipped it over my wrist, admiring how the tiny green beads looked pretty against the white cotton of my dress. I hadn't worn it since Polly had presented it to me. Sheila had said that she'd invested it with the power of protection. What did that mean? I made a mental note to ask Polly when I next spoke to her.

By this magical practice… Wasn't that what we'd chanted? And what was it Polly had said about a love spell in the bar later? *If you want to bring a lover to you, do it on a Friday.* Well, today was a Friday. Experimentally, I whispered *By this magical practice* and then again, louder. I said it again and then again. And I kept on saying it as I let myself out of the house. Making up the lines as I went along, I found myself creating my own do-it-yourself spell which I mouthed under my breath, all the way down Wimbledon Hill until I reached the restaurant.

Ed was already sitting at the table when I arrived. And he looked good. The pale blue shirt he wore was open at the neck. The colour suited his tanned face and the darkness of his hair. He looked masculine and competent and solid. I liked that. He stood up and kissed me lightly on the cheek as I slid in opposite him.

"Hi. You look lovely, Clarry." His eyes scanned my face and I felt a bubble of excitement fizz in my chest. "I've ordered some Chablis. Is that OK for you?"

"Sounds great," I said. "How are you?"

"Good," he replied. "Not been a bad week. I've put in two quotes for neighbours in the street where I'm working on a complete redesign. Don't know if I'll get either job, but referrals are always nice to have. That's actually one of the hardest things about what I do. Getting new business. I'm not very good at the marketing side. I should be much more proactive."

The wine arrived, and he paused until our glasses were filled.

"Cheers. Good to see you."

We clinked glasses and he continued.

"I'm not particularly comfortable with selling myself. All I really want to say to a potential customer is that I'm going to do a decent job at a fair price and that I believe they will be happy with my work. That's it. But when it comes to flyers and the website, I feel I should come up with something more interesting."

"I don't see why," I said, after taking a sip of the chilled wine. "I think a simple approach is often the best. It's honest and reassuring and gets straight to the point. But I suppose, with referrals, it's a lot easier as your work speaks for itself. By the way…" Aware that I was leaning forward across the table, I sat back as if just getting comfortable. "…thank you again for my jasmine. It looks fantastic. Like a foaming waterfall of stars. I love it."

"That's a nice way of putting it," he said, handing me a menu. "And you're welcome. It seemed to me that you have quite a lot going on. And, as it's what I do, I thought I'd help."

"Well, all the same," I said, "it was really sweet of you."

He looked about to say something but gestured instead to the menu.

"What do you fancy to eat?"

The restaurant was busy but, tucked away in our corner seats, I hardly noticed how the tables around us filled up as the evening progressed and the light outside darkened from indigo to a soft smudgy black. The food was Italian and delicious. Tealights flickering in stubby china holders created a warm intimate atmosphere that was perfect for two people getting to know each other. We'd found common ground when we'd first met, but now we talked more personally. I told him about growing up in Dorking and I learnt that he had two older sisters.

"Even though they've both got families of their own, they still think of me as their little brother who needs to be organised. I got a call from Tessa today – she's the eldest – reminding me to get a birthday present for my father next week. It would never occur to her that I actually might remember without her prompting."

"And would you have?" I asked, forking up a mouthful of my seafood risotto.

He grinned. "Maybe not. And you? Do you think you missed out by being an only child?"

I thought about it for a moment before answering.

"No, I don't think so. I've been lucky in the friendships I've made, and Mum and Dad were great parents. *Are* great parents," I corrected. "Mum can be tricky, though. She's not a big fan of what she calls my ad hoc lifestyle. Waitressing is definitely not a proper job in her eyes."

"And what about the investigative work?" asked Ed, topping up our glasses. "How does she feel about that?"

"Haven't told her," I said simply. "She wouldn't understand and she most certainly wouldn't approve. Mind you, I'm not sure many people would approve of what I've been up to in the last couple of days."

He looked at me questioningly and, when I didn't immediately respond, offered, "Go on. You know you want to tell me. Is it to do with that girl's case? The one who interrupted our last evening together?" He raised an eyebrow. "She's not going to show up again tonight, is she?"

"No," I said. "She's safely occupied." Idly, I wondered how Vanessa's evening was going with Jonian, and then brought my mind back to focus on my own date.

"OK. Well, last night, I broke into... and out of a shop and today... today, I gatecrashed a funeral."

Ed put down his forkful of tagliatelle.

"This I have to hear. Start at the beginning."

I remembered from our last meeting how much I liked the fact that he gave his full attention to a conversation. He didn't look about him or scan the room for something or someone more interesting but listened, apparently absorbed and amused. I found myself telling him more about the case than I'd planned to. I had only just finished recounting that day's bizarre encounter with the remains of Mrs. Florence Paige and the traumatising of a South American nanny with the erroneous idea that her employers had been killed, when the waiter brought us our raspberry pannacottas.

"This looks great," I said, but spooned up only a meagre mouthful, wary of spilling it down my white dress. "I'm usually very clumsy," I explained, "especially when I'm on a…"

"On a what?" asked Ed.

"I was going to say *on a date* but…" I flushed and broke off.

This time it was his turn to lean forward across the table.

"Well, we are, aren't we?" he asked evenly, "because I don't know about you, but I definitely am."

He looked directly into my eyes and I swallowed. "Me too."

"Good to know," he said, and in the pause that followed, I felt a charge of consciousness flash between us. We continued to look at each other when I became aware of a tingling sensation about my wrist. I looked down at my bracelet. The tiny green beads seemed to dance and shimmer in the candlelight. I blinked. *Don't be ridiculous*, I told myself. *You're imagining it.* What's happening here, if there *is* anything happening, is nothing at all to do with the bracelet. Or the spell.

"This friend of yours, Flan, sounds remarkable. To have got down that staircase at… how old did you say she was? Seventy?"

"Yes. She's amazing," I said. "Actually, I can't believe that it was only last night that we went through all that."

Suddenly I was overcome by the memory of Flan's face in the secret room when we'd heard the tinkling of the wind chimes. Of how she'd trembled. And of how afraid we'd both been. And of my guilt at having put her in that position.

"She really is amazing," I repeated hoarsely. "When I think what might have happened." Tears pricked at my eyes. "What so easily could have happened, I…"

I hadn't realised that I'd closed my eyes until I felt the touch of a hand upon mine.

"Are you OK?" Ed asked softly.

I blinked and nodded a little too emphatically.

"I'm fine. I'm sorry. It was all pretty scary, and Flan is such a trooper that I feel awful at what I put her through."

And to my horror, the tears I'd been repressing started to trickle down my cheeks. Embarrassed, I tried to check them, but they kept on coming.

"You should have heard her today. Talking about it as if it had all been nothing. When really last night…" My voice cracked. "Up on that tower, with the ground such a long way down, she looked like an eagle."

"An eagle?" queried Ed, concern written plainly across his face.

"Yes. And she doesn't usually. She's very elegant. She's known for it. She's glamorous."

I took a large gulp of wine. "I'm sorry. You must think I'm a complete mess." I wiped the back of my hand over my eyes. "I'm not normally like this."

I took another sip and laughed unconvincingly. "Right now, I bet you are wishing yourself far, far away from this crazy person."

"I don't think you're crazy," said Ed firmly, and then added, with a smile which made his eyes crinkle, "unusual, yes. Crazy, no. What I think is, that you've been through a hell of an experience. Don't worry about it, please. Shall we order some coffee?" He looked around for the waiter and I hastily excused myself from the table and headed for the loo. Downstairs in the cubicle, I stood in front of the mirror trying to blot the mascara runs from my face. I couldn't believe that I'd cried in front of Ed. He'd been nice about it but what must he really think of me? Overemotional and needy. Just what every guy loves. Well, that's that, I thought dully, smearing on some concealer beneath my eyes. He won't want to see me again now. So much for the bracelet. I glanced down at the beads, which appeared dim and lustreless now. And so much for my spell.

I studied myself in the glass. The concealer hadn't helped but only served to emphasise the pallor of my complexion. I rooted about in my clutch for my lip gloss. What did it matter now if my lips looked too sticky? He wouldn't want to kiss me anyway. I straightened my shoulders.

"Sorry again about that," I said as I returned to the table. "It has been quite a couple of days. And whilst there is no reason for you to believe that I'm not some neurotic emotional nutter that cries all over people in restaurants, I can assure you that this is not my normal behaviour." My words came out in a rush. "Usually, I do it in the street in front of an even bigger audience… No, I'm joking…"

"Clarry," Ed smiled, "drink your coffee."

Nodding mechanically, I took a few sips. Careful not to look at him, I kept my eyes fixed on my cup. When I finally raised my gaze, it was to find him steadily regarding me. He wasn't smiling but his eyes were warm.

"Better?" he asked.

It could have sounded patronising, but it didn't. I smiled gratefully across at him.

"Yes, much."

"Right." He spooned sugar into his espresso. "We're going to talk about other things."

"We are?"

"Yes, we are. My fallback topics of conversation are rugby and gardening. And as I don't think that rugby is quite your thing, then gardening it's going to be. OK?"

And he was off. As he talked about looking for the hidden potential in a site and how a house and garden need to harmonise, I listened happily, gradually forgetting all about my embarrassment and distress. I found myself fascinated. Not just by what he said but by the way that he said it. As he described the importance of creating an element of mystery in a garden; the gradual unfolding and discovery around a bend in a path or under a trellised arbour, of some unexpected feature, I could see that he'd made the right decision in turning his passion into his business.

"I like old stone walls," he said. "I like pergolas. And deep generous borders packed with shrubs and flowers that complement not only the style of the house but also that of the owners. And whether they're formally or informally set out, it's native British plants that I really love. I have made Japanese gardens but they're not my style. Too many straight lines."

He reached for the last of his wine and grinned wickedly. "Because, you see, I like curves…"

"Hmm," I said, feeling altogether better, "I bet you do."

*

He walked me home. And I found that lip gloss doesn't put all men off. Some have no problem with it at all.

CHAPTER TWENTY-NINE

I'd gone to bed, alone, with my mind full of Ed and of the strength of his arms and the taste of his kisses, but my first thought on waking was of my meeting with Diana Maitland.

After my shower, I slipped on the leaf bracelet. Last night hadn't exactly proved anything about its powers but it was pretty, and I was growing accustomed to it.

I dressed with care in a cream pencil skirt, heels and my favourite pale pink cardigan. Not my usual Saturday morning attire, but Diana was intimidating enough without giving her even more ammunition to judge me. For this same reason, I had decided against inviting her to meet me at my home. It was too personal a setting and I didn't want to witness her summing me up based on how I lived. Although, of course, that was exactly what *I'd* done when I'd visited her house. I suppose it's what we all do. I'd finally settled on Kendall's, which is open all day at the weekends and where I could be pretty sure of securing a secluded booth.

It was ten o'clock as I greeted Phil, the younger Kendall brother, where he stood behind the bar arranging a stack of cups and saucers.

"Hi, Clarry. Good to see you. Brett said you were in the other night. How's everything at Abbe's?"

"Crazy as usual," I said, "but when isn't it? And at least I've not needed to be on the scrounge for anything for a while."

There's an unwritten agreement between a few of the Village restaurants that if one or other of us runs out of something, then we help each other out. It works well for all of us. The ice machine at Abbe's can be temperamental and so I regularly cadge bucketfuls of the stuff from Kendall's, and, just last week, Phil had dashed in to us looking for a crate of Prosecco as their delivery hadn't turned up.

Phil has the same high cheekbones as his brother but, without the low sideburns and cool specs, he wasn't quite as good-looking. Still, he received his fair share of female attention and, unlike his big brother, he was single so at least he got to enjoy it. He flirted mildly with me as a matter of politeness; this is the currency between restaurant staff, but I knew I wasn't his type. Petite brunettes were more his style.

"May I take a booth at the back?" I asked. "I've got kind of a business meeting."

"Sure. So, branching out, are we? Good for you. Do you want to order something now?"

"I'll wait," I said, just as Diana walked in. She was in another of her perfectly cut shift dresses, this time in black with an olive fitted jacket, which flattered her expensively dyed honey-coloured hair. She was carrying a black leather handbag and, whilst I'm not usually one of those girls that suffer from handbag envy, I did feel a flash of something close to it, because hers, with its signature Aspinal shield lock, was a classic. She may not be an easy woman to get on with but, I had to admit, she had taste.

"Do you know this place?" I asked as we sat down, becoming aware that, just as I had taken a careful inventory of how she looked, she was coolly assessing me. It made me feel that I was only with her on a form of approval and that, like a jumper with a pulled thread, she would return me back to the shop or wherever I'd come from, without a moment's compunction. In answer to my question, she glanced around the room, dismissing the great jazz musicians of the past depicted on the walls with a slight shrug.

"I've been here once. Some years ago as I recall. Isn't it more of a late-night place?"

"Yes, but…" I broke off as Phil approached the table.

"What can I get you?" He smiled at Diana. "We have some homemade chocolate croissants to tempt you, or apricot ones if you prefer?"

"I never eat pastries," she said, cutting him off curtly. "Just coffee. Black."

"As you wish," said Phil, "and what about you, Clarry?"

"Oh, I'm all about the breakfast goods," I said, noticing a slight pursing of the lips from Diana. "A latte and an apricot croissant please, Phil."

"Coming right up," he said and left us.

"Now," said Diana, "tell me everything that you've found out."

Steadily, and loosely in order of discovery, I talked her through my findings of the last few days and through the questions those findings inevitably raised. I glossed over the episode in the tower and was careful to make no mention at all of Flan. Diana had made it clear at our first meeting that everything between us was to be strictly confidential, and I had no intention of letting her know that I had broken that agreement. She listened intently and didn't interrupt as I briefly sketched out my own impressions of what I'd seen when spying on Zoë, when following *Loafers* to the address in Putney, the photographs and the money accumulated by Sarah for the Wellness Centre, but a stillness had settled over her. A stillness and a silence that unnerved me.

"Well," I said when I was through and she hadn't yet said anything at all. "That's it. And so, now what would you like me to do?"

She didn't answer. Her gaze was steady but unseeing. The lines about her eyes and mouth seemed to have become more pronounced as she'd sat opposite me, and the straight Maitland nose, now, like Vanessa's, seemed too large for her face. She looked not only older but less crisp about the edges. It was clear that something I'd told her had caused her habitual confidence of demeanour to slip, revealing the fragility of the woman behind the expensive clothes and privileged lifestyle.

"Diana?" I said softly. "What is it? Are you OK?"

She cleared her throat. "Do you have the photographs on you?"

"Yes. Here in my bag."

"I'd like to see them, please."

I drew out the stained brown envelope and passed it to her. Wordlessly, she flicked through the photographs and then handed them back to me. I waited.

"It's Miles," she said eventually.

"To where?" I asked, confused.

"The man in the photographs," she said woodenly. "His name is Miles Cavendish. Caroline's husband, my son-in-law." I expelled a long breath. I would never have guessed that. No wonder Diana looked shocked. Caroline Maitland was Mrs. *Loafers*. She was the shadowy figure standing in the doorway of the house in Putney. Those had been her two boys waving their father goodbye. I thought back to that elaborate tea in the Maitlands' elegant sitting room. Caroline, tall and lean, wisps of straggling hair, and clothes that looked like they didn't belong to her, had seemed nice and well-meaning in a vague kind of way. I remembered her too at the anniversary party and the way she'd defended the institution of marriage when I'd joked about women losing themselves in complacent togetherness. Well, I knew just how together she and *Loafers* were, but did she?

"That's both of them," Diana said.

"Both of them?"

"Both of my daughters to worry about."

And I took her point. "Will you tell her?"

Diana looked down into her empty coffee cup. "Not yet." She raised her eyes and glanced about her before looking at me. "And perhaps not at all. Many marriages survive infidelity. There are worse things to bear."

That may be, I reflected, but shouldn't it be Caroline who got to decide that, and not her mother? I kept this thought to myself and offered what I hoped was reassurance.

"Try not to worry too much about Vanessa. I think this white witch thing is just a phase. Apparently, there's another meeting tonight, at midnight, but I've no idea if she will be there and not that I know where it's even being held. I suspect that Vanessa has a little too much time on her hands and is looking to fill a gap. The minute she gets a job or a new boyfriend in her life…"

I thought briefly of Jonian but decided against mentioning him. Her daughter's interest in an Albanian pot washer, albeit one taking a business studies course, was not something Diana needed to hear right now.

"And of course, if she learnt of Zoe's involvement with your son-in-law, she'd be horrified. It's just such a weird coincidence, isn't it? I mean how odd that…"

I hastily swallowed down what I was going to say, overcome by a sudden memory. Something I had completely forgotten now flashed up as a red warning sign in my mind. The night of the do at Cannizaro, when I'd gone with Vanessa to the pub to meet her friends, Sarah had asked why I was so dressed up and I'd been about to mention the anniversary party, when Vanessa had cut me off. I'd thought it strange at the time. Why hadn't she wanted Sarah to know that she'd been to her parents' party? Had she thought that Sarah would resent not being invited? That didn't make any sense. Diana didn't know her. Perhaps it was just that Vanessa wanted to keep that side of her life private. After all, how often is it that casual friends get to meet one's parents? Or was there more to it than that? Again, the image of her being shepherded away by Zoëeand Sarah after the white witch meeting surfaced, and the hideous thought that Vanessa might know about Zoe and Miles Cavendish forcibly struck me. *Did* she know? I couldn't believe it of her. My list of questions had just doubled in size.

Diana was looking at me and, concerned that she might have followed my train of thought, I started to mouth platitudes about Vanessa finding herself, when she interrupted me.

"You asked me what I want you to do. I'm now ready to answer that question."

She paused and shifted her teaspoon, which was lying flat on the table, a millimetre to the left. And when she spoke, her tone was authoritarian. The worst of the shock appeared to have passed and the old Diana was back.

"I wish to continue with our arrangement. You have done well, Clarry."

"Thank you," I said uncomfortably. My discoveries had just dealt this woman a body blow but here she was, politely, if stiffly, thanking me.

"You may not have brought me welcome information but, nevertheless, it is information that I am now the possessor of. No matter how unpalatable it is."

A shadow crossed her face. "But that is hardly a fault of yours. The question now, is what to do with this information." This time, it was her cup and saucer that got fractionally repositioned. "However," she continued, "before you go any further, you must be paid for the time you have already spent. I believe that you have not yet received anything. I had planned to leave Caroline to deal with the financial aspects of our transaction, but now, that is out of the question."

She opened her Aspinal bag and drew out a cheque book and a fountain pen.

"How much is it that I owe you?"

"Really, Diana," I protested, "we don't have to do this now."

"You have done a job of work and executed it well. You should be paid."

I thought of the couple of unpaid bills on my desk. She was right.

"Well, if you're sure."

I dug out from my bag the list that I'd compiled yesterday of the hours I'd spent, and handed it to her.

"We hadn't actually agreed on a rate," I said, as she scanned it.

She didn't answer but just wrote out a cheque. I blinked at the amount.

"Diana, that's very generous of you. I'm not really sure that I should…"

She waved my protests away and I let her. The money would cover my bills for the next three months and also leave me enough to treat Flan to something lovely.

"I'd like another coffee," said Diana. "Find that young man and order some, would you? Then we will discuss how you should proceed from here on in."

CHAPTER THIRTY

Diana and I parted at eleven thirty. I needed to nip home and change before executing my plan on how to discover the location for the white witch ceremony. Diana had been very clear in her instructions. She wanted me at that meeting. If I couldn't talk my way into an invitation, and I'd explained to her how that simply wasn't on the cards, then I'd have to attend illicitly. In addition to following the trail on Sarah, the money and the Wellness Centre, I was to seek out more information on Zoe. Diana felt that the special meeting was a starting place to do so. I was sceptical. What more could it reveal? A fresh batch of spells and further bucket-rattling for the cause? But, as I was being paid, and being paid generously, I wasn't going to argue.

I pulled on a pair of jeans and sneakers and headed out.

Even through the Saturday morning traffic, it only took me thirty minutes to get to Merton Abbey Mills. Once the grounds of a medieval priory, it had then, in the eighteenth century, housed a textile factory which was later taken over by William Morris as workshops for his design business. There had been silk and carpet weaving, tapestry and even stained glass made on the site, with water from the River

Wandle to drive the watermill and rinse the fabrics. Today, many of the original warehouses and showrooms are used as retail outlets and restaurants and, at the weekends, there's a busy craft and bric-a-brac market.

I made my way through stalls selling everything from handmade cards to baby clothes. There was a strong smell of hot salty dough from a booth offering oversized pretzels which had me reaching for my purse, but remembering the croissant I'd already eaten that morning, I had just decided to resist, when a burst of clapping and whooping rang out. I looked around, hoping that my own personal Diet Police had finally materialised and were cheering me on, when I realised it came from the Colour House Theatre where a children's production had just come to a close. A girl with long blonde hair extensions, dressed in a gauzy outfit in varying shades of pink and wearing a plastic tiara, was handing out flyers for the next performance. She offered one to me, but I thought that I was probably a bit old for *Princess Petunia and the Magic Garden*.

Mums and dads trying to control hordes of hyped-up children were now exiting the theatre when one of their little treasures, whose face had been painted to look like a cross between a lion and a zebra, cannoned headlong into me, smearing make-up all over the legs of my jeans. I was glad that I'd changed out of my cream pencil skirt.

Strolling through the market, I looked at a collection of wooden artisan-style toys for young children, some pleasing ceramics and a selection of hippy-dippy clothes that I couldn't imagine anyone ever buying, before remembering Sheila from The Nook. She had probably filled her entire wardrobe from here. But what struck me the most was that I had never seen so much hideous jewellery all in one place before. It was everywhere. Heaps of ugly stones in even uglier settings. Whether bracelets, necklaces or rings, they were all equally an eyesore. They could, by the more generously disposed, be described as having a certain naïve charm, but not by me. When I'd first seen Polly's designs, I'd thought them an acquired taste, but in comparison to these monstrosities, hers were right up there with Tiffany's. I remembered her saying that she believed everyone was creative in some form or other. And that's probably true, but creativity can be released in all kinds of ways; in the preparation of a meal or the baking of a cake, in growing vegetables or making a home warm and welcoming. Why then was it that self-expression so often took the form of clumsy misshapen jewellery that people were expected to pay for?

A stall selling crystals attracted the most custom. Semi-precious stones with, reportedly, healing or empowering properties were being sold almost exclusively to women. As I watched hunks of faux quartz and amethyst being exchanged for hard cash, I wondered just how much the purchasers really believed in the power of the stones. Then I remembered the spell I'd muttered on my way to the restaurant last night. I glanced down at the leaf bracelet that I had, quite deliberately, put on that morning and felt my face flush. Who the hell was I to knock what anyone chose to believe?

At a stall close to the Pottery Wheel, I spotted Jo-Jo from the white witches' meeting. Her stack of printed tablecloths, aprons and laundry bags were carefully arranged and looked attractive. A couple were just paying for half a dozen cushion covers, and I waited until they had left before I made my way over.

"Hi, Jo-Jo," I said brightly. "I'd forgotten that you said you had a stall here. This stuff looks great."

"Clarry," she said, with a broad smile and a flash of her tongue stud. "Welcome Be. How are you? Lovely to see you."

"You too," I said and meant it. There was something refreshing about her frank, open face, but I did feel rather small knowing that I was only there to pump her for information.

"I'm just on the lookout for a present," I improvised. "This tablecloth is really pretty."

I picked up a square of plain white cotton with a design of flowers on each of its four corners and asked, "How much is this?"

"£20 usually but…" she grinned, shook her brown curls and whispered, "…to one of us, it's fifteen."

"I'll take it," I said, wincing inwardly at the words *one of us.* "I have a friend who'd love it."

I would be treating Flan to a lot more than a tablecloth, but I felt I ought to buy something and I could see Flan using this in her kitchen or in the garden when she had people around to lunch.

"Great night on Tuesday," I remarked as she wrapped the cloth in some brown paper. "I was blown away. Especially when Polly told me that Bonnie was found safe and sound."

"Wasn't that amazing?" said Jo-Jo, "and all thanks to the Lady. We are so lucky and have so much to be grateful for."

"And so does the dog," I said. "I bet she enjoyed her meaty-chunks that day. Do any of the other girls have a stall or shop here?"

"Polly used to, and Elaine has a weekly slot on a Thursday at the cafe across the square."

"Slot?"

"For her performance poetry. You should come one time. It's a good night."

"Shame," I said, "but I work most Thursday evenings. So, people actually pay to hear her poetry?"

Jo-Jo laughed. "Yes, but she doesn't make much out of it."

Now to get on to what I had really come for. "I can't wait for the meeting tonight. Really exciting, especially being at midnight."

"Oh, you're coming, are you?" Jo-Jo looked surprised. "I am glad. It's pretty advanced for a new member, but I think we all felt that you really fitted in."

Not quite all, I thought, remembering Sarah's look of malevolence.

I opened my purse, drew out some cash and then added as casually as I could, "Where are you guys meeting again? I know I've written it down, but I can't…"

Jo-Jo took the money I proffered.

"In the car park at quarter to. Not on the windmill side but the other one."

Where was she talking about? The only windmill I knew was on Wimbledon Common. She couldn't possibly mean there, could she? I knew from my jogging that there were a couple of other places to park by the common. I took a guess.

"Oh, that's right. Is it the one past the Fox & Grapes and then down that little track? What's it called again?"

"Camp Road." Jo-Jo nodded and reached for a ring bound folder where she wrote up my purchase. "Are you coming on your own tonight? I promised to give Sheila a lift and I think Polly and Vanessa are coming together."

"Haven't made any firm arrangements yet," I muttered, anxious lest she question me further.

A woman with a pushchair approached the stall.

"It looks like you have another customer," I said. "I'd better leave you to it. Thanks a lot for this." I indicated the brown paper parcel and then lowered my voice. "And thanks again for the discount."

"Merry Part until we Merry Meet again," said Jo-Jo with a wave.

CHAPTER THIRTY-ONE

It was after two o'clock when I got back. I felt that my next step should be to contact Vanessa but, as I had no idea how to get her to reveal if she knew about Zoe and her brother-in-law, I prevaricated and made myself a mug of tea. I tried to concentrate but found my thoughts straying to Ed. His rugby game would have just started. He'd invited me to watch him play, and the thought of him in shorts, storming about the pitch, felling his opponents with a thrust of his powerful shoulders, had been tempting, but we'd deferred arranging another date until I knew where I was with the case. I'm practically a workaholic, I thought sanctimoniously.

Flan, when I answered the phone on the fourth ring, barely gave me time to say hello.

"Darling, Mary Cunningham has just telephoned me with some very interesting news. This morning, before nine o'clock, Ron, who had been raking the leaves up from their front lawn, spotted Sarah Gaitskill getting into her car. Now, they had the idea that she didn't usually work on a Saturday and so they dropped what they were doing and took off in their car after her."

"Oh," I groaned, "I hope they were careful. I don't want them getting into any kind of confrontation with her."

"Don't worry about that, Clarry. They were very discreet. Where was I? Oh yes, they followed her into Epsom town centre and parked in the multi storey. Once they were on foot, they had a bit of a job not losing her because of Ron's hip, but this Sarah person is a big woman, they said, and doesn't walk fast. Anyway, Sarah went into a travel agents, where she spent nearly an hour. Ron and Mary kept a lookout from a bookshop across the road and then Mary decided upon a closer inspection. She casually strolled past the travel agents' and saw Sarah sitting opposite a young woman at a desk in the rear of the shop. She then went back and waited with Ron until Sarah left the shop—"

"This is all very interesting, Flan," I interrupted, "but what does—?"

"Clarissa," scolded Flan, "what have I said to you before about rushing me?"

"That I must never ever do it," I answered with a laugh. "Go on then. What happened next?"

"Mary pulled off something rather impressive. She went into the travel agents and sat down with the same young woman that Sarah had been talking to and found out that Sarah has booked a one-way ticket to the Dominican Republic. What do you think of that? Jolly good work, I'd say. Actually, I feel a little jealous. I thought my detective skills were second to none, but I have to hand it to Mary Cunningham. And you'd never think it to look at her. Tiny little white-haired old lady. She looks ancient and yet she's only a year older than me. But then I look after my skin and only use the best—"

"The Dominican Republic?" I interrupted before Flan proceeded to outline her full beauty routine. "And a one-way ticket. Are you sure?"

"Perfectly," replied Flan. "Mary was quite clear about it."

"But I can't believe the travel agent told her. Isn't there's such a thing as client confidentiality? Surely, they don't just dish out that kind of information to…"

"Ah!" said Flan with a spike of triumph in her tone. "This is where being old, or at least older," she corrected, "has its advantages. Young people discount us. They think we are all just part of a faceless formless Grey Army, whiling away our time until death. Mary Cunningham played the part magnificently. She asked to see some brochures as she wanted to go on a trip and had been chatting this morning to her friend, Sarah, who hadn't been able to make up her mind between Greece, Egypt, America, etc. Mary speculated in exhausting detail as to where Sarah had finally settled upon, until the young woman, no doubt to get rid of her, simply told her the destination. Mary then, after much backwarding and forwarding about not wanting to be away at the same time as Sarah or else who would put out the bins, managed to extract the fact that Sarah leaves on the 20th, that's this coming Monday, and has no return date booked. One-way only, apparently. You see? Impressive, as I said."

"She's done a hell of a job. Will you please thank her for me? And her husband."

"Mary admitted that she was very nervous at first," continued Flan. "But she thought of Freddie, that's their cat, you remember? And the stone that Sarah had thrown at him, and so she held her nerve and persevered. Actually, they are coming for tea on Monday on their way back from Kingston and the choosing of their caskets at Harold's undertakers."

"Funeral directors," I corrected automatically.

"If you are free, darling, I think it would be nice if you could thank them yourself."

"Absolutely," I agreed. "I will. But don't you think it odd, Flan, that Sarah booked her ticket through a travel agent? Why not just do it online?"

"My generation wouldn't, of course," replied Flan. "However, Sarah is very much younger and so yes, the whole net-thingy would be the natural choice for her... but not..." I could hear the mounting excitement in her voice. "Not if she were covering her tracks.

"Darling, I believe I've got it! You know how much I enjoy those American TV cop shows?"

"You may have mentioned it. They're your guilty TV pleasure."

"Guilt, Clarry, is not part of my repertoire, as I thought you would have known by now. Well, the FBI, or whomever, always find something incriminating on the suspect's computer. When they do a sweep."

"A sweep?"

"I believe that's what it's called. I'm a mine of information. Really, I don't know what you'd do without me."

Neither did I.

"Oh," she continued, "I forgot to say that Mary, once she'd got into her stride, thoroughly enjoyed her sleuthing experience. I have a feeling that, like me, she and Ron might get a taste for this line of work."

"Yes, and that's what worries me," I said darkly, before filling her in with the news about the identity of *Loafers*.

*

Trawling the net, I could find no sign of Sarah's house on the market, and when I'd called all seven local estate agents, none of them had a property in her road up for sale or for rental. Perhaps she was selling it privately. The one-way ticket to the Dominican Republic made me think that she would be unlikely to rent the house out; too much hassle, I would have thought. Either way, she was clearly leaving the country and in three days' time. This now made sense of what the Cunninghams had seen when they'd spotted her shifting her belongings. And what about The Nook? Had she sold the shop? I wondered if Shelia knew that she might soon be out of a job. And the centre for wellness, and the donations she had collected? How would that work? How would she run it from the other side of the world?

I stood up and paced about the room. So many questions. I'd give it up for now and take another tea break, but it was just as I was shutting down the computer that I felt the gears in the back of my mind shift, and then come together in a moment of clarity. When first discussing the Wellness Centre with Polly, I'd been sceptical about the whole project, but had partly dismissed my suspicions as a knee-jerk reaction to my instinctive dislike of Sarah. But now, I had a new theory. There would be no Wellness

Centre. There was no property. No deposit had been put down. I'd already suspected that there was no bank account, which explained the fact that her records were handwritten, leaving no trail for a computer sweep to unearth. Sarah had no intention of using the money to provide a haven for women to find spiritual and creative release. She was keeping it. And Zoe? She had to be in on it, but why then, were the incriminating photos of her and Miles Cavendish locked up in Sarah's secret room? Had my original idea of blackmail been correct? Or was Sarah using it as insurance to ensure that Zoe kept her mouth shut? Because, as we all know, there is no honour amongst thieves.

My head swam at the repercussions if my conjecture proved to be correct. Sarah, either alone or in cahoots with Zoe, had conned everyone into giving her cash for a project that would never see the light of day. Poor Helen had coughed up £250,000, a staggering amount of money, but Jo-Jo, Polly, Sheila, Vanessa and the rest of the group had also placed their trust in her. Maybe they had been a bit naïve, but they were contributing to something they believed in. And that was admirable. My mind flicked back to Vanessa. Her mother was my client. It was her to whom I was responsible. But the truth was that I felt a sense of responsibility to all the women. They didn't deserve this. I felt pretty sure that Sarah Gaitskill was a liar and a thief. And, in just two days' time, she would be on her way to the other side of the world and scot-free.

CHAPTER THIRTY-TWO

I dialled Vanessa's number.

"It's Clarry. How was last night with Jonian? I want to hear all the juicy details. Are you free now, for coffee or something?"

She laughed happily. "I've got loads to tell you but I'm just off for a hack. Why don't you join me?"

"What, me? Ride?" I squawked. "No. I don't think so. I haven't been on a horse since I was about ten years old, and anyway, I'm not very good with…"

"Oh, come on," she persisted. "It'll be fun. And they say you never forget how to ride."

"A bike, Vanessa. Not a horse." But I was wavering, and she knew it.

"It'll be my treat, Clarry. I'll see you at the stables in twenty minutes," and she rang off before I could protest any further.

Oh, well, I thought, how bad can it be? We'll have a quiet plod around on some steady old nag and, as we bond on the trail, I'll fish for information.

*

The smell of warm dung hit my nostrils as soon as I entered the yard. Vanessa, in jodhpurs and smart brown leather boots, was there to meet me.

"You'll be needing this," she said, proffering a black felted helmet. This was the second hat I'd been obliged to wear for the sake of the case. On tightening the chin strap, I decided that, for comfort, I preferred the funeral director's topper.

"You're looking very professional," I remarked, as we crossed a cobble-stoned quad edged with individual stalls, from which some twenty or so horses looked down their long silky noses at us. Stablehands were busy mucking out and sluicing down with buckets of water. They were all young girls and appeared to be enjoying their tasks. One was lovingly curry combing a magnificent bay mare, who submitted to her ministrations with dignified gravity. As we passed, I could hear the girl talking softly to her in time with her brush strokes.

"I've been riding since I was a child," Vanessa said. "Caroline never took to it like I did. That's her hat you're wearing."

I'd been wondering how to bring up the subject of her sister and here was an opening.

"I'd like to have had a sister," I said. "Someone to swap clothes, boyfriends and confidences with."

"I definitely didn't swap clothes with Caroline," Vanessa shrugged. "We have completely different tastes. And as for men... no... nothing in common there either."

"I didn't get to meet her husband at the party. What's he like?"

An expression I couldn't read rippled across her face.

"Like a lot of men, I suppose. Selfish."

"Sounds like you don't like him?"

"I simply don't think about him." She shrugged again. *Does* she know about him and Zoe? I wondered, and was just trying to come up with a line of questioning which might reveal this, when she changed the subject of the conversation.

"I ride most weeks. I know a lot of people do it for the exercise and the fresh air, but it's the connection between the horse and the rider that I love. It's such a special communication."

"Is it?" I asked dubiously, as a stable girl in a grubby pair of overalls approached us, leading two horses.

"Vanessa, you booked Mackie, right?" the girl asked. She was about sixteen years old with a freckled face and short brown hair which had pieces of straw in it.

Vanessa greeted the chestnut gelding with a neck rub and a carrot.

"Hello, boy. Hello, Beauty," and moved around to check the girth straps before putting her left leg up in the stirrup. With one graceful fluid movement, she then swung her right leg up and over the saddle.

Mackie, who had stood quite patiently as he was mounted, gave a little whinny as if eager for the off.

"OK, Clarry," said Vanessa, sitting straight backed. "Now it's your turn. I took a guess at your weight. No, it's all right…"

She broke off as she caught sight of my face. "I reckon you're somewhere around…"

"Don't say it out loud," I begged.

She laughed. "You've got Cleo. She's seventeen hands and mostly very placid."

"What do you mean, *mostly*?" I eyed the strawberry mare with caution. She looked awfully big and there was something about the baleful stare she gave me that I didn't quite like.

"Can you manage on your own?" asked the stable girl. "I can give you a leg-up, or there's a mounting block on the other side of the yard if you'd rather use that."

I swallowed, aware that Vanessa was watching me.

"I'll give it a try," I said eventually. "Hello, Cleo. Good girl. Nice horsey."

Cleo flicked her ears dismissively by way of reply. Gingerly, I patted her flank and raised my leg up to the stirrup.

"Now, be a good girl and just let me put my foot in there…" I broke off as Cleo took a pace sideways and I found myself stepping down into thin air.

"She's moving. She's moving," I yelped.

"Try again," said the stable girl. "You'll soon get the hang of it."

But I wasn't getting the hang of it. Just as I'd got my foot in the stirrup, Cleo took another sideways step, leaving me hopping up and down on one leg before managing to extricate my foot.

"You made it look so easy," I called to Vanessa.

"Cleo senses that you're not comfortable around horses," she replied, and I swear there was a suggestion of a smirk.

"Then she's pretty smart," I said with feeling, "because I'm not. Right, where's that mounting block?"

It took three attempts and it may not have been elegant to watch but, at last, I was on. All I had to do now, was stay on.

I was given a quick refresher on the basics of riding by Briony with the freckles, as she led me across the quad and out onto Wimbledon Common. She then assumed her own mount, Dolly, a steady-looking piebald mare with a white star on her nose.

"Do you think you're ready to take control now?" she asked. "Don't worry if not. I can easily stay alongside you and keep you reined in."

"No, I think I can take it from here." I was conscious that if I was going to get anything out of Vanessa, then we had to talk in private. "As long as we stick to a walk. I don't think I'm up to trotting. I'll go on ahead with Vanessa."

This proved easier said than done. Cleo was an independent-minded beast. Mackie and his rider had taken a path to the left of me and were some hundred yards or so ahead. Getting Cleo to aim in their direction became something of a challenge. I pulled gently on the left rein, but she went right. I wasn't wearing gloves and so it wasn't easy to keep the reins looped through my fingers. Each time, Cleo responded by veering repeatedly to the right before eventually coming to a complete standstill.

"Left hand down," called Briony from behind me. "And use your heels."

I applied a gentle pressure with my heels, but the horse was having none of it. Not an inch did she budge.

"Come on, Cleo," I coaxed. "Work with me here."

In answer, Cleo merely turned a deaf ear. Focussing in on some tasty-looking grass, she then dropped her head and placidly began to graze.

I leaned forward and, somewhere above her neck, hissed into the air, "Listen up, horsey. This is no time for snacking. I'm on a case. Try and cooperate, will you, please?"

And maybe because, unbeknown to myself, I actually *am* a secret horse whisperer, or because the thistle that she now, with great delicacy, spat out of her mouth wasn't to her taste, Cleo deigned to walk on. I drew up beside Vanessa.

"All good?" she asked, and this time there was absolutely no doubt about the smirk.

"Couldn't be better!" I agreed heartily.

*

As Vanessa described, in glowing terms and at great length, her date with Jonian, I found myself becoming accustomed to the motion of the horse. Maintaining a sedate pace, we picked our way along paths lined with buttercups and cow parsley. The tang of wild garlic mingled with Cleo's own signature honeyed scent and, from somewhere in the trees above, I could hear the shrill tic-tic-tic of a bird scolding its neighbours. This isn't so bad, I decided, beginning to enjoy myself and the feel of the afternoon sun upon my face. I might think about taking this up regularly.

"So, when are you next seeing him?" I asked

"It would have been tonight because he's on the day shift at Cannizaro, but I can't make it."

Ah, then she would be at the meeting later.

"That's a shame. Can't you wriggle out of whatever it is that you're supposed to be doing?"

"I wish I could." Her voice dropped. "But, no. I promised. I can't explain…"

I took a swift glance at her. It was difficult to be sure, under the rim of her helmet, but her face had lost all its previous animation. This is the time, I thought, to get her to open up; however, I was determined to tread lightly. The last thing I wanted was to antagonise her.

I took a punt and instantly regretted it. "You're seeing Sarah? Or Zoe?"

"No!" she shot back. "Well, yes, I am. And what's so wrong with that?"

"Nothing." I kept my tone placatory. "Nothing at all. It's just that you look so…"

"Look so what?" She was still very much on the defensive.

I took another punt.

"So reluctant. And I'm guessing that it's not just about being unable to hook up with Jonian. The last time I saw you look like that was when, after the meeting, you went off with Sarah and Zoe… so I just guessed that it was them that you couldn't bail on."

I half expected her to flare up again, but she didn't answer, and we plodded on for a while in an awkward silence, only broken by the soft clip-clop of the horses' hooves.

When she did speak, her voice was subdued. "It's complicated."

I didn't make a response, willing her to continue.

"They've been good to me. And, it's through them that I've met Polly and the others."

"Polly's great," I said. "I really like her. And Jo-Jo seems cool, but what do you mean, that they've been good to you?"

"They've opened my eyes. By introducing me to The Craft and the power of The Lady, they've helped me understand how the world works. Or at least how it should work."

"Not sure I'm following you."

"They've made me realise how privileged I am to have been born into a society, a family, where I have had so many advantages just handed to me on a plate."

"Right," I said dubiously.

"Don't you see, Clarry? To really be able to be present, to maximise the moment and live each day as if it's one's last, one has to free oneself of the trappings of privilege."

"Ah." I now had a sense of where this was leading. "And that's what you are doing?"

"You won't know this, Clarry, but I am rather…" She broke off as Mackie, clearly bored by our slow pace, made a sharp thrust forward. Vanessa reined him back in.

Rather what? I wondered. Mixed-up? Lost? Changeable? Haughty and more than a little petulant?

"Rich," she said glumly.

I laughed. "You say that like it's a bad thing."

"It is, if I don't use it wisely."

Cleo, picking up on Mackie's restlessness, then gave an experimental lurch and I shifted uncomfortably in the saddle.

"You thank The Lady for your gifts and graces?" I said. "Isn't that what you all chanted the other evening?"

"Exactly that."

"So, you're donating your *gifts* in the form of some spare cash to this centre for wellness?"

"Considerably more than some spare cash," she said. "This project can do so much good and it needs serious investment. It's going to be a place for…"

"It sounds great, Vanessa. It does. But what do you really know about it? The hard facts, I mean. Like where exactly it is, and how much it costs and how secure the money is, that's been given by you and…"

It was on the tip of my tongue to say Helen, but I stopped myself just in time.

"I don't need facts," she retorted. "I know what the real heart and purpose of the venture is."

I wanted to shake her. How could she be so naïve? And then, I remembered that she was only twenty-one years old, and felt grateful that the five years I had on her had rendered me infinitely less gullible. Endeavouring to keep my tone reasonable, I answered, "All I'm saying is that it might be a good idea to make a few enquiries. To seek advice maybe."

"I don't know why I'm talking to you." The haughty petulant side to her nature was making a comeback and beginning to irritate the hell out of me. "You simply don't get it."

"I'm trying to, Vanessa. And I'm not criticising," although, of course, I was. "It's just that something doesn't seem right to me and I'm concerned about—"

"Oh, *concerned.*" She was deeply sarcastic. "I can't tell you how fed up I am at hearing how concerned people are about me. I don't *need* anyone's concern. Not yours. Not my mother's. Not my sister's."

I tried to interject but her voice was rising higher and higher with every word.

"I'm perfectly fine without this patronising concern. And perfectly able to run my own affairs, thank you very much, without interference from you or anybody else. It's my life and I'm happy."

Yeah right, I thought. *You sure look happy.* But I said nothing.

After a moment, she twisted in her saddle, shooting me a look of blistering condescension. "As I said, you don't get it."

"It's not that I don't get it," I snapped. "It's more that I just don't bloody well buy it."

I'd well and truly blown it now. So much for treading lightly.

"No one's asking you to *buy* it," she shouted, pushing Mackie on with a kick of her heels. "You don't know anything about us, or what we do, or what we believe in, or who we are. So why don't you get off your high horse and mind your own fucking business?"

Cleo, registering either the fiery atmosphere or simply expressing a desire to follow her four-legged companion, started to pick up speed.

"I would get off this high horse right now," I yelled back, as, at a fast trot, we headed towards a belt of low hanging trees, "if I could do so without breaking my damned neck."

"Good luck with that!" Vanessa laughed over her shoulder before taking off at a thundering gallop.

Cleo, participating now in a game of equine follow-my-leader, instantly ramped things up from a trot to a fast canter. As I closed my eyes and clung desperately about her neck, I thought, way to go, Clarry. Way to go. Could you possibly have handled that any worse?

If I hadn't thought myself up to a trot, then how I managed to stay on as Cleo broke into a canter, I really don't know. I'd lost both of my stirrups and the reins were looped over one of my shoulders, when Briony caught up with me just before we met the road. She helped me dismount outside the stables and led Cleo off to her stall and her dinner, whilst I, with shredded nerves and wobbly legs, walked home.

CHAPTER THIRTY-THREE

My shoulders and neck muscles ached, and my inner thighs would probably never be the same again. I felt flat and defeated. Who on earth did I think I was, believing that I could pull off this private investigation stuff? I'd never really been much good at anything before in my life; why should things be different now?

Staring listlessly into my kitchen cupboards, my gaze fell upon the family-sized packet of mini meringues I'd picked up in the supermarket the other day. I reached for them and ate three in a row. I studied the back of the packet for the calorie content. It was loads. I had another.

Until now, I'd always been such a quitter but, after my first case, I'd really believed that I could make a go of this new line of work. And look what a mess I was making of it. I'd nearly got Flan and I killed on our perilous descent from the Tower, and I'd only just narrowly escaped breaking my neck whilst careering headlong over Wimbledon Common on a runaway horse. Oh, stop being so overdramatic, I told myself. You're perfectly all right. You've got a job to do and a long night ahead of you. So get a hold of yourself... and, whatever else you do, put down the mini meringues.

*

There were still forty-five minutes until midnight when I parked the car outside the Fox & Grapes pub. Inside, the lights were blazing, and the comfortable background hum of late-night drinkers and diners seeped out through an open window. That's where I should be, I thought, or someplace like it. Doing what normal people do on a Saturday evening, not skulking about in the shadows, spying on a coven of witches. Who does that? Me, I guess. My career really was on the up and up. Mum and Dad would be so proud.

The air felt fresh and sharp and I was glad of the heavy dark sweater I had on over my black jeans, but I found that I missed my baseball cap, lost somewhere on the steps in the Tower. I hadn't realised how much it had made me feel anonymous and, oddly, braver. Like I was someone else.

A car door slammed from somewhere behind me and, at the gate of one of the cottages, goodbyes were being shared by a couple and their departing guests. The school on the corner, which in the daytime radiates the energy and noise of four to eleven-year-olds, sat eerily silent. A very few lights burned in the neighbouring houses, but these were soon left behind as I made my way swiftly down Camp Road and into the small tarmacked car park. With accommodation for less than a dozen vehicles, this space, from sunrise to sunset, was much in demand by the regular dog walkers. Now, it was empty.

My plan had been to hide myself until Zoe and her followers arrived, and then, keeping well back, slip after them unnoticed, but an almost overwhelming reluctance had taken hold of me. The full moon, under whose brilliant gaze I had left home, was now veiled by cloud and a light mist. I eyed some bushes just off to the left of a well-used dirt track and only six paces or so ahead of me. It would make ideal cover, but my legs didn't seem interested in receiving the command from my brain to move.

I'm not sure how long I hesitated but suddenly I heard vehicles approaching. My legs were all obedience now. I ran and, pushing through the shrubbery, squeezed myself into position. Twigs tugged at my hair and thick, damp rubbery leaves pawed at my face. I peered out. Six cars had pulled up. Doors then opened, decanting robed and hooded figures, talking in low excited voices. *Robes.* I suppose that I should have expected it, given the sense of theatre that I had noted in Zoe. Each one carrying a lantern, they stood in a clutch, until one of their number took the lead and they advanced towards the path. I shrank even deeper into the bushes and then peeped out. The robe worn by the woman at the head of the group was of some pale silky material, girdled about the waist and edged in a thick band of silver. The fabric's rich sheen gleamed in the light from the lanterns. I caught a glimpse of long black hair spilling out from under the hood. Unmistakably, Zoe. Behind her, the other women, wearing robes of soft blues, greens and browns made of heavy cotton, whispered together about how much they had been looking forward to tonight, about how keyed up and yet how nervous they were. The odd giggle was shushed and then suppressed, only to instantly bubble up again.

Elaine's beaky nose protruded from under her peaked hood, and I caught a glimpse of Mary's pale pink fringe from under hers. Polly was there, as was Shelia, Jo-Jo, Vanessa and four other women I didn't recognise. Helen came next, walking alone and speaking to no one. The diamante clip she'd been wearing when I met her secured the hood of her robe, revealing her face fully. In her clear sea green eyes, I detected a blend of wistfulness and fear and I felt a stirring of anxiety for her. Did she know something about the upcoming proceedings that Polly, Vanessa and the others did not?

Bringing up the rear, I recognised Sarah's substantial frame. Instinctively, I closed my eyes and held my breath until she had passed by. Thirteen women in total. I didn't know whether a coven required a certain number, but the number thirteen didn't strike me as accidental.

I let them get a good fifteen paces ahead of me before extracting myself from the bushes. Having been unwilling to secrete myself amongst them, I now felt a strong disinclination to quit the security of their cover.

The dirt track was soft beneath the soles of my trainers, and I made no noise as I stole swiftly in their wake. The moon was still bedimmed by cloud, and there was only a faint glow from the lantern light ahead of me. This disappeared altogether as the women turned right at a plot of pine trees.

I hesitated. The path through this section of the common, well known to me from my morning jogs, ran open and exposed, until it narrowed once again through a tunnel of overhanging vegetation. I held back and waited, aware that in this stretch, if one of them turned to look behind, I could well be spotted.

It was at this point I realised that, ever since the cars had pulled up and the group had arrived, I'd been operating on automatic pilot, concentrating only on not being seen and on observing whatever I could. Now, I had a moment to fully take in what was about me.

At my back lay Caesar's Well and, for just a second, standing all alone in the darkness, I imagined that I could hear the ghostly tramping footfall of long-dead legionnaires. Above me loomed the tall inky spires of the pines. From within the surrounding woods echoed the lonely hoot of an owl. And, as I listened, I became aware that the night was alive with sound. There was a faint rustling from all about me. It wasn't just the branches of the trees whispering together as they shifted in the wind but, at ground level, stirrings from the nocturnal creatures of the woods; foxes, shrews, stoats and voles, up and out and hunting for prey.

I didn't want to go any further. Why did I have to go any further? Yes, it was what I was being paid to do, but that didn't mean I had to like it.

Tentatively, I stepped out. The group were out of sight, once more lost under the drooping foliage of lime and birch trees, but I could just make out a faint glow ahead. I broke into a jog until they were back within view. They were walking single file now and the talking had all but died down. Occasionally, one would start at the sound of a twig cracking or a faint pitter-pattering from the undergrowth. Twice I had to duck behind the trunk of a tree.

We crossed another open stretch and again I hung back, only to catch up when they reached the sheltering camouflage of the woods.

Patches of the common, so familiar to me in daylight, had taken on a threatening disguise and I was losing my bearings.

Where were the women making for? These woods seemed endless, boundless, a place occupied by shadows, nocturnal creatures and thirteen women dressed in hooded robes. Nerves were getting the better of me. Get a grip, I told myself. Yes, I dislike Sarah and Zoe, and suspect them of a financial scam, but don't forget about the others. There's Polly and Jo-Jo, Mary and Vanessa out there, having one hell of an unconventional night out. A very weird, totally bizarre night out. In fact, right now, ahead of me, Elaine was probably busy composing some more of her truly terrible poetry about it. This thought cheered me, and I pressed on.

I had reached a belt of trees when, just ahead of me, I could see that the ground sloped down dramatically. Although I hadn't come this way for some years, I knew exactly where I was now. Below me, down a flight of rough-hewn steps, lay Queensmere Pond, although, due to its size, it was more of a lake than a pond. Grandma P. had first told me its history, when as a child, I'd fed the ducks and the swans on Sunday afternoons. Impounded in a small valley, it had been excavated, in the 1830s, for the diamond jubilee of Queen Victoria. Once it had been a place where men in frock coats, cravats and stovepipe hats fought duels to satisfy matters of honour or revenge. Gaming debts, character slurs, even political differences had been settled by a lead musket ball taken in the shoulder, the leg or the heart.

In the light of their swaying lanterns, the group picked their way carefully down the steps, which were deep set and,

I knew, could be treacherous. If I followed them, I'd almost certainly be seen. There was no option but to strike off and away from the path and try to work my way down some other route.

I hugged the tree line and veered off to the right, on the lookout for an alternative track, but there didn't seem to be one. In the darkness, all I could see were clumps of bushes spiralling down into the valley's basin. Another mental debate with myself, but one of less intensity this time, because my curiosity was beginning to override my fear.

I made my descent. Hands groping, I clutched at the splintered limbs of silver birch, at the boughs of ash and rowan. Sprays of leaves swiped me, spiky twigs poked at me, ferny fronds glanced off me as I lurched and tilted my way down. Thick tree roots, thrusting up through the earth, tripped me. I stumbled and slid on loose soil, pitching drunkenly forwards until, at last, the gradient evened out and I could stand steady on my feet again.

It was then that the moon decided to stage a comeback. As I squinted out from behind a screen of bushes, my breath caught at the beauty of the scene before me. From an indigo sky, a waterfall of moonlight poured directly down into the shimmering waters of the lake. A glittering passage connecting Earth to the heavens above, it was luminous, iridescent.

I understood now why this place and this night of a new moon had been chosen for whatever rite was about to be performed, and, despite myself, I couldn't help but feel a little overawed.

CHAPTER THIRTY-FOUR

The women, hushed and solemn, positioned their lanterns along the eastern curve of the lake and then formed a loose circle. The silver hem of Zoe's robe, as she stepped within its centre, flashed as if it had been dipped in the radiance of the waters. Turning to face the lake, she spread her arms out wide and began to speak, but the wind, light yet persistent, made her words only partially audible to me. I had to get closer.

Stealing from my hideout, I slipped, ghost-like, through the trees and concealed myself behind a clump of weeping willows which grew almost up to the water's edge, until I was positioned directly behind the women. Their hoods were all drawn back as they chanted thanks to The Lady for their gifts and their graces, and in the brightness, I could see that the figure with her back to the lake, at the south of the circle, and directly facing Zoe, was Helen. On either side of her were Elaine and Sheila. The positioning of the others meant that I couldn't see their faces, but from her outline, I suspected that the person at the north of the circumference and therefore right in front of me, was Sarah.

I watched and I waited. I didn't know what was coming but somehow, I didn't think that tonight's spell was to be for a lost dog. Once again, the haunting hoot of an owl pierced the silence of the night, and from out of the shadows around me flitted a family of bats, their rapid upstroke wingbeats wheeling and dipping low until they were lost from sight.

"We must tune into the shifting energies around us and from deep within us." Zoe's voice rang out clear and sonorous. "Our bodies are miraculous gifts in harmony with the moon and which we may choose to share."

Oh no, I thought, hastily shutting my eyes. Don't tell me they're about to strip off their robes and get naked. I gave it twenty seconds before opening them again, to find that, thankfully, they were all still fully dressed.

"I call upon the power of the Triple Goddess, Hecate. Goddess of the Moon, of the Night and of the Underworld," intoned Zoe. "You stand at the crossroads of our world and the world of the spirits. This night, I call upon you."

An uneasy shuffling broke out amongst the women at this.

"Tonight, I ask you to open the doorway to the world of the spirits. I am your vessel. Through me, let them come forth."

Again, the women stirred in confusion.

"Goddess, Overseer of the World of the Dead, you can give, and you can destroy. The owl is your messenger and the willow your healing staff. I feel that you are near."

Further consternation amongst the women and whispered mutterings of "What's going on?" and "This doesn't seem right."

Precisely what I was thinking. Here I was, standing directly beneath a willow tree, the Goddess's healing staff, apparently, and only moments before I'd heard the call of her messenger, an owl. I didn't believe in magic, or witchcraft, or any of this stuff, and Zoe's performance was over-egged, too theatrical; but nevertheless, I was beginning to feel spooked.

"Ah, Hecate," continued Zoe, and her voice had risen as she lingered over each word. "I hear the howling of the black dog. A sure indication that you are near. Come to us."

I stiffened, straining my ears. If I caught even the faintest of howls, I was out of here. But I heard only the wind rippling through the trees.

What on earth was happening? I'd thought that tonight's meeting would just be a ramped-up version of the last one, but this was next level freaky. This ceremony was morphing from oddball whimsy to seriously sinister.

The circle was loosening; everyone seemed confused and alarmed. Everyone, that is, except Sarah and Helen. Sarah's stance hadn't shifted. Her body displaying neither surprise nor alarm, she kept silent, remaining fixed and stolid before me. Helen stood perfectly still as if mesmerised. The diamante clip in her hair shone brilliantly in the moonlight, and upon her face was a look of such longing that I could only gaze at her.

Beside her, Sheila took a tentative step forward, but Zoe, ignoring the general discomfort, commanded, "Stay in position. It is vital that you keep the circle."

Her presence and authority were such that the women re-formed the circle. Zoe, her arms still spread wide, raised her face to the moon and began to sway. "She is here. She is here. I feel her. The Goddess is here."

Instinctively, I span around, the long willow fronds slapping at me with a loud dry sibilant rustling, but there was no one there. Of course, there was no one there. I knew that.

Exhaling, I turned back to face the group, only to see Sarah peering behind her and straight in my direction. I froze, snapped my eyes tight shut and held my breath. I heard a movement. Was that her coming towards me? Don't let that be her coming towards me, I prayed, expecting at any second to feel a heavy hand claiming me as a human sacrifice. A minute went by, maybe two, before I plucked up the courage to reopen my eyes. Sarah had her back to me once more. Breathe, I told myself, just breathe. And whatever happens, don't make a bloody sound.

The group's restlessness intensified as Zoe, still swaying, cried,

"Hecate, you bring with you from the world of the spirits, Gregory, departed brother of your devotee, Helen. We welcome him."

Helen gave a low moan and staggered forward but instantly righted herself, shaking off Elaine's arm, which had shot out to support her.

Sheila spoke up, her West Country burr stronger and more forcible than I'd heard before.

"Stop this, Zoe. Beware harnessing the dark energy."

"Yes, we have to stop," piped up other voices. "I don't like this," said someone who may have been Polly. And whomever she was, I had to agree with her.

"No!" Helen almost screamed the word. "Proceed. I must hear his message. I must! Proceed."

I'd been right; she *had* known what was to happen tonight.

I looked beyond the women to the lake. Its gleam was duller now. The light had dimmed. Radiance spent, the passage from the heavens to the earth was narrowing, closing. The moon was turning her face away from us, as if in sadness or in shame.

"It's dangerous," persisted Sheila. "Power is sacred to the Goddess and must not be misused."

"Count me out." I recognised Vanessa's high-handed tone. "I want no part of this."

There were assenting calls of "Me too" and "Nor me." The circle had once again broken form.

I looked at Sarah, still facing away from me. Would she intervene? Would she back up Zoe and insist that this crazy ritual went ahead? But she did nothing. There was something of the guard dog in her stance, I noted, but not that of a protector. More dispassionate warden, sentinel, watchman. She was of this group but apart from them.

"You must stay," pleaded Helen. "We need thirteen. Make them, Zoe. Make them do it. You promised me. You promised me a message from Gregory. You promised!"

She was crying now. Jo-Jo made as if to comfort her but halted in her tracks as Shelia, raising her right arm high, cried, "An it harm none, do as ye will."

There was something so compelling in her tone that everyone fell silent.

"An it harm none, do as ye will," she repeated severely.

"But they promised." Helen dropped her head and would have fallen had Elaine again not put out an arm to

273

save her. This time she wasn't shrugged off. "Sarah," Helen's voice was weak, "you promised that Zoe would do this in return for all the—"

Sarah instantly cut her off. "Enough!" She clapped her hands together. "I think that's more than enough for one evening, don't you, Zoe?"

She looked meaningfully at Zoe who answered, "Yes, for tonight we have lost the ear of the Goddess. We should—"

"*You* should all make your way back to the cars," interrupted Sarah. "Zoe and I will follow shortly."

"I don't need telling twice," said one of the women I didn't know. "Quick, let's get out of here."

Polly, in whose face I could read real distress, said, "Yes, do let's go. Come on, Vanessa. I could do with a drink."

Couldn't we all? I thought. I felt exhausted and, shifting awkwardly on my feet, I stumbled and fell back against the willow's trunk. The encircling branches all about me shifted noisily before settling, and Sarah, catching the sound, swung around to face my direction. Again, I froze. Surely, after all this, I wouldn't be discovered now?

CHAPTER THIRTY-FIVE

I wasn't. No one else appeared to have heard anything and I saw Sarah's stance relax as she turned back to the group. The mood had lightened. Whether relieved to simply be going home or that the ghost of Helen's dead brother, Gregory, was not to be summoned from his grave, I didn't know or very much care. All I wanted was to get out from beneath this tree, sprint back to my car as fast as I could and be quit of this place. I was cold; I was tired; I was scratched, bruised, filthy dirty and longing for a glass of wine.

Mary and the four women I hadn't met, having picked up their lanterns, started to make their way back up the rough-hewn steps and, although there were protestations of tiredness and comments on how disturbing the ceremony had been, it seemed that they were recovering themselves well. Not so, poor Helen. She was crying softly to herself as Sheila and Jo-Jo helped her negotiate her way. The others followed, with Elaine bringing up the rear. Only Sarah and Zoe remained, standing roughly in the middle of the circle that had so lately been disbanded. They didn't speak until the noise of the others' departure had faded. Now, this should prove interesting, I thought.

It was Sarah who broke the silence. "Got a little carried away, didn't you?" Her laugh was unpleasant. "You frightened them off. Next time, I'd take it down a notch if I were you."

"Well, you're not me," Zoe snapped back. "You don't command the power that I do. It's my gift, not yours."

"Save it." Sarah's tone was contemptuous. "The punters have all gone home. You don't have to keep spouting that crap."

"How many times do I have to tell you that my gift is real?" With the fading moonlight glancing off her high cheekbones, Zoe was very striking.

"It's late. I'm tired," she said. "There's no point in having this argument with you again. I just feel bad, that's all. Helen deserved to receive her message. I really thought it would come tonight. I felt it *was* coming… until everything unravelled."

"We got her to hand over the rest of the money, didn't we? So what if old Gregory didn't get to rattle his chains?"

Zoe shook her head. "We owe it to Helen. You know that. Never mind. We'll try again at the next full moon and it might be better to bring in the other group; what do you think?"

"You can if you like. I won't be here."

About to pick up her lantern, Zoe turned in surprise. "What do you mean?"

Sarah shrugged. "We've had a pretty good run, wouldn't you say? But, like all good things, it must come to an end." She smiled nastily. "So, I think it's time to say… goodbye."

The emphasis she placed on the word *goodbye*, didn't sit well with me. What exactly did she mean by it? How final, for Zoe, was this goodbye to be?

"That's OK," said Zoe. "You don't have to come to all the meetings. I think it's better that you don't. Your energy is all wrong. I've felt it block me. But it's hardly goodbye." She stooped again for her lantern. "There's the Wellness Centre, remember? Or has our million-pound project just happened to have slipped your mind?"

A million pounds. That was double the figure recorded in the papers Flan and I had taken from the Tower.

"It's not on my mind at all. Never has been," said Sarah.

"What do you mean?"

There was no response. Zoe was looking fully into the other woman's face now. "Sarah, what's going on?"

"Maybe I should have mentioned this before, but there *is* no Wellness Centre. Sorry and all that." Her words were at odds with the coolness of her tone. "It's bound to be a bit of a disappointment for you. I do understand. But you'll get over it."

"What? You told me you'd put down the deposit. We'll lose the property if we don't go ahead."

Sarah shook her head in mock contrition. "Not strictly the case. Not the case at all, in fact."

"What are you saying?"

"I'm saying," Sarah made a palms-up gesture with her hands, "that there never was a property."

"But you showed me the estate agents' details. We talked it all through."

"A set of property details are easy enough to pick up."

"You tricked me!" Zoe shouted. "You absolute bitch!"

Sarah's voice was calm and her posture utterly relaxed as she answered, "You're not very smart. Decorative, yes. But smart, no."

"Don't speak to me like that," Zoe snapped back.

"Why play the innocent?" Sarah asked. "You were just as instrumental as me in getting those suckers to shell out their cash."

"Yes," Zoe admitted reluctantly, "because people like Helen can spare it. They don't need it and so, yes, I encouraged her to donate."

"Yours is a flexible take on morality," Sarah remarked.

"And yours isn't?"

"I make no claim to a moral code. Far too restricting. But look at you, quivering there in righteous indignation. It's pathetic. Don't pretend that it was ever anything other than a hustle."

"I'm not pretending!"

"And *encouraged*?" Sarah jeered. "Extorted more like. The pitch you hit her with was dynamite. You know how to reel them in, I'll give you that. It's why I brought you along. You can be very convincing."

A look of calculation flashed across Zoe's face and her voice hardened. "The money. All that money. You just said that you couldn't have got it without me. We were partners in this. And still are. I'm prepared to forget all about the Wellness Centre as long as I get my share of the cash. And, as a favour, I'll accept just fifty perc ent, even though I could quite justifiably demand more."

"Demand all you like, love. There's nothing in the pot for you, I'm afraid."

Sarah's sharp chin looked more pronounced than ever. "I have need of it, you see. So, how about you chalk this one down to experience, Zoe? Consider it one of life's lessons. Isn't that your philosophy? Isn't it just what The Craft teaches? Do *that*. Give it a go. I'm sure you'll find the disappointment easier to bear."

"You fucking cow!" Zoe's hand shot out to slap the other woman across the face, but Sarah was too quick for her. And too strong. She grabbed Zoe's arm and then laughed as the other woman tried to shake her off.

"I'll tell on you," yelled Zoe. "I'll go to the police. I'll report you to…"

"No, you won't." Sarah twisted Zoe's arm painfully.

My mind raced and I felt slightly sick. The last thing in the world I wanted to do was show myself and go to Zoe's rescue. But should I?

"There are those lovely intimate photos, remember?" Sarah's height and bulk in the dark robe appeared menacingly powerful.

"I'm sure that Miles's rich wife would be very interested to see them. And we both know that he'd drop you like a shot if he thought he might lose his affluent lifestyle."

"Get off, you're hurting me." Zoe again tried to break free. "You have to destroy those photos. Please, Sarah, I'm begging you. I can't give him up. I can't. I should never have agreed to letting you take them in the first place."

"You should never have fallen in love with a mark! If you'd stuck to the original plan, we'd have taken him for every penny he's got."

"I couldn't help myself. I'm meant to be with Miles. I see it, I feel it…"

"Do shut up. You're boring me. Do you really think I give a damn about your dreary little romance? Oh, and just to be absolutely clear…" Her grip tightened on Zoe's arm. "Don't for a moment think that I'd be naïve enough not to have secured some spare copies."

The photos. It seemed that Sarah thought that it was Zoe who had broken in and stolen them.

"What?" Zoe had started to cry. Shock had registered now, and her eyes were black pools within the whiteness of her face. "I don't know what you're talking about."

"Sure, you don't." Sarah's tone was sceptical as she shook her head. "It doesn't much matter now anyway. No time for it. I've things to do, planes to catch. You know how it is. And packing really takes it out of a person."

"Planes?" Zoe looked completely bemused. "You're going away?"

"Far, far away," replied Sarah as she looked the other woman up and down. "And so, *partner*, what am I going to do with you?"

"Please, please don't hurt me," whimpered Zoe. "I won't tell anyone. I promise I won't."

"Yes, but I do need to be sure of that."

Bloody hell, this is it, I thought. This is the moment for me to dash out and… and what? Hope that Sarah's undeniable strength would be no match for two of us? I hesitated and as I did so, Sarah released her hold on Zoe.

"There, there." She traced her finger against Zoe's cheek. "I'm not going to harm a hair on your head. Although I could," she reflected almost to herself, "but you're right; it's late and I too am tired."

She focussed on the other woman again. "The reality is that you can't open your mouth about me without facing charges of extortion. And with me out of the picture, you'd take all the heat."

She laughed. "I have a feeling that you'd be a very popular girl on D wing. So, this is where we're at. I get to keep the money; you get to keep the man. Do we have a deal?"

Zoe stared at her dumbly.

"Special offer. One night only." Sarah glanced at her watch. "Actually, not one night. One minute. So, what's it to be? Be quick, before I change my mind." The threat in this was only too clear.

Zoe, squirming within Sarah's grip, shouted, "Yes! Yes, all right. You win."

"Oh, my dear." Sarah took a step back and laughed. "How could you ever have imagined that I wouldn't? Let's call it a night then, shall we?" Her tone was back to light, conversational almost.

From beneath the shelter of my willow tree, I let out a long, slow breath as they both picked up their lanterns and Zoe meekly followed Sarah over to the steps.

I waited until they were nearly at the top before poking my head out and gingerly emerging from my hideout. I crept my way after them. Once clear of the steps, I hung back. I could just make out, in the faint glow of the lanterns, the outline of the two women as they reached the open section of the common.

I was nearly done and would soon be home, but the distance back to the car suddenly seemed immense. I closed my eyes for a second, drawing on the last reserves of my energy. As I opened them, a dark robed figure detached itself from the clump of trees on my left and, with obvious stealth, followed Sarah and Zoe along the track. I gasped. I'd not been the only one out spying tonight. Someone else had been watching and listening in the darkness.

CHAPTER THIRTY-SIX

It was the ringing of my mobile that woke me at just after 9am.

As I groped a hand across the bedside table to pick up the call, I knocked onto the floor the bracelet Polly had given me. It had only been after my return from Wimbledon Common, as I'd stripped off my filthy clothes before stepping into the bath, that I'd realised I'd still been wearing it. Perhaps there was something to be said for that Spell of Protection after all? I stretched down to pick it up before answering groggily. "Hello."

"Hi, it's Vanessa."

I heaved myself up into a sitting position. "Hold on," I said and shoved a pillow behind my back.

"I know it's early, Clarry, but I think I may owe you an apology."

"You mean for nearly getting me killed by a stampeding horse?"

Vanessa laughed. "Cleo didn't stampede; she just got a bit of a spurt on."

"*Bit of a spurt on?* That was a galloping rampage. I was lucky not to have been killed."

"Briony did say that you made a pretty good job of hanging on."

"Hmm," was all I said. I allowed the pause that followed to develop. My head felt foggy, I was desperate for a cup of tea and I was in no mood to make things easy for her.

"The thing is," she said eventually, "I've been thinking about what you said about the Wellness Centre and how little I know about it." She broke off but as I didn't respond, continued. "Things have got a bit… well… weird."

Now, there's the understatement of the year, I thought.

"I'm sorry that I snapped at you, Clarry. Really, I am. You've only ever been nice to me and all I've done is throw it back in your face."

You've got that right, I agreed, but wisely, left it unsaid.

"And, Clarry, I need advice about something. Someone, actually. You remember Helen? You came to the meeting at her house."

I was wide awake now. "Sure, I do. What about her?"

"I'm worried about her. We had one of our meetings last night and… Oh, it's difficult to explain over the phone, but I've just called her to see how she is, and she sounded odd. Like she's in shock. I'm going over there in about an hour and I'm not sure how to handle it. I suppose I could ask Polly… and I don't know why you should, but I wondered if you might come with me."

I thought hard for a moment. The job I'd been commissioned to do was basically done. All I needed to do was to report back to Diana and that would be that. But was my work as a *detective* complete? What about Sarah and the money? If I did go to the police, how would I explain away the fact that I had stolen the photos and Sarah's record of donations? I didn't know what to do for the best.

Although I hardly knew Helen, I too felt worried about her. And that wasn't all. Who was that mystery robed figure? One of the group must have doubled back, and whilst I didn't think Helen had been in a fit enough state to do so, she might have noticed something that could put me on the scent.

"Make it an hour and a half and I'll see you there."

That would give me enough time to have some breakfast. And after last night, I deserved a belter. I'd have a pile of toast, maybe some eggs, and there might be a handful of mushrooms in the back of the fridge. Or did I have some croissants in the freezer? That would be…

"Thanks, Clarry." Vanessa interrupted my food reverie. "I told you before that I had a feeling that I could trust you."

I did wish that she wouldn't keep saying that.

*

If Helen was surprised to see me accompanying Vanessa, she didn't express it. She didn't express very much at all. I recalled the kindness of her greeting the last time I'd been here. Today, although polite, there was a wooden quality to her welcome.

In her Sunday morning outfit of navy cotton trousers and linen blouse, she was again wearing her diamante clip. She led us through to the sitting room where the French windows, open to the garden, allowed in the sweet fragrance of some climbing plant, whose nodding heads of tiny pale pink blooms drooped over the casement. Was it a variety of jasmine? Ed would know. The thought of him sent a little frisson of happiness through me. This beautiful May morning, rich with the scent of flowers and pierced with the fluty melodious song of a blackbird, was exactly what I needed to dispel the legacy of last night's menacing visions. That, and the prospect of a hot date with Ed sometime very soon.

"This is a beautiful room," I said, taking a seat on the sofa beside Vanessa and glancing up at the portraits of Helen's younger self, and those of her dead brother, Gregory.

"Thank you," was Helen's only reply. On a low walnut table, a tray had been set with a pot of coffee and two cups.

"Excuse me one moment," said Helen. "I'll just fetch another."

Vanessa and I exchanged a look.

"She looks upset," I volunteered.

"Exactly," hissed Vanessa.

Helen returned with the cup and poured us all coffee. Whilst it lacked the ceremony of Diana Maitland's afternoon tea ritual, there was a similar formality in Helen's offering of milk, sugar and shortbread biscuits. She took a seat in a comfortable-looking armchair opposite us.

Vanessa and I hadn't had a chance to confer on the doorstep, and so I waited for her to take the lead. But she didn't. Instead, she asked about the painting that Helen was working on and made various inconsequential remarks about the weather. I gave her a nudge.

"So," she offered hesitantly, "I was worried about you. After what happened last night."

Helen, setting her cup onto its saucer, didn't respond.

Vanessa flashed me a look.

"What *did* happen last night?" I asked disingenuously.

For a moment, I thought that Helen wouldn't answer, but when she did so, her statement was delivered in a flat monotone.

"Hope was lost last night."

"What do you mean?"

"My last hope of communicating with my brother. I wanted so much to let him know that I understood why he did what he did and that I didn't blame him."

"Blame him?"

"For killing himself."

At these words, tears began to slip quietly down her face. Vanessa crossed to her and placed an arm about her shoulders, and then Helen, remaining very calm throughout, disclosed the whole sad story. Gregory had battled schizophrenia all his adult life. He, like Helen, had been a gifted painter. The portraits hanging upon the walls were mostly his work. In his later years, the medication that he had been taking for so long began to affect his concentration, and his painting suffered. This he could not bear. He was found hanging from a lamppost in the backstreets of Kennington.

"He chose somewhere that would not hold memories for me. Somewhere unrelated to our lives," said Helen. "It was his way of protecting me."

As she went on, with some colourful asides from Vanessa, to describe last night's events, I worked hard to feign an appropriate level of surprise, before asking, "Did you genuinely believe that Gregory would appear? That he would materialise in some form?"

The diamante clip glittered in the sunlight as she dipped her head before replying, "No. But I wanted to."

Vanessa stood up and began to pace the room.

"And that's what's so wrong." She was bristling with indignation. "Zoe and Sarah should never have allowed you to. It's… it's exploitative. They've capitalised on your grief and they've…"

Although I knew the answer, I threw out my question anyway.

"Profited?"

"I have given them a great deal of money if that's what you mean," Helen said in a low voice.

"As payment?" I asked gently. "That was the deal?"

"I didn't see it like that at the time," admitted Helen. "But yes, I suppose you could call it that. Do you think they could be persuaded to give it back?"

"Probably not," I said, as Sarah's one-way ticket to the Dominican Republic crossed my mind.

"Well, I'm through with them," said Vanessa decisively. "Done. How they have treated you is shameful. I'm never going to speak to either of them again."

This would come as a massive relief to Diana, I knew.

Vanessa stopped her pacing.

"I wonder how the others feel. I think that they should be told."

She turned to Helen. "Do you agree?"

Helen was silent for several moments. "Yes, you're right; they should be told, but I'd rather not tell them myself. I just don't feel up to it. Would you be kind enough to do it for me?"

Vanessa instantly agreed. "Of course! I've got Polly and Jo-Jo's numbers and I think that Jo-Jo has Mary's. Do you have Elaine's or any of the others?"

"I think that Shelia has the others, but I do have Elaine's. She left her jacket here once, and we exchanged numbers when she called to collect it."

"Great. How about you make some more coffee, Clarry, and I'll start ringing round."

Helen provided Vanessa with Elaine's number and then insisted on helping me, and so we went to the kitchen together. As we put out fresh cups and more biscuits, I could hear across the hall, Vanessa talking first to Polly and then to Jo-Jo.

Now I was alone with Helen, it was time to put out feelers as to who the mystery woman might have been.

"I can't begin to imagine how distressed you must have been last night. I hope that you weren't driving home."

"No, thankfully, Jo-Jo drove me."

"And the others," I asked, "did they carpool?"

"I think Pam and Beth might have come together, I'm not sure."

These were two of the women that I hadn't met. Try as I might, I couldn't think of any way to extract further information and so I asked, "What drew you to this... umm... witch business? Sorry, I mean, The Craft?"

"I can see how it must seem to..." She broke off and then smiled for the first time that morning. "I was going to say to an outsider like you."

She crossed to the window and looked out at the garden for a long moment, before turning back to me. "An outsider like me, I should have said. My parents were both academics. Gregory and I were brought up to be freethinkers, encouraged to hold a deep reverence for nature. I think it's one of the reasons that we both became artists. As children, we were alone much of the time. We would play in the woods. For us, they became a place of enchantment. We would re-enact the old legends of King Arthur and Merlin. We'd decorate our camp with flowers and garlands of ivy, making sure to ask permission of the nymphs that lived in the tree before cutting down their boughs. It was just pretend; we both knew that. But later, those games, those rituals provided an escape from the fear that Gregory's condition, developed in his early teens, engendered in both of us."

The shrill of the kettle coming to the boil brought us both back into the present.

"And so, to answer your question," she said as she refilled the coffee pot, "when Gregory killed himself, it felt natural to re-look to the comfort of that childhood belief in magic. It was a connection to him, you see."

I could see that. Or at least, I could understand the desire to offset grief with hope, no matter how tenuous that hope might be.

"And you have no other family?"

"No. I'm alone. An outsider, as I said."

There was something so bleak in her utterance that I couldn't stop myself from leaning in and giving her a hug, to which she submitted awkwardly.

"I think most of us are outsiders," I said, disengaging myself. "It's just that we do everything we possibly can to avoid recognising that fact."

As we brought in the coffee, Vanessa was still on the phone. She shifted her mobile from one ear to the other and called, "Clarry, I've already spoken to Polly and Jo-Jo. I'm just talking to Elaine... what?" She spoke into the phone again. "Sorry, Elaine… I was just saying to Clarry… you remember Clarry? She came to the meeting we had at Helen's house. Yes. Tall. Blonde. That's her." She flashed a grin at me. "Yes, she is quite well built."

I rolled my eyes at her as she continued talking to Elaine.

"What? Well, Clarry happened to be with me when I dropped in on Helen and so… no, she won't tell anyone. Yes, I know we don't want this getting out. It's weird enough without… " I could hear sounds of protestation coming from down the line. "Look, don't worry about that. Clarry won't breathe a word of it to anyone. She's very discreet. I trust her."

Again, with the trust, I thought.

CHAPTER THIRTY-SEVEN

I turned down an invitation to have lunch with Vanessa. There were things I had to do. I needed to let Diana know that Vanessa was safely out of Sarah and Zoe's clutches, and I should call Flan to update her, but firstly, I wanted time to process everything that had happened over the last thirty hours or so. And I really should call Dave at Abbe's to find out what shifts I would be doing in the week ahead.

Back home, I started to make notes on all that I'd seen and heard. Totting up the hours I'd spent, in order to invoice Diana, made me feel almost like a professional.

I put down my pen and rubbed my eyes. I wasn't even remotely a professional. Firstly, because I spook easily, and secondly, because the case had become personal. That was something a professional would never allow. The fact that Sarah was leaving the country tomorrow with Helen's money bothered me enormously. Hadn't Helen lost enough? Why should Sarah get away with it? I still couldn't decide whether I should contact the police, and time was running out.

Then, there was the matter of the mysterious figure on the common. I couldn't shake off that unsettling image. Who was she?

I got up and let myself out into the back garden, where I sat down at the old stone table. The garden always had a steadying effect on me. I wasn't often on top of the weeding, but I did manage to mow the lawn every month or so.

Gazing at the lilac tree, at the pale pink sweet peas snaking their way up a wigwam of ancient canes, and at the lily of the valley, Vanessa's words about her good fortune having not been earnt came back to me. Well, neither had mine. Should I, like Vanessa, feel therefore that I owed something back? And if so, what? Standing up and picking off a stem or two of the apricot roses that clambered up the back fence, I decided that this was a matter for another day. For the moment, I'd park it.

As I arranged the flowers in an old enamel jug, something else bothered me. I still hadn't established whether Vanessa had known about her brother-in-law's affair with Zoe. Although she could be a bit of a brat, I couldn't help but like Vanessa. And, given all she had said about trust, I shrank from the idea of suspecting her of a cover-up. Or worse, of complicity.

*

By late afternoon, I'd made my calls. I was due at the restaurant for the evening shift on Tuesday, Thursday and Friday, which meant that I'd be free for a date with Ed on Saturday. All I needed now was for him to ask me.

Diana, when I got through to her, was, as I'd anticipated, very relieved. "Thank goodness for that!" she breathed. On being told that although I didn't know exactly how much money Vanessa had already contributed but that I guessed it was a significant amount, she merely said, "But at least she's come to her senses now and won't be handing across any more. I've always thought that coming into the family trust fund at only twenty-one years of age was a mistake, but there was nothing I could do about it. I would much rather she'd had to wait until she was at least thirty. Wouldn't you agree?"

"I've not much experience of these things and so I wouldn't know."

There was a pause before Diana continued. "As you are aware, Clarry, I did have some doubts about this arrangement at the beginning. However, I must say that I am very pleased with the results. Thank you. I will contact you sometime over the next few days and we will arrange for your payment. Now, I must fly; there's a car coming to take Clive and I up to London, to the theatre. We're having early drinks with friends at the Goring Hotel before seeing Roger Allam at the National, in some play I've never heard of, but it's had good reviews."

"Just one thing, Diana, before you go," I said quickly. "If you don't mind me asking, have you had any more thoughts about the situation with Miles? Are you going to tell Caroline?"

Diana left it a beat before replying. "I don't mind you asking. The truth is, I simply don't know what to do. I've even been toying with the idea of speaking directly with Miles and insisting that he finish his sordid little affair, but I need a little more time to decide."

Flan, predictably, was very disappointed not to have witnessed the scene on the common herself.

"You should have asked me to accompany you, darling, really you should have. It sounds like the most tremendous fun. And how fascinating. To have witnessed a charmed circle. A witches' line-up. No, I've got it. A conspiracy of witches. That's much better."

"The only ones conspiring, Flan, were Sarah and Zoe."

"And that other sinister figure you mentioned, Clarry. Don't forget about her."

"If only I could."

"It's over now, darling, and so you soon will. Besides, congratulations are in order. The Love Detective has closed her second case. Now, may I suggest an early night, Clarry? You've had an eventful week."

"Yes, I have," I agreed warmly, "and I do feel a little wrung-out. I wouldn't be a bit surprised if all this stress has even affected my appetite!"

She was laughing as she rang off.

*

I didn't get my early night. Keyed up and restless, I found myself unable to relax. I wanted to be doing something, something proactive, and so I called Flan back and obtained the Cunninghams' phone number.

Ron Cunningham provided me with the colour, model and registration number of Sarah's car. A tan-coloured

Volkswagen Polo, he told me it was currently sitting in her drive.

At seven thirty, as I drove down to Epsom, I wondered if planning might be overrated. Isn't it better, occasionally, to trust to the inspiration of the moment and simply wing it? Probably not, I decided. And who did I think I was kidding with, *occasionally?*

I didn't know what I was expecting to discover. Absolutely nothing, most likely, but it felt good to be on the move.

I parked at the other end of the street from Sarah's and then made my way through a side gate that had been left unlocked for me, to Mary and Ron Cunningham's back door. They made me very welcome. Armed with tea, chocolate biscuits and a pair of Ron's binoculars, I set up position.

The Cunninghams' home was detached from that of their neighbour. This was the elderly man in carpet slippers and stained brown cardigan who had slammed the door in my face and that of Mr. Babcock, when we'd been carrying out our fake survey on the correct attire for funeral directors. Next to him was the detached side of Sarah's house. As the Cunninghams occupied a corner plot, it was possible, through a leaded mock-Tudor window on the far eastern side of their sitting room, to obtain a fairly good view of Sarah's front door.

"This is just what we needed." Mary's watery blue eyes gleamed with excitement. "Things have got a little stale around here lately and I've been looking to take up a new hobby. I find that I no longer get the satisfaction out of bridge that I once used to. Do you play, dear?"

"Don't be plaguing her with questions," Ron cut in. In impeccably pressed grey flannel trousers and red V-necked pullover, his manner was stately but courteous. "She needs to concentrate. Now, as I said, Clarry, if you need to…" he coughed delicately, "use the facilities… I'll take up your post. Or even if you just need a break."

"No, I'm fine for the moment, thanks. You've already done so much, and I'm really grateful for the help."

"No trouble at all. We've never liked that Gaitskill woman, even before her assault upon poor Freddie. There's something malign about her. I've always said so, haven't I, Mary?"

"Indeed you have," agreed his wife, smoothing the collar of her mauve cardigan. "Malign; that was your exact word."

"Freddie certainly seems to have recovered," I remarked, putting aside the binoculars and glancing at the corpulent marmalade cat stretched out upon a rug. "He certainly looks comfortable."

*

An hour went by with no movement from Sarah. The upper storey of the house was in darkness and, on the ground floor, only a light in the hall was visible.

"She may well have bedded down for the evening," I said to the Cunninghams, who had now settled themselves on the sofa.

"This is thrilling," said Mary. "An actual, real live detective sitting right here in our living room."

"I'm not really…" But why disappoint them with the truth and confess to the fact that I was merely a bumbling amateur? It would be cruel to curtail their enjoyment.

"It's unlikely that anything will happen tonight, and I will have wasted your time. There's a lot of sitting around and waiting on a stake-out, I've learnt. But, if it's OK with you, I'll give it another hour or so."

*

Time ticked on. By ten thirty, Ron had exhausted his stories of his career in the civil service, and Mary was covering her mouth with her hand in an attempt to stifle some increasingly deep yawns. "I should go," I said. "I'm sorry to have…"

A car had pulled up outside Sarah's house and a woman got out. I adjusted the binoculars. About five foot five or six with mid-length dirty-blonde hair; it was Vanessa.

CHAPTER THIRTY-EIGHT

I let out a long breath. What on earth was she doing here? I watched as she walked up the path, brushed past the miniature bonsai trees and lifted the lion's head knocker. Several minutes went by. I could see by the set of her shoulders that she was getting impatient. She gave the knocker another rap and, on still getting no response, was just turning away when the door slowly opened. I fiddled again with the binoculars' central focussing knob until the image, sharp and crisp, revealed Sarah dressed in one of her long linen shapeless dresses. There followed a brief conversation and the two women disappeared into the house.

Putting down the binoculars, I found that the Cunninghams were standing one on either side of me.

"What's happening?" asked Ron. "Do you recognise the Gaitskill woman's visitor?"

"Yes, I do. I'm just very surprised to see her, that's all."

"What are you going to do now then?" Mary asked sharply, all trace of her former sleepiness dispelled.

"Umm… I'm not quite sure."

"If this was an Agatha Christie story…" she said.

"Which it isn't," observed her husband.

"If it was," Mary persisted, "then you'd try and get into that house to discover what was going on."

"*Would I?* Hmm, well, perhaps you're right,"

She fixed her watery blue eyes upon me. "I'm quite sure that I am, dear."

*

Ron, carrying a portable step ladder, led the way to the back of their extensive rear garden.

"I could have hoisted you up," he whispered, "but with my hip, I daren't risk it." He set the step ladder into position against a tall fence that separated his house, on the eastern side, from that of his elderly neighbour. "Now then, Clarry. You just hop on over."

I looked from him to the step ladder. "You make it sound so easy. I'm just wondering what's on the other side. I'm rather hoping for a soft landing."

"Nothing to it," returned Ron. "I'll pass the step ladder up to you. But best be quick. We don't want old Lionel to see you. He doesn't sleep much and his mind's as sharp as a tack. He'd be sure to come out and investigate."

Once sitting astride the fence, I peered down. Directly beneath me was a gravel path flanking an expanse of lawn.

"Do you want me to pass the ladder back to you?" I hissed.

"No, keep it. It might come in handy. Good luck."

The step ladder made a soft crunching sound as its feet hit the gravel, but within seconds I was over. I unclamped it and looked about me, studying the stretch to the opposite fence. I didn't want to trip over a rockery, twist an ankle or tumble into a water feature, but the way looked to be clear.

There were only a few stars out and just one dim light showing on the ground floor of the old gentleman's house. I waited for any sign of movement and then, my heart giving a warning thump, I shot across the lawn and reached the fence, on the other side of which lay Sarah's garden.

I was very glad of the step ladder. This fence was even higher than the one I'd just come over. Again, once astride, I peered down. There, beneath me, was a deep flower bed. I lowered the ladder, where it settled unevenly into the soil, making my descent a little wobbly. I was about to collapse it back into a portable position when I hesitated. It might be a good idea to keep it as it was, in case I had need of a swift exit. That thought was very unnerving.

Sarah's garden was on a similar scale to her neighbour's, except that instead of a gravel path running alongside a lawn, the grass was set in a rectangle, with a courtyard abutting the house. I dropped to a crouch and crept my way forwards. There were lights on in two of the ground floor rooms. One, with curtains fully drawn, I guessed to be a sitting room and the other, with blinds only partially lowered across three sash windows, proved to be the kitchen. The lower sash to the middle window was open.

I swallowed. What I most longed to do now was shuffle back the way I'd just come, let myself out of the Cunninghams' back gate, leg it to the car and get myself the hell out of there. I should do that. That's what any sane person would do. But it appeared that any semblance of sanity I'd once possessed had completely deserted me, because I did none of those things. I'd come to feel a certain responsibility for Vanessa. Her trust in me imparted a weight of obligation.

I peeped through the window and into a farmhouse-style kitchen with a central island and a door that opened onto the hallway. There, I could see a large suitcase and matching holdall. Sarah had her back to me, but I could see and hear Vanessa quite clearly.

"I can't understand why you are refusing to accept that what you and Zoe have done is just plain wrong."

Sarah tried to interrupt her, but Vanessa was in full imperious Maitland mode now. "Stop trying to talk your way out of it. Just do the decent thing and give her back her money. I don't care about mine. You can keep it. I want nothing more to do with you. Keep it to build this Wellness Centre," she sneered, "if indeed you ever had any plans to do so at all, which I now seriously doubt."

I winced. Vanessa had made a mistake in coming here at all, but now she was making a more serious one by treating Sarah with such obvious contempt. She didn't know what Sarah was capable of. Neither, for that matter, did I, but I'd seen enough of her treatment of Zoe last night to believe that she wasn't a woman likely to tolerate interference or submit to reproof.

"So," insisted Vanessa, "are you going to give Helen back her money?"

"No." Sarah's refusal was flat and cold. "And yes, I'll be holding on to yours too. So, thanks for that. Very generous of you. Now, if you've said all that you came to say, do trot off home. I've a few last things to do and you're starting to grate on my nerves."

"But you can't keep her money!" Vanessa shouted. "I won't let you. My family won't let you. We have solicitors and lawyers who will make sure that it's returned. *I'll* make sure of it."

Sarah let out a long sigh and then shrugged. "That's not going to happen."

"Oh, yes it will! My father is…"

She broke off with a cry as Sarah hit her hard across the face.

"You and your breed. That sense of entitlement you all possess. The arrogance. I'm betting that you've never had to want for anything in all your pathetic sheltered little life. Well, here's one time that you won't be running back to Daddy."

She raised her hand to strike Vanessa again, just as I slithered my way through the open window and sprawled down with a thump onto the tiled floor.

Sarah swung around in surprise and then laughed. "Ah, and here's your irritating prying little friend, just in time to join you."

As I pulled myself upright, I caught just a glimpse of Vanessa's gaping blood-streaked face before Sarah pounced and struck me with a karate chop to the neck. Pain exploded through me and I slumped to the floor.

Vanessa screamed, only to be grabbed by the hair and flung up against the wall. "Phone," Sarah demanded.

"I don't have it," Vanessa whispered.

Sarah slapped her again. "Don't fuck with me."

Weeping now, Vanessa reached into her shoulder bag and dragged out her mobile. Sarah took it, threw it to the floor and stamped on it.

"Now hers." Sarah gestured to me. "Come on. Quickedy quick. Time is money, as they say."

Vanessa patted me down and found it in the back pocket of my jeans. It met the same fate as hers.

I tried to raise myself from my knees, but I felt sick, dizzy, like I was going to pass out. Sarah looked from me to Vanessa, cowering by the central island.

"I have to leave in thirty minutes. These early-morning flights do mean that one has to check in at an ungodly hour." She put a finger to her cheek, feigning contemplation. "And so, what to do with you two?"

I tried to speak. Tried to tell her that the Cunninghams knew I was here, but the feeling of faintness had intensified, and I couldn't get the words out.

"What a nuisance you are. Let me think. Let me think. Well, as I only need to ensure that you are both kept quiet for a limited amount of time, and because I never like to leave behind more complications than are strictly necessary, then I'll show you to the guest quarters. I can't promise that you'll be comfortable, but at least you'll be out of my way."

With that, she propelled Vanessa back into the hall, opened a door under the stairwell and shoved her through it.

"Now you," she said, advancing towards me. I tried to fend her off, but I was no match for her. She manhandled me up onto my feet and steered me roughly into the hall. I was then thrust through the same door to join Vanessa. As it slammed to and the lock turned, I found myself standing at the top of a short flight of steps leading to a dank, dark airless cellar. Panic seized me. Vanessa and I were prisoners in a soon-to-be-abandoned house. When I didn't return, would the Cunninghams raise the alarm or merely assume that I'd gone straight home? We could be trapped down here forever.

CHAPTER THIRTY-NINE

I sank down heavily onto the top step, dropped my head between my knees, and for some moments tried to concentrate on regulating my breathing. In and out. In and out. It was working. I raised my head experimentally. I no longer felt sick, but I was still weak.

I became conscious of Vanessa standing a few steps below me. She was snuffling softly to herself.

"Are you OK?" I whispered.

"Yes, are you?" she whispered back.

"Just about," I said, and then added in my normal voice, "but I don't know why we're whispering."

At that, she stopped snuffling and gave a little laugh. "Neither do I."

Somehow, hearing that laugh made me feel better. I stood up gingerly and ran my hands across the rough enclosing walls about me until I found a light switch. I flicked it on but either it was dead, or the bulb was out.

"Should we bang on the door?" Vanessa sounded more like herself. "Do you think she'll let us out?"

"Not a chance. I think our best bet is to wait until she's gone and then try to smash our way out of here. Change places with me, will you? I want to see what's down here that we might be able to use."

"As a weapon?" she asked.

I thought about it. *Should* we try to escape whilst Sarah was still here? No, too risky. If we did manage to get through the door, we might walk straight into an ambush.

"Let's explore first," I said. "I don't suppose you have a torch? Have you still got your bag?"

"Yes, but I don't own a torch."

We swapped places and I counted the steps until I reached the bottom. It wasn't pitch-black; a tiny trickle of light permeated from somewhere off to my right.

"There's thirteen steps in total," I called, groping my way about the room. It was only eight paces wide and there was a tall shelving unit located on the left-hand side. Wary of cutting myself, I carefully ran my fingers over its contents. Some old paint brushes, a jar of screws and nails, a couple of large books or albums, jugs of varying sizes, a garden trowel, some bits of rope and other odds and ends. Inadvertently dislodging something with my foot, my heart nearly jumped out of my chest as something long with sharp edges narrowly missed hitting me in the face.

"Christ!" I spluttered, patting it down and discovering it to be an upturned rake. "Keep hold of that." I passed it, right way up, to Vanessa, who now stood on the bottom step.

Tripping over cartons and several plastic bags containing something lightweight and soft, I stumbled fourteen paces along the cellar's length until my hands met a wall of stacked wooden crates. It was there, in the right-hand corner, from somewhere behind the crates, that a sliver of watery grey light winked at me.

"I think there might be a window back here," I called. "Vanessa? Are you there?"

"Shush," she whispered. "I can hear something."

I inched my way and joined her at the top of the steps, where we pressed our ears to the door. Vanessa was right. We could hear raised voices. Not coming from above us but from somewhere on the ground floor.

"They're not in the kitchen. They're at the front of the house somewhere," I whispered. "Can you make out any of what's being said?"

"No, but I don't think either of the voices are male. How long do you think we've been down here?"

Instinctively, I glanced at my watch, but it was too dark to make out the dial.

"Not more than fifteen minutes. I think we can presume that Sarah's still here."

"And that her visitor is pissed off about something," said Vanessa, at the sound of shouting.

We caught a couple of words: "*Liar!*" And "*you never…*"

"That's not Sarah," I hissed. "And although the voice is quite deep, I think you're right; it's definitely a woman."

We strained our ears for more but all we heard was, "*You…*" And then something we thought might have been "*…used me,*" followed by a muffled crash.

We listened intently but all had gone quiet.

"Whoever the hell she is," I said, "she can get us out of here."

I pounded loudly on the door and yelled, "Help! Let us out! Please help us."

Vanessa joined in but there was no response, but I thought I detected a slight creaking from the other side of the door.

"Help!" I called again. "Call the police! Tell them that Clarry Pennhaligan and…"

I broke off, certain that I'd heard footsteps walking away and off through the hall. My suspicions were confirmed when, seconds later, we distinctly heard the front door close with a muted bang.

CHAPTER FORTY

Vanessa started to cry again, and I felt a return of my previous dizziness.

"Come on," I said eventually, giving her a hug. "Let's have a rest for a few minutes."

We sat down two steps apart from each other and remained in silence for a while, until she asked, "How did you know I was here? I couldn't believe my eyes when I saw you come wriggling through that window."

"I like to think of it as more of a shimmy," I replied, ignoring her question. "Actually, I wasn't sure I'd fit through it. It was a pretty tight squeeze."

"Didn't Sarah call you my irritating prying *little* friend?"

I snorted. "She can't be all bad then. Right, half an hour must have passed and so let's hope that Sarah's gone. How about we get the hell out of here? We'll start with the door."

But, despite all our efforts kicking and shoving, the door wouldn't give.

*

I'm not sure how long it took to shift the crates away from the back wall, but it felt like forever. Some of them were light, but others took the two of us to get them down onto the floor. Part of the problem was placing them so that we still had room to move. We had to keep rearranging and restacking them, and this wasn't easy in the dark. I kept hoping that the more boxes we transported, the more light would be revealed, but this didn't prove to be the case. As we removed the lowest level of boxes, we found that this end section of the cellar's floor hadn't been concreted over. We were standing on compacted soil.

Once we had exposed the full extent of the back wall, disappointment and a developing sense of despair enveloped us. This wasn't a way out. It wasn't even a window. Grimed with dust and streaked with cobwebs, it was merely a two-foot square aperture, positioned three quarters of the way up the wall, and which had been in-filled with thick glass bricks.

"What are we going to do?" Vanessa's voice cracked as she sank down onto one of the crates. "We're going to die down here."

"No. We're not!" I retorted as I suddenly remembered something that my mother used to say when I was a child. That it's amazing how much braver you can feel when there is someone else to take care of. And that one day, if and when I became a mother, I'd understand what she meant. "I feel like that about Pepe," I'd said. He was our spaniel and I'd adored him.

"Good girl" she'd said. "Then you understand already."

"Vanessa, get up. I've no intention of starving to death down here. Although, given that I'm heavier than you, you'll probably die first and then I'll be forced to eat you."

There was a long silence which she broke with, "I can't believe that she hit me! How dare she!"

"That's good. Anger is good," I said. "Now, can you please channel it into action?"

"OK." She got up and stared at the glass bricks. "I think this might once have been a coal-hole. My grandmother had one in her house in Godalming. In the old days, coal was delivered and poured down a chute and it would have been one of the housemaid's first jobs of the day to bring it upstairs and lay the fires."

"I'm not sure everyone had a housemaid, Vanessa, but you're probably right, as the height would make sense. Although how it helps us, I don't know. These glass bricks are thick."

"Budge over, Clarry." Vanessa ran her hand over them. "Yes, but the mortar surrounding them is crumbling." She took my hand. "Feel. It's disintegrated completely along the top in one section."

"You're right!" I exclaimed. "We might be able to dislodge the bricks. Let's try bashing it with the rake, shall we?"

Vanessa took the first go as I stood well back and out of the way. She gave it half a dozen hard thwacks. The ringing of the metal rake head hitting the glass was very loud in the confined space.

"I've loosened it a bit," she said, "but this rake is too unwieldy. We need something smaller."

"There's a trowel on the shelf unit," I said. "I'll get it."

It was laborious work, and we took it in turns bashing and scraping until we finally managed to knock out all the mortar. Our movements had kicked up a lot of the dirt beneath our feet, and at one point I tripped over something pale, thin and tree root-like.

Vanessa shoved hard at the glass bricks. "It's shifting," she exclaimed and pushed again. "It's definitely moving."

At last, after further manoeuvring, the complete block of bricks fell forward and landed with a thud on the other side of the wall.

"We did it!" Vanessa was jubilant. "We're going to get out of here. If you think you can fit through the hole, that is!"

"Yeah, yeah," I said, peering through it. "Piece of cake. Ah… I thought you said this was an old coal-hole?"

"Yes." Vanessa poked her head through beside me and then groaned. We were looking into another dimly lit cellar.

"I'm an idiot not to have realised before." I rubbed my eyes. "This is the semi-detached side of the house. They couldn't have delivered coal on this side, unless maybe the house next door was built later."

"What bloody difference does it make?" Vanessa was close to tears again.

"We're not giving up." I was adamant. "That cellar belongs to the house next door. All we've got to do is…" I broke off, recalling the look of shock on the South American nanny's face when she'd thought that Mr. Babcock and I were delivering news of the death of one or both of her employers, the Scarboroughs.

"Fuck!" Vanessa, withdrawing her head from the hole, stumbled awkwardly and fell backwards onto the dirt floor. Scrabbling to right herself, she pushed one hand down into the dirt and then let out a high-pitched shriek.

"Oh my God!" She screamed again. "Clarry, I think there's a…"

"What?" I yelped. "Have you hurt yourself?"

I bent down to help her. Vanessa stared up at me, her eyes wide with horror. In her hand was something that looked suspiciously like human bone.

CHAPTER FORTY-ONE

O ne after the other, we pitched our way out through the hole. The idea of spending even another minute in the company of a skeleton, or part of a skeleton, was unbearable to us both.

Groping my way, I found a set of steps, and taking them two at a time, I reached a door at the top. It was locked and the house was quiet. I hadn't the remotest idea of the time but guessed it had to be somewhere in the early hours of Monday morning.

"Help!" I shouted and thundered hard on the door with my fists. "Please help."

Long minutes passed until I heard sounds of activity. "Someone's coming," I called down to Vanessa. "They've turned on a light. I can see it shining under the door."

"Who eeees it?" called a frightened female voice with a marked South American accent. The Scarboroughs' nanny gasped and clutched her chest as, on releasing us, she caught sight of me. "*Ay Dios Mio!*"

*

The two police officers, when they arrived ten minutes later, at first struggled to comprehend our story. Vanessa and I kept talking over each other and interrupting. Both of us filthy dirty, our clothes snagged and rent, we were sitting at the Scarboroughs' kitchen table. Her employers, away with their children for the weekend, had left the nanny, Maria, alone in the house, and she'd nearly died of fright at hearing shouts coming from the basement. Listening to us explain ourselves, as she now handed around mugs of tea, I noticed that when we got to the part about the human bone, she kept darting looks at me and making furtive signs of the cross.

"*Ella trae la muerte*," she whispered.

Vanessa, who'd taken Spanish at school, translated, "She's saying that you *bring death*."

Adding tonight's episode to our previous encounter, when I'd been wearing a funeral director's top hat, I was forced to concede that she might just have a point.

Officer Smythe, a blunt-faced man in his forties with shrewd brown eyes and a thick neck, made us repeat our tale several times, whilst his colleague radioed through to the station.

"You're not going to ask us to go back there and show you, are you?" Vanessa was shaking now. I looked from her tear-stained and blood-streaked face to that of Officer Smythe. He shook his head.

"No. If it does prove to be human remains, then our forensic team will be brought in, but I don't want to call them out only to discover the bones of a family pet. Officer Brody will investigate first. He's leaner than me. Ready, Stuart?"

Stuart Brody, a wiry guy in his thirties, nodded and turned to Maria. "Got any lights down there?"

Five minutes later, he reappeared, a serious expression on his face.

"Yep, human all right."

Leaving Vanessa slumped at the kitchen table, her head pillowed on folded arms, I followed Officer Smythe out into the street, where a second squad car had just turned up. "Inspector Tindall and MIT are on their way," a young female officer with white-blonde hair clipped back from her face and wearing a high viz jacket informed him. "We're to check the house for occupation before we cordon off."

The bustle generated by the police presence had brought many of the neighbours out into the street. Mary Cunningham, in quilted dressing gown, was there, as was her husband, although he was fully dressed. Under the street light, he looked grey with exhaustion and with concern.

"I've been so worried about you, Clarry, but I didn't know what to do. I'd just decided to give it five more minutes before calling the police myself, when…" he looked at the officers conferring on Sarah's front doorstep, "…they arrived." He took in my dishevelled appearance. "Are you all right, my dear?"

I reassured him and then turned my attention back to the action as Officer Smythe knocked heavily on Sarah's door. At getting no response, he then applied force and I edged down the path for a better look. Having gained entry to the house, he turned on the hall light, and I could see that Sarah's suitcase and holdall were where I'd noticed them earlier.

Hesitating on the threshold, I watched the female officer and her partner make their way to the upper floor, announcing themselves as they did so. No one was paying any attention to me and so, warily, I followed Officer Smythe into the first room off the hall, a sitting room. There, with her linen dress splayed out around her, lay Sarah, face down on the carpet, a large bloodied wound to the back of her head.

She wouldn't be making that early flight now. For unless one counted the crossing over to her final resting place, Sarah's travelling days were well and truly behind her.

CHAPTER FORTY-TWO

I spent the next two days going through everything with the police. They were firm in their questioning and very thorough indeed. I kept painstakingly to the truth, with one notable exception. I left out the fact that Flan had been my accomplice when breaking into The Nook. I handed over the papers and photos from the Tower and they were placed in evidence. I shared my thoughts about the donations, informed them that the Wellness Centre had been a scam, and told them everything I'd seen and heard at the midnight meeting on the common. Of the mystery robed figure, I confessed to having no clue as to who she might be.

I told them of Sarah's one-way ticket to the Dominican Republic and about the two passports she possessed, one in the name of Gaitskill and the other Perry, but that I couldn't remember the differing dates of birth.

Throughout, they were polite but very formal, and it wasn't until Inspector Lawson of the Wimbledon force, the senior officer I'd met whilst on my first case, confirmed her previous dealings with me, that the suspicion in which they held me appeared to relax.

It was through Inspector Tindall, of the Epsom Police, a tall, trim black man with a silver-grey buzz cut, that I learnt all the women who'd been present at the ceremony on Wimbledon Common, were to be called in for questioning. And, although I wasn't told much else directly, I did gather, whilst going from interview to interview and from hanging about the break room, that they were still working on identifying the body in Sarah's cellar, but it was confirmed to be that of a male who'd been dead for approximately ten years.

*

Diana Maitland was contacted to support my claim of being hired by her, and there then followed a difficult scene between Vanessa and me.

"I thought you were my friend," she'd cried. "I trusted you."

"I am your friend *now*," I'd insisted. "It just didn't start off like that."

But she remained sullen and angry. She did reveal, however, that she knew of Zoe's relationship with her brother-in-law. They'd met through her, quite accidentally, and she'd not been insensible to the palpable tension of physical attraction between them. Miles had then questioned her about Zoe in a manner that he'd thought casual, but was, in fact, quite transparent, and later, Zoe had fully confided in her.

"Not only was she eager for details of his marriage to Caroline," Vanessa said, "but I think that she just wanted to talk about him. It put me in a terrible position. I wanted to tell Caroline, but I kept hoping that the affair would fizzle out and that she'd never learn of it. Never be hurt by it."

"So, you'd agree that it's not always easy to disclose the truth?" I'd asked with a grin. "That means you have to forgive me."

"No, I bloody well do not!" she'd spat at me before storming out.

I didn't contact her again. She'd either come around or she wouldn't. I was simply too drained and dispirited to care. I was having trouble sleeping. When I did drop off, it was only to have terrifying nightmares where witches ripped apart skeletons and hurled their bones into a lake, and where I retched and tried to spit out the clods of earth under which I was being buried alive. I'd awake from these dreams shaking and sweating and my face wet with tears.

My mobile's sim card had been recovered undamaged and, once I'd replaced my phone, I was back in contact with the world. Polly phoned late on Wednesday morning.

"It's not like on TV, is it?" Her voice was bright with interest. "I'm not sure whether to be disappointed or relieved. How was it for you…? Oops, sorry…" She laughed. "That sounds weird."

"Gruelling."

"I can imagine. I've spoken to Vanessa. You've both been through a lot."

"And it's not over yet. It won't be until they catch Sarah's murderer."

"I just can't take in that she's dead," said Polly. "That someone killed her. Murdered her. It's so terrible."

"Believe me," I said, "I saw her body and…"

"I refuse to think that it's one of us," she replied. "One of the group, I mean. Besides, there's the three-fold law of return to consider."

"The *what?*"

"The Craft teaches us that if we cause harm, then it ultimately causes harm to ourselves. The power and energy expended is returned to the sender at three times the level it was sent out."

"Polly! You can't still believe all that stuff! Not after what went down on the common?"

There was a pause. "Actually, I'm not going to have as much spare time to devote as I used to. And although nothing can shake my belief that there is magic all around us, because it's only too evident in nature, in the—"

"Yes, you said before," I interrupted, recalling our late-night drinks at Kendall's, and her rhapsodies about raindrops and spiders' webs.

"But, yes, as you say," she continued, "after what happened on the common, I do feel differently. I understand that you were there that night? Hidden away."

"I was."

"There's something else." All Polly's brightness had dissipated, and I wondered what was coming. "I heard from Elaine that her friend Nadine got the result of her breast biopsy. You remember that we sent out our positive energy for her?"

"I do."

"Unfortunately, that wasn't enough. Nadine has been diagnosed with cancer."

"I'm sorry to hear that, poor woman."

I was about to add that all the positive energy in the world could never be expected to influence the outcome of a cancer diagnosis, when she announced, "So… I'm ditching The Craft."

I laughed. "Great news. But why am I sensing that there's more to it than you're saying? What's keeping you so busy?"

"Adam." She practically sang out the name.

"No! Not Adam from work?"

"The same. I'm so happy! I took your advice, Clarry, and vamped it up a notch. It turns out that he's been into me for ages, but thought that I'd placed him strictly in the friend-zone."

"I'm so pleased for you." And I genuinely was. Whilst, as far as I knew, the identity of that mystery figure on the common had not yet been established, I couldn't for one moment believe it to be Polly. I liked her and wanted to keep in touch.

"I'm guessing that you now know why I tried to infiltrate the group?" I asked. "I'm sorry, Polly. I hope that, like Vanessa, you don't hate me too?"

"Of course not. You and I are friends. But there is a way that you can make it up to me."

"There is?" I asked dubiously.

"Definitely there is. Elaine is performing tonight, and it doesn't look like even half the tickets have gone."

"Not her poetry? Please, no," I begged. "Anything but that."

"It won't just be her on stage. Not that there is an actual stage, because it was once a greengrocer's. Kingston Council have agreed that one night a month we can use this empty shop, which they haven't been able to let because it's in a back street, as a venue for open mic nights."

I remembered that she worked in the publicity department for a local arts charity.

"And this month, it's Performance Poetry."

"Really?" I groaned. "Do I have to?"

"It will be fun. We've decorated the shop with posters and flowers. And there'll be candles on the table. No bar, because we don't have a licence, but there'll be herbal teas and cordials."

I sighed. Listening to Elaine without a drink to take the edge off? Why was I being punished?

"I'll be going straight from work." Polly was brisk now. "And so I'll meet you there. Seven thirty."

Allowing me no further opportunity to wriggle out of it, she gave me the address and rang off.

CHAPTER FORTY-THREE

I parked in an alley behind the greengrocer's. I'd kept it casual tonight in jeans, stripy pink and white T-shirt and trainers. My body had taken a fair amount of punishment over the last week. I was bruised and scratched along my arms, legs and hips and so I covered up. I'd also slipped on the bracelet Polly had given me, partly because I thought she'd like to see me wearing it, but also because it looked good against the pink cuff of my T-shirt.

I followed the alley down to the corner and walked up the street to the venue.

"It's £5 to get in," apologised a long and lanky guy of about nineteen years old with shoulder-length frizzy hair.

"It's only to cover the costs. We don't make a profit. But I promise you, it will be worth every penny."

I felt my eyes cross at this but dutifully passed over my fiver.

He rolled the ticket stamp over the back of my left hand, leaving a purplish smudge. "Enjoy!"

Polly, pretty in a flowery off-the-shoulder dress, sneakers and her dangly silver and turquoise owl earrings, was looking pleased with herself as she greeted me.

"How cool is this? Come on, you have to admit it looks great."

And, surprisingly, it did. Part of the original shelving was still in situ. Where once cauliflowers, lettuces and apples would have been displayed, there were now canvasses of varying sizes, depicting an eclectic range of images, propped up alongside items of handmade pottery and ceramics. Old theatre posters had been blu-tacked to the walls, and flyers for current and upcoming music gigs were fanned out along a trestle table that also bore a giant hot water urn, cannisters of fruit teas and a mixed assortment of mugs. Twenty or so scuffed chairs, which might once have belonged to a school, had been placed in rows facing the rear of the shop, where a space had been set up as a makeshift stage. Behind the stage, Polly told me, was a small and spotlessly clean bathroom and a rear exit.

"The numbers are better than I'd thought," said Polly, lowering her voice and looking around as the room filled up. "Quick. We'll sit in the front; it's more supportive."

More difficult to feign an expression of enjoyment, I thought, but took my place next to her on the last seat in the row and, with deep mistrust, sipped at my nettle tea. It tasted exactly as I expected it to.

Long & Lanky turned out to be our compere for the evening.

"We all love words, don't we? That's why we're here."

On getting no response, he gave an awkward laugh and shuffled his feet. "I should explain first, that although this is an open mic evening, our performers won't be using a microphone." Another nervous laugh. "It would be deafening in a place this size." More foot shuffling. "So, ladies and gentlemen, we're about to meet some performers who really know how to use their words. Get ready to hear them roll, hum, boom and bust their rhymes."

He was getting into gear now and starting to relax. "Please, give it up for our first wordsmith of the evening… Steve."

We all clapped as Steve, a man in his thirties wearing an oversized check shirt and a cap, ambled out from behind the stage. Steve proved to be a ranter. Perplexed and pissed off about everything, from the latest trend in artisan gins to mobile dog groomers, he thundered his discontent in intricate, undeniably clever, word patterns. It was exhausting to listen to.

A handful of latecomers arrived halfway through his set. All the seats were now full and there was a clutch of people standing and blocking the entrance. Polly muttered something about Health & Safety but looked gratified.

Up next was Sandra. In her mid-twenties, dressed in a black and white midi-skirt, a hot pink T-shirt and leather jacket, she took us through the highs and lows of becoming a mother aged just seventeen. Laced through with humour, humility, irony and a seam of sadness, her free verse, delivered simply but with a quiet power, drew us all in. She was wonderful, and I found myself clapping quite as enthusiastically as Polly.

Sandra was a tough act to follow. I felt a little sorry for the couple of also-rans who came after, one of whom was a protest poet. He made the best job he could of finding words to rhyme with *Fracking,* but by the time he'd exhausted *hacking, lacking, snacking* and *smacking,* he'd lost my attention.

Then, it was Elaine's turn. She didn't walk out onto the stage; she drifted, her arms and long thin hands undulating slightly as if preparing for lift-off. Wearing a dark green cotton dress that was a little too large for her, she positioned herself dead centre and regarded us. There was a silence. Were we supposed to clap before she'd even begun? No. She finally spoke, her deep voice rich with a portentous solemnity.

"I present my latest work... *The Elements of Betrayal.*"

No comedy moments to come, I was guessing. I just hoped that it wouldn't be as graphically sexual and embarrassing as her last poem. I hoped in vain.

You took me
You shaped me
You led me into the sweetest garden of ecstasy that I
*   have ever known*
You touched me, you teased me, your caresses made me groan
You offered your breasts, you offered your thighs
Never did I dream that you'd feed me with lies...

This was new. I'd made the sexist assumption that the plasterer she'd so longed for in her previous poem was male. It appeared I'd been wrong.

You used me.
You discarded me.
You weaved such a spell of seduction and of hope that
*   I believed*
You fashioned a plan that promised me recognition but
*   I was deceived*

328

You offered me a role, you offered me a home
Never did I dream that you planned to leave me all
alone…

This has to be the worst poem ever written, I decided, just as something stirred in the back of my mind. What was it she'd said that I thought I'd heard before, and recently? I tried to grasp hold of it, but Elaine was now stretching her arms out wide and declaiming…

I loved you
I trusted you
You used me
You lied to me
Never had you cared for me

That pricking sense of the familiar was still with me. And it felt important. Elaine's beaky nose twitched, and she stroked at her long ashy-grey hair before dropping her voice to a cadent whisper…

You used me
You tricked me

I felt suddenly cold. The memory I'd been searching for leapt to the forefront of my mind. I knew where I'd heard those words… *you used me…*before. But then, they hadn't been dramatically declaimed and lingered over; they'd been shouted. Trapped in the cellar, Vanessa and I had heard them. *Elaine*. Elaine had murdered Sarah.

329

Never should you have used me
Never should you have denied me

I had to get hold of Inspector Tindall. And I needed to do it now. I took a swift glance behind me. With the people collected by the front door, I'd cause a commotion if I tried to get out that way. Hadn't Polly said that as well as a bathroom, there was a rear exit behind the stage? If anyone thought it odd that I was getting up mid-performance, it would just be supposed that I needed the loo.

I gave Polly a nudge and whispered into her ear, "Sorry, but I've got to go. I can't explain, but I really have to."

"What, *now*?" Polly hissed.

"Yes, so sorry," and with that, I slipped out of my seat. Aware of several pairs of eyes on me, I sidled along the flank wall. Elaine had noticed me too. Her voice had risen again, and I feared the audience was in for a big finish.

Never should you have used me
Never should you have discounted me

As I passed and her eyes fixed upon mine, it hit me with absolute certainty. She knew… that I knew.

CHAPTER FORTY-FOUR

The rear door led me out into a loading area that serviced the small row of shops. Deserted, there was a whiff of overfull bins. It was dark except for the reflected light of a street lamp positioned somewhere out of sight. I looked at my watch. It was nine fifteen. Even if Inspector Tindall wasn't at the station, they might be able to contact him, or, if not, put me through to one of the other officers on the case. About to rake through my tatty old leather messenger bag for my mobile, I was startled by the sound of the door behind me, opening and then closing.

"Wait," a voice commanded.

My heart thudded hard in my chest as I swung around to confront Elaine.

"Of late, The Muse visits less frequently, but when She does come, her touch is divine." She stood quite still, her gaze unwavering. "My work has become truer, more beautiful and more powerful... as you, yourself, have just heard."

She dipped her head as if waiting for acknowledgement.

It's like she's still performing, I thought. And although unnerved by the sight of her, I felt a spark of irritation. Who on earth says... *of late*?

"What is it that you want, Elaine?"

"Ah." She raised her head, her eyes glittering. "That's the eternal question, isn't it? What is it that we all want?"

"A vodka shot is top of my list right now," I said, turning to leave.

"It's a basic human desire," she pronounced.

I turned back. "What is? Alcohol?"

"To love and be loved in return."

"I can't argue with you there."

"I *gave* and Sarah took."

"Is that why you killed her?"

Her laugh was knowing, insulting. "You have a small, inelegant way of thinking."

I wasn't going to rise to the bait. "The police found traces of Sarah's blood and hair on the table lamp, but you'd wiped it clean of prints. Clever."

"Clever? Not particularly." Elaine ran a slow, thoughtful hand through her hair. "Although I do seem to find myself hemmed in by inferior minds."

"I'll be taking my inferior mind off home now, then," I retorted. I had risen to the bait after all.

"No!" She took three rapid paces towards me and I retreated a step. I was closer to the bins now, closer to the stench of rotting food and ammonia.

Attempting to appear in control of the situation, I asked, "Given your supreme cleverness, I assume that you knew it was me locked in the cellar?"

She gave a bark of laughter. "Your mind isn't just small; it's positively puny. You announced yourself! You shouted your name out when you were banging on the door. Your recall skills are remarkably low for someone so young."

Perhaps she was right. At least about my memory. I had completely forgotten calling out my name when asking Sarah's unseen visitor to call the police.

"And whilst we're clearing things up," I said, "the body in Sarah's cellar, know anything about that?"

"No." She was looking bored now. "And why you should expect me to be interested, I really don't know."

I stared at her.

"I was to have led a creative writing group at the Wellness Centre," she continued. "Did you know that?" I shook my head. Her self-absorption was staggering. "With that as my platform, my work would have had the recognition and the respect that it deserves. I would have been published, celebrated. I would have won awards, been looked to for inspiration and advice. I would have dazzled them."

Them who? I wondered. She took another pace towards me, effectively blocking my path, and her voice rose. "It was my due."

She's quite mad, I thought.

"It was," I agreed, "and it still is." Hoping this might appease her, I made a tentative step to my left, my eyes fixing on the exit to the alley.

"But Sarah destroyed that dream." Elaine wore her bitterness with relish. She was sad, lost, mentally ill possibly. Or was she still performing?

"She lied about the Centre. She lied about everything." She was looking through me now as if communing with an unseen entity. "Lovers should never lie to one another."

"No, they shouldn't!" I agreed stoutly. I could outrun her, I thought. I'm twenty years younger. The immediate problem was getting past her.

"I had planned to call the collection *Poetry from the Centre*. You see the play on words, of course?"

"I do. Catchy." I edged another step to my left. She was making that weird flapping movement with her hands again and I felt my body tense, anticipating an attack. Why was she stretching this out? Was her *superior* mind working on a way to take me off balance? If I wasn't going to let that happen, I needed to keep her talking and distract her.

"Sarah didn't just lie to *you*, Elaine, she cheated all the women. She cheated them out of their money. Particularly Helen. But I don't suppose that, with your pursuit of truth and beauty, you would have stooped to anything so shabby as to have been in on that?"

The paddling motion came to a halt. "Certainly not, I despise the mercenary; I wouldn't taint my soul with avarice. But Sarah? Sarah had been brought up in poverty. She was obsessed with money; she believed that it gave her security. And yet it appears she wasn't good at managing it. The rent hadn't been paid on the shop, I gather."

"You knew that and yet you believed her about the Wellness Centre?" I couldn't disguise my incredulity.

"I didn't know. Sarah rarely spoke about the shop. She despised it, that much I did know, but that it was failing came as a surprise to me."

Elaine obviously hadn't been there. The image of those fairy figurines floated across my consciousness and I blinked them away as she said, "To learn that she was looking for a way out of the mess she'd created, that she was making a plan to— "

"To leave her financial worries behind?" I interrupted.

"It must have given you quite a shock overhearing her telling Zoe on the common that she was leaving the country."

Elaine looked blankly at me.

"You stayed behind that night," I reminded her. "You listened in on Sarah and…"

"I don't know what you're talking about!" Her voice was shrill, and she was growing agitated. "Why must you bother me with these details? It was only after The Reading that I realised I knew almost nothing about Sarah."

The Reading? Was she talking about one of her poems? And if she wasn't the mystery figure on the common, then who was?

"That's why I went to Sarah's house," she explained. "I needed to hear it for myself. To hear from her own lips that she was leaving. I'd only ever been to her home once before. She always stayed with me, at my flat; and so I had no idea that it was being repossessed and that she'd been gradually getting rid of her possessions."

"I don't understand." I tried to cut in, but Elaine spoke over me.

"And then she told me that she had never loved me. *You don't matter*, that's what she said to me. *You don't matter.*"

Even in the dim light, I could make out the tears brimming in her eyes. "Why don't I matter? Why have I never mattered to another living soul? Why is that?"

Her distress struck me with such force that I couldn't help but feel a strong flare of natural sympathy, human being to human being. A murderer she may be, but no one should feel like that.

335

"I'm sorry, Elaine. That must have been hard." My mouth felt suddenly dry as I offered, "But you know what you have to do now, don't you? You have to turn yourself in to the police."

"No!" The violence of her opposition propelled her forward until she was only inches away from me. Now was the moment when compulsion might outweigh risk. Now she would strike.

I braced myself and balled my fists but, again, she looked through me.

"I won't be shamed. I won't be degraded, peered at, prodded, manhandled. I won't allow my talent to wither away and decline. It's all I've ever had."

I thought that I understood. Her grandiosity masked a life defined by a sense of worthlessness, a sense of fear, and I felt a rush of pity.

"What other choice do you have?" I asked gently.

Her focus returned to me and for a split second I could see her weigh up the one choice I hadn't wanted to mention. That she could try and silence me.

"Don't even think about it," I said with more firmness than I felt. "I won't let you."

Pointing her right foot, ballerina style, she started to tap the toe of her shoe in a steady rhythmic beat, but she said nothing. I waited, wondering what was coming. Was she going to attack me or launch into the *Dance of the Nutcracker*?

"I will treat myself with honour," she said at last, and her voice was more natural, more real than I'd ever heard it.

"Always a good plan," I said, but she wasn't listening. She was running.

Blinking in surprise, I stared after her as she shot full pelt across the loading bay, reached the alley and turned right. I gave chase. Within seconds, I had my phone out of my bag and was dialling 999.

"You need to get some officers out here now! And let Inspector Tindall, at Epsom, know. Tell him Clarry Pennhaligan…"

I'd been confident I could outrun her, but Elaine was fast. Driven by desperation to escape capture, this woman could move like a whippet.

I sped up and reached the end of the alley as she went streaking off down the thoroughfare, her long ashy hair streaming behind her.

I raced after her, accelerating, but my progress was checked by passers-by, obliged to jump out of my way.

I had the police controller still in my ear. "What direction is she heading?"

"North. Towards the centre of town, I think." I thundered past a pub where drinkers spilled out onto the street, past a fast-food restaurant where wafts of fried chicken competed with the aromatic scent of curry from the balti house next door.

Aware that I was gaining on her, Elaine flung a look over her shoulder at me and came to a shuddering halt, before dashing straight out into the middle of the road.

To a furious honking of car horns, she threaded her way through the two lanes of oncoming traffic until she reached the central island, where she turned to face me. Panting, I reached the pavement and stood directly opposite her.

"There is always a choice," she shouted, and placed one foot deliberately down into the road. "I choose this."

She *had* been trying to escape but not in the way I'd thought. She wasn't running away from the police; she was running away from her own life. Escaping her demons, her sadness, her deep-rooted belief that she would never count to anyone.

"No!" I screamed. "Elaine, don't!" I looked about wildly. Dimly, I registered the sound of sirens but there was no time to be lost. I couldn't just stand by and watch a woman kill herself.

A transit van was moving fast in the outer lane and a saloon car more sedately on the inside. Breathlessly, I darted forward in front of the saloon, jumping back behind the transit, and wrenched hold of Elaine's arm, just as she took another step out into the road. With a screeching swerve, a Jeep narrowly avoided hitting us. I leapt onto the central island, dragging her back with me.

As she tried to shake me off with her left hand, her right hand gripped my shoulder and I felt myself being pulled closer to the edge of the kerb. Frantically, I struggled to shrug her off. If she flung herself out in front of a car now, I would be dragged with her.

At last, I managed to free myself and stood back as far away from Elaine as the narrowness of the central island would allow.

For a moment, she stood there staring at me before turning purposefully back to face the traffic. I couldn't bring myself to watch and covered my face with my hands. She was choosing a truly terrible way to die and there didn't seem anything I could do to stop her...

"Elaine, wait! You can still dazzle them," I yelled into her ear. She hesitated and I pressed my idea home. "You're sure to be published now. Think of Oscar Wilde and his *Ballad of Reading Gaol*. Yours could be the *Ballad of Wandsworth Nick…* or wherever. The world will have to pay attention. You'll be famous."

As two police cars came into sight, blue lights flashing, sirens screaming, Elaine turned to me with a look of ecstasy upon her face. "*From Behind Bars*, that's what I'd call it. That's what I'd call my first collection." In that moment, her nose no longer appeared beaky; it was aquiline, distinguished.

"That's great!" I said. "You hold on to that thought and very soon…"

She shook her head. "It's too late. I feel the Muse desert me, and without her, I'm just ordinary. That's not enough for me. It never has been."

And with that, to a frantic squealing of brakes, she stepped directly out into the path of an oncoming lorry.

CHAPTER FORTY- FIVE

Four police officers had witnessed Elaine's suicide, but it still took several hours to go through my statement. Once finally home, I downed two large glasses of red wine in quick succession, hoping that they'd knock me out cold. They didn't. The sickening thud as the lorry hit Elaine's body, followed by her agonising scream as it ran over her, haunted and tormented me. The horror of the scene replayed over and over in my mind; the ghastly images seemed burned on my retinas.

Finally, I drifted off to sleep around dawn, and when I awoke, it was with a realisation that somehow, through my dreamscape, I'd managed to join the dots that still puzzled me in this investigation. It might not be the full picture but it was, at least, a rough sketch.

*

The Nook was not a place I'd ever planned to revisit. The window was empty of its oversized onyx hand, its lavender and rose soaps and artificial blooms. The closed sign was up but I could see movement within. As before, the scent of resin and flowers met my nose and the familiar peal of

340

wind chimes announced my arrival. Sheila looked up from behind the counter, where she was wrapping individual ornaments in newspaper and placing them into a large cardboard box.

"Welcome Be, Clarry." She was wearing the pale blue cardigan with the corsage brooch that I had last seen hanging over the back of the shop's only chair.

"I wondered when you would come by to collect it." She pulled my baseball cap out from under the till.

"I've given it a wipe-down," she said, and handed it to me. "Got rid of the worst of the dust and the cobwebs."

I stared at her open-mouthed. "But how could you possibly have known that it was mine?"

She ignored my question. "You've missed it. It's part of your protective colouring."

I *had* missed it and the sense of anonymity it gave me, but again, how could she know that?

"But you've not just come for your hat." Her West Country burr was coaxing. "You've come to complete your reading."

"I've come for information, Sheila."

"It's the same thing. The reading will bring to the surface matters that you want to pay attention to. You have already chosen *The Fool*; I can guide you in interpreting its meaning."

I shuddered. A week ago, when I'd broken into the shop with Flan, I'd picked that card at random from the pack on the table in the Bedouin room.

"And the *Tower*," Sheila continued, "the card that brings sudden awareness, a necessary process to awakening. Your old ways must be destroyed before…"

A creeping repugnance stole over me. The white stone tower, bodies falling, lightning zigzagging across the night sky.

"Enough!" My voice was strident and not quite steady. "This is all crap and you know it."

"Is it?" Sheila asked, "and yet, sensing The Divine, you tremble."

"I'm not trembling," I retorted. "I'm shuddering… which is… a completely different thing."

"Disenchanted with your life, you're a Hunter of the Truth, Clarry. And what makes you interesting is that you don't just seek for yourself, but you seek the Truth for others."

Her complacent assumption that she knew anything at all about me was beginning to get on my frayed nerves. Exhausted, drained, shocked by last night's events, I felt strung out, irritable and on the verge of tears.

"Oh, knock it off, Sheila." Irritation was dominating. "If you know about those two cards, then that can only mean it was you that night coming up the stairs to the secret room."

"It was. I had a late reading. When I realised that someone was in the upper room… Sarah's secret room, as you say… I went to investigate."

I thought of Flan and I making our terrifying descent down the open-sided steps as the wind and rain lashed at us, the vision of a vengeful Sarah in pursuit and, this time, I really did tremble.

"But how did you know it was me?" I repeated.

"I can't explain. Sometimes, I see things. And I had a feeling when you came here on that Sunday afternoon with your older beautiful friend, that you would be a balancing force." Wasn't that exactly what Polly had called me? A balancing force? Well, I wasn't feeling all together balanced now. My hold on what was real, solid and certain was slipping. I didn't believe any of this supernatural business, but why then was I experiencing a queasy sensation of dread?

"Why don't you pick a third card, Clarry? Or better yet, let's do a full reading. It will help you. It unlocks the door to the subconscious."

"Really? And what about the door to Elaine's subconscious?" Not troubling to disguise my scepticism, I was determined to turn the subject away from me and to the reason why I'd come to the shop. "Perhaps that door would have been better left firmly closed?"

Sheila's deep blue eyes were fixed upon me, a benign smile playing about her mouth, but she said nothing. As she picked up another ornament to wrap, I caught the spiteful gaze of *Serenity*, one of the ghastly fairy figurines.

"Elaine chose the Five of Pentacles repeatedly over the last few months," she said eventually as she covered the fairy's pointy little ears with the yellowing pages of an old copy of the *Guardian*. "And in a love reading, it indicates a feeling of isolation and the need to let go of a toxic relationship."

"She's done that all right," I flung back at her. "Four nights ago, she bashed Sarah's head in and then, last night, she killed herself."

Sheila's hands shook slightly as she placed *Serenity* into the cardboard box. "I didn't know that Elaine had killed herself."

"And I'm wondering," I pressed, "whether her actions were a direct consequence of your so-called reading?"

"The choice of card is exactly what the Higher Self already knows." She had recovered herself immediately. "Tarot is a conversation with the Higher Self."

"And in Elaine's conversation with her *Higher Self…*" It was impossible not to lay sarcastic emphasis on the word. "What role did you play? Commentator? Prompter waiting in the wings? The Greek bloody chorus?"

"I merely helped Elaine flesh out her reading, as I do for all who come to me."

Composure fully regained, she picked up a small pottery jug and calmly began to wrap it. I wanted to shake her.

"But then waiting in the wings is very much your style," I remarked. "That was you, the other night, on the common, listening in on Sarah and Zoe?"

She raised her eyes and looked hard at me.

"As were you. No, don't trouble to deny it. I sensed your presence. You and I have an affinity, Clarry. You have gifts that you aren't aware of, that you haven't tapped into. I could show you how."

"Save it," I snapped. My irritation was now battling with an increasing sense that I had wandered into a menacing surreal landscape, and that I might not find my way back out. "It was you who told Elaine that Sarah was preparing to skip the country. You who told her the true state of Sarah's financial affairs," I insisted. "Who else would have been in a better position to know? There would have been letters, phone calls here about the rent arrears, and probably about the foreclosure on her house. Debt collectors are persistent; they would have tracked her down to the shop."

"The Five of Pentacles also indicates financial loss, poverty." Sheila still appeared completely unruffled. "Elaine, whilst she earnt very little, was not herself in financial trouble, and so she knew that it referred to Sarah."

"And you were only too happy to fill in the blanks. The question is, why?" I took a step nearer to the counter. "Because it occurs to me, Sheila, that you might have steered Elaine's actions. That perhaps, for some private reason of your own, you wanted Sarah gone and so you manipulated Elaine's vulnerable state of mind."

"You credit me with far too much influence, Clarry."

"What was it you said on the common?" I asked. "Something about not doing harm? Is that why you wanted Sarah gone? Because she was making a mockery of your beliefs?"

"Misusing the sacred power of the Goddess," she corrected me. "No, and if that were the case, Zoe would also be dead. And she's very much alive and well, although she will be punished for her part in both the ceremony and her treatment of Helen."

"What do you mean?" I demanded. "Is that a threat?"

"Zoe's punishment is getting what she most desires."

"I don't understand."

"No, but in time you will. And besides, you're forgetting something in all this." She pushed back one of her salt and pepper plaits from her shoulder. "You're forgetting that Sarah *was* to be gone. And gone completely of her own volition. Her flight booked, she was preparing to leave those persistent debt collectors you mentioned, far behind her."

That silenced me. My rough sketch was disintegrating, leaving just a pencilled question mark. I made one last attempt. "You've not expressed sadness over Elaine's death. Why is that?" She didn't respond. "Don't you feel any sense of responsibility for what happened?"

She placed the wrapped jug in the cardboard box. "Elaine chose her own cards and ultimately her own path. In her response to the symbols on her cards, she brought her own narrative and fulfilled a cycle."

"A cycle?" I asked, not really interested now in the answer. I was getting nowhere. My theory had been wrong, and the scent of resin and flowers was sickly and starting to give me a headache.

"The cycle of nature. Of birth and rebirth. Of Life and Death. And Sarah had more secrets."

"Yes, I know all about them," I said wearily. "The money, the scam over the Wellness Centre."

The feeling of dread had evaporated, and I simply didn't want to hear any more.

"Life and Death," Sheila murmured. "The cycle repeats itself. Life and Death… Life and Death."

"Yes, you've just mentioned that."

"Life and Death."

"Why do you keep saying it?"

"You'll get there, Clarry."

"You're obviously trying to tell me something. Why don't you just tell me what's on your mind, like a normal person?"

"Life and Death," she said again, and her eyes bored into mine.

I turned to leave. "We're going around in circles here."

"Going around in *cycles*," Sheila corrected.

"All right, have it your way." I turned back. "Cycles. The cycle of life and death. But whose life and death are we talking about?"

Sheila didn't answer but just nodded encouragingly. "I hope no one puts you in charge of organising the party games at Christmas. You'd be a bust. Is there a prize if I guess right?"

She shook her head, but she was smiling.

"No? Typical. OK. The cycle, blah blah. Life and death, blah blah. Let me think. Elaine kills herself after murdering Sarah. A cycle of a sort, I suppose, but you're suggesting there's more to it. Right. Sarah is murdered in her own home, but I know that she wasn't born there so that doesn't work... But," I exclaimed, "did she also *take* a life in that house? That would complete a cycle. That's what you mean, isn't it? You knew about the body in the cellar!"

"I told you you'd get there." Sheila stretched a hand out to me. "You have a gift. You're like me."

"Stop saying that! I'm nothing like you." I felt my head swim. I was back in the menacing, surreal landscape. "But wait... let me get this straight. To expose a murder... you... you *orchestrated* one?"

"Again, you credit me with too much influence."

"Just tell me, Sheila! No more games."

"Sarah sat for a reading only once, but it was enough. Enough for me to know what she had done."

"Then why the hell didn't you go to the police?"

"And say what?" She shrugged. "That I read it in her cards? What do you think they would have made of that?"

She was right, of course. She would never have been taken seriously.

I shook my head. I was done. There was nothing further to be gained by being here. About to leave, I glanced down at the counter and there, waiting to be wrapped in newspaper, sat *Fairy Friends*, the figurine of the three fairies with their long garlanded hair and gossamer wings, entwined in one another's arms. I had disliked it intensely on my first visit but now it seemed to embody every sinister aspect of this case. Yielding to an impulse that I didn't even try to fight, I picked it up and threw it onto the floor where it smashed into thick, jagged pieces.

"How much do I owe you for that?" I asked.

"£25," Sheila returned smoothly.

Ouch. Yielding to impulse can really cost you, but it was worth it. I dug out my purse and handed over the cash. "Goodbye, Sheila. No offence and all that, but I hope that I never see you again."

I turned, strode to the door and yanked it open. As the wind chimes started up, Sheila called me back.

"You're wearing it."

"Wearing what?"

"The bracelet I invested with the Power of Protection."

I looked down at my right wrist. I was wearing the bracelet, but it was completely covered by the sleeve of my white shirt.

I let the door slam behind me and made my way down to the High Street where, slipping off the bracelet, I dropped it into the nearest rubbish bin.

CHAPTER FORTY-SIX

That Sunday afternoon, Flan and I sat at the old stone table in my garden, drinking Champagne and watching a pair of blue tits excitedly dunking and splashing in the bird bath. Between us was the tall long-necked Champagne bottle in an ice bucket, and the pale green jug I'd crammed with apricot roses and sprigs of frothy white cow parsley.

"In that American TV cop show I so enjoy," Flan clinked her glass against mine, "they celebrate the successful end to a case with a tray of doughnuts. This is so much more my style."

"And mine," I agreed, "although normally I can't afford it, but Diana Maitland was very generous in her final payment. So, there's another three bottles of bubbly for you to take home."

"Darling, you shouldn't have, but thank you."

"And, Flan, whilst the case is over, I'm not sure it could be considered a success."

"You mean that poor woman killing herself?"

"I keep thinking that maybe there was more I could have done. Something else I could have said that would have…"

Flan reached across the table and patted my hand. "Darling, she made her choice. She would have done that with or without you."

She took a thoughtful sip of Champagne. "I've been thinking about something you said at the start of all this. About how *love* in the Love Detective's second case appeared not to have played a part. Well, you were wrong. This case began and ended with love."

"Don't you start banging on about cycles," I begged. "I had enough of that from Sheila."

"Diana's love for her daughter opened the case, and Elaine's tortured love for Sarah closed it."

"There was quite a lot of other stuff going on in between," I acknowledged, "but I do take your point."

"Top us up," Flan said, "and tell me if you've heard anything more from Vanessa Maitland?"

"Yes," I said. "She's finally cooled down."

"It sounds like she's still got a lot of growing up to do," Flan observed. "Mind you, haven't we all? I'm still locked into my rebellious teenage years."

"She's come clean to her mother about dating Jonian, the Albanian guy, and Diana's taken it pretty well." I poured some more bubbly into our glasses. "Vanessa also told me that her sister, Caroline, kicked out her cheating husband. He's moved into Zoe's flat in Raynes Park, where apparently not only is he extremely bitter about the change in his financial circumstances, but he's also discovered that he is highly allergic to Tabitha, Zoe's cat."

Sheila's words about Zoe came back to me. That her punishment would be getting what she most desired.

Would Zoe now have to choose between her lover and her witch's familiar? I'd met the cat and hadn't taken to it, and whilst I'd not been formally introduced to Miles, I hadn't liked his black suede loafers or his old-school rock music. If I were Zoe, there'd be no contest. I'd get rid of them both.

"My turn to catch you up with some news," Flan grinned before taking another sip of Champagne. "The Cunninghams tell me that Maria, the Scarboroughs' nanny, has given notice. She's developed a morbid dread of their house and is convinced that Death stalks the neighbourhood."

Recalling her fervent signs of the cross whenever she looked at me and the events of the last week, I really couldn't blame her.

"Oh, and I haven't told you, darling, how the Cunninghams and I got on at Harold's undertakers."

"Funeral directors," I corrected automatically. "You went with them?"

"Yes, I thought it might be fun."

"And was it?"

"It began well…" She was the picture of innocence.

"Ah," I said, "what happened?"

"I was sitting in the showroom with the Cunninghams whilst a perfectly pleasant middle-aged woman, in a perfectly dreadful paisley blouse, went through photographs and samples of different styles of coffins. They opted for a cherry wood by the way, which wouldn't have been my choice. So ageing, practically Victorian. Anyway, I was just thinking of asking the woman about that Viking funeral idea of mine and being floated into the Thames on a burning pyre, when

I heard a knocking sound coming from the floor below. "I'm so sorry to interrupt," I said, "but what's down*stairs*?"

The woman did look a little put out at the question. "That's where our Dearly Departed lie at rest," she said in that hallowed whispery tone these people use and which I assume they consider suitable for the job but isn't.

"Well," I remarked as the knocking sound began again, "I think one of them might just be trying to get a message through."

I laughed. "What did she say to that?"

"She tried to explain it away by saying that they were having work done on the central heating, but the Cunninghams and I weren't convinced."

I picked up my glass and gazed at the tiny bubbles fizzing and popping before asking, "Flan, do you think that there is anything in the supernatural? Tarot cards, witchcraft, all the rest of it?"

Flan settled herself more comfortably in the ancient Lloyd Loom basket chair before answering. "I think it's natural, Clarry, to look for certainties in a world that offers none. We all do that in our different ways, I think. Perhaps that's the reason why organised religion, of all faiths and denominations, continues to be so popular? It offers answers, or, at least, it claims to." Her voice was serious as she continued. "I don't think it matters what we as individuals believe, as long as we don't try to inflict those beliefs upon others. My personal feeling is that there are no answers, no certainties. We are owed nothing, and we own nothing. All we possess, right now, this very minute, in this glorious garden on this beautiful day, is just the breath we draw. This breath, this moment, is all we can count on. Who knows if we will take another? The past is behind us, the future can't be relied upon and so the present is to be lived in… fully. And so, how about we concentrate on doing just that?"

I felt such a rush of affection for her that I had to get up and give her a hug.

"You're very wise," I said, sitting back down and taking a slug of my Champagne. It was ice cold and delicious.

"Yes." Flan's satisfaction was evident as she crossed one elegant cream-trousered leg across the other. "I am surprisingly sagacious."

*

We sat in companionable silence for a while. The sun felt warm on my skin and a feeling of contentment gradually stole over me. A third blue tit had joined its fellows at the birdbath, and their sheer joy in the water and in the moment reinforced Flan's words about celebrating the present.

"That's the bottle done," I said, pouring the dregs into our glasses. "So, which of the two men in your life will you be enjoying the other bottles with? Isn't Mr. H. due back from his daughter's tomorrow?"

Flan grinned. "Yes, I'm looking forward to seeing him. But what about your love life, Clarry? That's far more interesting than mine. Didn't you have a date last night with that caveman garden designer? How did it go?"

I sighed happily. "Fanbloodytastic."

"How perfectly lovely for you, darling. Tell me all about it." And so I did.

Thank you for reading *The Love Detective: Next Level.* I do hope you enjoyed it. If you did, I would greatly appreciate it if you could leave a review on Amazon. They really do make a huge difference helping budding Authors be found by new readers.

I'd like to give special thanks to Sarah Jellema and Nicole Birkett for the rousing case they each made for The Old Frizzle to win my characterful venue competition, hope it earned you a couple of freebies!

Did you know you can visit my website www.angeladyson.com for lots of goodies?

Here, you can sign up to my newsletter for the chance to WIN book 3. And no need to worry about being spammed. I use my newsletter sparingly, primarily emailing to let you know about new releases and with a handful of exclusive offers each year.

On my events page you can also see what stores I'll be visiting on my Book Tour. Do come along to any spots local to you, it would be so lovely to meet you in person and sign your copy!

Do connect with me on Facebook @AngelaDysonAuthor or Twitter @AngelaDysonAuth or reach out by email angela.dyson@hotmail.co.uk as I love nothing more than chatting to readers. I also use social media to share the occasional competition and news about my events and activities

COMING SOON...

THE LOVE DETECTIVE: IN DEEP

IF YOU MISSED BOOK 1 IN THE SERIES, THE LOVE DETCTIVE, WHY NOT ORDER IT NOW?

THE LOVE DETECTIVE:NEXT LEVEL

READING GROUP GUIDE
NOTES FOR DISCUSSION

1: One of the central themes of the novel is that many of us (but not all) need to believe in something.

2: Part of Clarry's job as a Private Investigator involves lying. She is paid to befriend and spy on Vanessa. This professional betrayal presents a dilemma for her.

3: Is Diana Maitland right to employ Clarry. At what point does parental protectiveness become interference?

4: The pressure on women (and particularly young women) to conform to a physical stereotype can be intense. Here's Clarry on her appearance: "I'm not bad looking in my way. I hover somewhere between a size 14 and 16. I have the occasional very good day but mostly I'm about a 6 -7 on the scale. And I'm OK with that."

5: Clarry is aware that she is very fortunate to have been left a house by her grandmother, and questions whether she owes something back to society.

6: In praise of older women. Why Flan is a great role model.

7: Female friendship....... and the power of the group.

8: "The Rules of Dating say never accept an invitation made on the same day. It makes you come across as too eager." A wise policy or just game-playing?

9: The relationship between Clarry and Flan is a very special one and treasured by both.

10: Clarry says to Helen "I think most of us are outsiders. It's just that we do everything we possibly can to avoid recognising that fact."

11: When trapped in the cellar with Vanessa, Clarry remembers something that her mother used to say, "It's amazing how much braver you can feel when there is someone else to take care of."

12: Flan reminisces about an old flame "It would never have worked out between us, long term. He wasn't a sensual man. Sexual but not sensual. An important distinction, wouldn't you agree, Clarry?" Are you with Flan on this or not?

Author's note: This should make for an interesting discussion!

13: Flan believes that is important to live fully in the present. This is not always easy to do.